PLAGUE LAND

LAND

ALEX SCARROW

Published by Sourcebooks Fire, an imprint of Sourcebooks, Inc.
P.O. Box 4410, Naperville, Illinois 60567-4410
(630) 961-3900
Fax: (630) 961-2168
www.sourcebooks.com

Originally published as *Remade* in 2016 in the United Kingdom by Macmillan
Children's Books, an imprint of Pan Macmillan.

Library of Congress Cataloging-in-Publication Data

Names: Scarrow, Alex, author.
Title: Plague land / Alex Scarrow.
Description: Naperville, Illinois : Sourcebooks Fire, [2017] | Series: Plague
land
; 1 | Summary: An unidentified virus wipes out most of the Earth's
population and Leon, his mother, and younger sister Grace, who just moved
to London from New York, must run for their lives.
Identifiers: LCCN 2016050933 | (alk. paper)
Subjects: | CYAC: Survival--Fiction. | Plague--Fiction. | Virus
diseases--Fiction. | Family life--England--Fiction. | London
(England)--Fiction. | England--Fiction. | Science fiction.
Classification: LCC PZ7.S3255 Rem 2017 | DDC [Fic]--dc23 LC record avail-
able at https://lccn.loc.gov/2016050933

Printed and bound in the United States of America.
VP 10 9 8 7 6 5 4 3 2 1

For Debbie...my partner in slime ;)
A big thank-you to James Richards for reading
through from a microbiologist's viewpoint.
Any errors are mine, not his!

PART

1

CHAPTER

1

West Africa

THE GIRL WAS ONLY TEN. HER NAME WAS CAMILLE. SHE WAS on her way to collect water from the drinking well—a large, battered, and dented tin jug dangling from each hand—when she spotted it just a few feet off the hard dirt track.

A dead dog.

Not an uncommon sight—except for the fact that it was only *half* a dead dog. Camille stepped from the road onto the rough ground, mindful of the clumps of dry earth. There were still plenty of old, rusting land mines to be wary of, half-buried in the sunbaked dirt...a regular reminder of the days of the civil war.

As she approached the dog, she could see that it was actually still alive. The tan-colored animal was whimpering, its front paws clawing at the earth as if it was trying to pull itself along the ground. Its head, chest, front paws—the whole front half of its body—were intact, then sloped away into a messy, shredded end of bones, tendons, and spilled organs. Its eyes rolled up at her as she stood over it. Its pink tongue lolled as it panted.

Camille squatted beside the dying animal. "You poor, poor thing," she said softly. The dog must have triggered one of the old mines, blown its hindquarters clean away.

She stroked its muzzle. It licked her hand, pitifully grateful for the company.

"You sleep, little lady." For some reason, she was certain the dog was a bitch. "You sleep now."

Female. In this troubled country, it was always the women and girls who did the suffering. The men did what they did, and everyone else endured. She caressed the animal's muzzle. It licked her fingers, leaving a slick of saliva stained pink with blood.

The dog quivered and blew froth from its nostrils. Then, with a final whimper, it died.

Camille stood up and looked around.

There was no hole of dark, freshly exposed earth nearby that would indicate a recent explosion. Maybe the animal had managed to crawl a ways after being blown up.

It seemed unlikely. And it had happened recently. Surely she would have heard the bang, wouldn't she?

Not that it mattered now. The dog was dead. Her suffering was over. At least Camille had been there to comfort her in the last moments of life. She wiped her damp fingers down her yellow shirt, leaving faint pink smudges on the material.

She winced. The fine cotton felt oddly coarse against her sensitive fingertips.

Which was silly, because she had skin that was thick from hard work, calluses on her fingers from carrying those water jugs every day. She looked down at her hand...

...and saw that the dark pigment had vanished from the tips of her fingers, exposing raw pink flesh that glistened wetly...like the tender, not-quite-ready skin beneath a freshly burst blister.

Camille was dead an hour later.

CHAPTER

2

Leon suspected this was something really different. It was the speed with which it all happened, the speed with which it had gone from being some curious little comment he'd heard tacked to the end of the morning news on the radio, to being the main item on the TV news, to being the end of the world. Three quickly taken steps all occurring within the span of a week.

His ears had pricked up over breakfast, catching those few words on BBC Radio 4, the very last item as he raced to finish his breakfast.

"...in Nigeria. There's very little information as yet coming from the region, but we do know some sort of containment procedure is already being put in place..."

He tuned out his mom and his younger sister, both of whom were talking, neither one listening to the other. Leon struggled to hear the radio beneath the shrill babble of their voices; he was sure he'd heard the word *plague* in there somewhere.

"...no confirmation that this is another outbreak of Ebola. In fact, we've heard that's already been ruled out..."

And then the newsreader was off, talking about the tedious world of sports: which new athlete was being outed for taking performance-enhancing drugs, which soccer team was in danger of being dropped from the Premier Division...

Just blah, blah, blah. The usual stuff that filled the 8:30 to 8:40 morning slot. Which was his handy daily cue to finish his bowl of Weetos and get going.

He pushed the bowl of now-chocolaty milk away and stood up. Done.

Bus to catch for school. Another day to endure. Just like the last, just like the next.

"Leon?"

He looked at his mom. "Huh?"

"I said don't forget to bring your gym bag home. Your uniform's probably growing mildew all over it by now."

"Uh, yeah, right," he mumbled. He grabbed his backpack from the back of the chair and headed for the hallway.

"Bowl?" Grace looked up from her phone. She was busy feeding her virtual pony on the screen. *Swipe-drop-munch-neigh... points!* Like it actually really mattered.

He sighed at his bossy younger sister. Twelve, and she nagged him like she was his mother, a mini-version but every bit as nag-some. He sighed again and doubled back, picking it up.

"And, Leo...you really shouldn't waste the milk."

He drooped his eyelids at her—his version of *shove it*—poured the milk down the drain, and dropped the bowl into the sink. Half an act of rebellion against his younger sister.

"Good boy," said his mom distractedly as she fiddled with the buttons of her blouse with one hand and held her phone to her ear with the other. He squeezed past her, around the kitchen table, heading for the hall.

"Leon?" she called after him.

He stopped and turned.

She smiled guiltily at him, the phone still pressed to her ear. "It'll be all right, you know? We'll all settle in soon enough."

He figured she was on hold, listening to crackly elevator music.

"I know it's been hard, Leo, but..."

He knew she felt bad about the way things had been, guilty about everything that had happened recently, sorry that she hardly had time for either of them.

"Yeah, well..." was all Leon could offer in reply. He shrugged. He couldn't even manage to find some sort of lame smile to give back to her.

"You've got friends now, haven't you?" she continued, half stating, half asking.

He nodded. "Sure." It was far easier to lie than tell the truth. The last thing he needed right now was his mom telling him how he needed to *engage*...to get out there and mix with the other kids.

"How's your head?"

Leon shrugged. He tapped his temples. "Fine."

"You got some aspirin? Just in case?"

"Yup."

"You going for the bus?"

"Uh-huh."

"Don't forget to pick your sister up on the way back."

"I won't."

Grace had broken her forearm playing basketball. She now had it in a cast and a sling, and his mom wanted him to help her home. Her arm ached, his head throbbed, he suspected his mom was on Prozac. Between the three of them, they were going through drugs like junkies in a crack house.

Leon's mom looked at him pitifully, and for a moment, he glimpsed her old self. Mom...before she changed her name back to *Jennifer Button*, almost *forensically* removing all trace of his dad. Mom from way back when she'd had time for him.

"Leon...honey, it's going to work out—" Her call suddenly connected. "Oh, yes. Appointments, please."

He turned and headed into the hallway, grabbing his jacket off the peg by the front door, and let himself out. If he'd known how this particular week was going to go, how the next few months were going to be...he would have told her he loved her, that all the crap they'd been through over the last year was OK...

I forgive you, Mom.

But he wouldn't know any of that. Today was only Monday. Just like any other Monday. Another stuff-just-rolls-along day, marked by nothing different except one word he'd just about managed to hear on the radio in the background.

Plague.

7

CHAPTER

3

LEON HATED THIS PLACE ALREADY. SEVEN WEEKS AT RANDALL Sixth Form College and he'd spoken to no more than a dozen of the other students. Coming in midyear, he might as well have arrived smeared with human excrement; every little clique, every little gang was already well and truly established, and they all kept him at arm's length.

No one seemed willing to admit the lanky new kid with the funny New Jersey accent into their little circle.

Mostly they left him alone. There were a few assholes who picked on him. Nothing particularly inventive—"Hank the Yank" and a few other no-brainers like that. There was a little dose of it every day, just five minutes of it usually; then they got bored and moved on.

When Leon's mom had first dropped the bomb on him and Grace—that she and his dad were splitting up and she was taking them both back home to live near her parents in England—he'd been shocked. Tears. Panic. The foundation of his world just ripped out from beneath his feet.

But also there'd been a hint of relief—relief from the fights, those barked exchanges in the hallway of their New Jersey apartment, from the lowered voices behind the closed bedroom door, from the murmurs from both of them that ended with a *screw you* and the click of a light going off.

Leon's mom had put a desperately positive spin on things. That London, England, was a "totally sick" place to live. (*Oh jeez...Mom, puh-lease. Don't even try that talk.*) She'd told him and Grace the other kids were going to love their "exotic movie accents" and all the other London kids would be fascinated by their interesting, new, stand-out-from-the-crowd American buddies, even though Leon and Grace were both British by birth.

She completely missed the point. No kid wants to stand out.

Just like no soldier wants to stick his head up out of the fox-hole, not if he doesn't want it splattered over the guy standing next to him. And that "cool" American accent had drawn fire for Leon all right. By the end of day one, he was *Hank the Yank.* By the end of week one, it had mutated into *Hanker the Wanker.* Hey, because, y'know, it rhymed.

Genius.

He wasn't a Yank, he'd explained far too many times. He was British. British born, British mother. It's just that he'd happened to have spent the first sixteen years of his life in the United States. Not exactly a crime.

There was another outcast in the class—someone else with whom Leon took turns being target of the day. *Samir.* He'd shortened his name to Sam because he thought it sounded cooler. He wandered over to Leon in the hallway at the midmorning break as Leon was sorting through the stinky tangle of damp clothes in his gym bag. His mom was right—it smelled like something was growing in there.

"'Sup, Leon."

"Hey," he replied, looking up at Sam. Sam's family had come from Pakistan, but the way he talked, dressed, and carried himself was more British than the rest of the students in their year.

"My dad just texted me."

"Yeah?"

"He said…" Sam pulled out his phone and swiped it. "He said did I see the news."

"See the news? Why? What's up?"

"I don't know," replied Sam. "Something must've happened, I suppose. A bomb maybe?"

A bomb? If there'd been anything like that subway bomb scare at Shepherd's Bush a few months back, he figured the school's PA system would have announced it.

"I'm going to the library. Want to come?" asked Sam.

The school library was more like an internet cafe than a place that stored books. One side had a row of computers, and the other racks of well-worn magazines and untouched newspapers. Oh, and a small spinner rack of paperbacks in the middle that the librarian optimistically refreshed daily with "The Latest Teen Must-Reads!"

Sam led the way inside. Some heads turned toward them from the various clusters of students in the room, tucked closely together and conspiring about God knows what. He hated entering rooms. Heads always swiveled. He much preferred leaving a room.

Leon hid behind Sam Chutani, who seemed to be one hundred percent bulletproof to the hallway sniggers, sideways glances, and curled lips. He dressed like an adult, like an IT consultant: department store suits, loafers, tie, shirt, and a fountain pen permanently nestled in his breast pocket. He simply did not give a crap about the others and the peer pressure to conform.

Leon envied that—Sam's rhino-thick skin.

Sam sat down at one of the computers and logged on to his student account. "My dad watches the Reuters news feed all day long at work. He's always the first to know if anything has happened anywhere."

As the Reuters website opened, Leon expected some large apocalyptic headline to grab their attention. But no bombs today, apparently. No crashed planes. No tourist shootings or shopping-mall massacres. Today, for once, there seemed to be an outbreak of sanity.

Sam pointed out a headline in the tech-business column. "That's what it is."

ForTel buys out silicon rival in Indonesia.

"Oh...right," said Leon. *Earth-shattering.*

Sam's dad ran a small high-end PC business, building to order—the price of silicon chips was *everything* to him. He knew Sam was building his own PC, a "monster-ninja-kick-ass rig" ready for the "final" *Call of Duty* due to be released just before Thanksgiving.

Final? Ha. Leon figured he'd die an old man before that gravy train stopped running.

Then he spotted another news item at the bottom of the page: *Quarantine...*and some place he'd never heard of.

Sam hit a link, and in a flash, the page changed to the ForTel homepage.

"Wait!" said Leon. "Can you go back?"

"Sure." Sam sighed and went back to the Reuters page. Leon looked for the small headline, but it wasn't there anymore; the page layout was different, displaying a new page of news stories.

"Crap, it's gone."

"What are you looking for?"

Leon shook his head. "Never mind. It was something to do with a... I don't know, just..."

Sam patted him on the back. "You OK, Leon?"

CHAPTER
4

Ionian Sea, off the West Coast of Greece

COMMANDER BENITO ARNONI STOOD AT THE PROW OF THE *Levriero* with a line ready to throw. The pilot cut the engines of the Guardia di Finanza motorboat as it closed the last sixty feet of choppy water.

The boat before them was one of the usual repurposed fishing vessels used by migrant traffickers, stripped of fishing lines and apparatus to make maximum use of the deck space. The vessel had first been spotted an hour ago, and Arnoni's patrol boat had been hastily dispatched to intercept it.

Even as a dot on the horizon, it hadn't looked quite right. Closer to it now, it looked decidedly wrong. No waving arms, no rows of malnourished faces, no painfully thin and terrified stick figures braced against each other to keep their balance as the boat bobbed and rocked on the water.

It looked utterly deserted. Arnoni had no one to toss a line to.

Their motorboat slowly approached the deserted vessel and Arnoni, standing at the prow, stretched and craned his neck to get a better look across its empty deck. No bodies to be seen, but the boat looked oddly *decorated*. Ribbons of bright pink, like streamers, were draped across the rusty, paint-flecked deck. Some of those streamers were wound up the side of the bridge, up the support stanchions, to a radio antenna where a large, pink streamer flared out and fluttered like a pennant. For a moment, Arnoni wondered if this boat was someone's idea of a joke or a publicity stunt. Maybe some concept artist's idea of meaningful "art." Crimson and sepia paint seemed to have been spattered everywhere, as if the artist wasn't quite satisfied that his ribbons were enough of a creative statement.

As the prow of his ship bumped against the front of the boat, Arnoni threw a leg over the safety rail and hopped across, onto its foredeck.

The first thing that hit him was the stench—a sickeningly sweet yet cheesy smell that reminded him of hanging joints of salted ham.

And no, they certainly weren't party streamers or decorative ribbons. He hunkered down and inspected the pink webbing more closely. It glistened wetly.

"*Merda.*"

The boat looked like a slaughterhouse, as if the contents of the building had been dumped on the boat from high above. Now he knew what he was smelling: the putrid, sickly sweet odor of rotting flesh. He covered his nose and mouth as he made his way down the side of the boat, shuffling along the narrow space, past the bridge, toward the open cockpit and the aft deck. A low, green canvas awning spread over the bow of the vessel rustled and snapped in the breeze. He took a deep breath through his mouth, steadying his nerves, his stomach, knowing, sensing, that there was more to see beneath it.

He ducked down under the awning.

"*Gesú Cristo!*" He crossed himself. His first thought was that he was staring at the handiwork of the devil himself, some barbaric, playful, diorama ingeniously constructed from the parts of humankind.

Commander Benito Arnoni threw up…and just over an hour later, he was dead too.

CHAPTER
5

School finished for Leon at two o'clock. There was a key skills class he was supposed to attend, taking him to 3:00 p.m., but he decided to skip it. He went to his locker and retrieved the gym bag. The clothes inside were all convincingly damp and muddy. He'd take them home tonight and give them to his mom to throw into the washing machine, and she'd dutifully ask him how the soccer game after school went. He'd tell her it went well, that sure, he was making friends. That the guys were, like, all totally cool. She'd smile as she stuffed his clothes in the washing machine and then get back to thinking about work, about herself, thinking about how her children's father had messed up all their lives so completely.

Leon's plan had worked twice so far. He took his gym clothes and tennis shoes to school, dragged them through a mud puddle, let them sit damp for a few days, then brought them home and told his mom he'd had fun kicking a ball around with the other lads.

Now he made his way through Hammersmith toward Grace's school, a secondary school that looked like a high-security prison from the outside, its small playground fenced high and topped off with wire. Leon's mom insisted he meet Grace right at the school gates, so she didn't have to walk home on her own. There had been a girl at another school nearby who'd been assaulted by a gang. That had happened a few weeks after they'd arrived from the U.S. and settled into their apartment.

Maybe when she was a little bit older, Grace could make her own way home but not yet, and not with her broken arm.

Her school finished at three thirty. Leon had some time to wander through King's Mall. He hung out here on Wednesdays and Fridays (when he was supposedly playing soccer). It was warm and dry, and he could usually make his hot chocolate from Starbucks last for a long time as he stared at the passersby.

He walked past a shop window flickering with the same image across a dozen widescreen plasma TVs: a reporter, and behind him, what looked like someone's cell phone video, pixelated and blurred. Leon could make out what looked like discarded piles of clothes left in the middle of some dusty street. He quickly realized they were bodies, dozens of them, scattered about randomly. The video lasted only a few seconds and then looped. Across the bottom of the various TV screens, a headline scrolled.

Unidentified viral outbreak in Nigeria

He wondered if this had something to do with the sound bite that had caught his attention this morning over breakfast. He looked around, expecting to see others beginning to gather to stare at the screens, but the mall was busy with people who had far less time on their hands than he, certainly not enough to hang around watching TV through a shop window.

He watched for another couple of minutes, until a commercial break came on. And then he realized he'd better get a move on to pick up Grace.

―――――――

"I'm worried about you, Leo."

"I'm fine, Grace," he replied.

"No. You're not. You don't have *any* friends. You spend too much time on your own."

"Jeez. What are you, my mother?"

Grace shrugged as she walked beside him, small and slight at half her brother's height. He took her pink schoolbag and slung it over his shoulder while she adjusted her sling.

"You can be really immature sometimes, Leo. *Somebody's* got to look out for you."

Grace was doing far better than him with the sudden move to London. She'd already been invited to several birthday parties, and from the snatches of chitchat he'd listened to while she was on her phone, she sounded as if she was already well on the way up her school's social food chain.

It seemed the whole exotic-accent thing was working in her favor, and of course, she played on it, hamming it up so much so that she sounded like some precocious Beverly Hills princess. Even before the move, back in New Jersey, she had been popular—queen of the playground, a member of every after-school club.

She placed a hand on his arm and looked up at him. "You're missing Dad, aren't you?"

"Dunno, a little...maybe."

"Don't! He was a complete jerk, cheating on Mom like that!"

Leon wasn't so sure it was *that* one-sided. Yeah, he'd had a *thing* with someone at work. But his mom wasn't entirely blameless. She pecked at him all the time, always seemed to have something to complain about, to blame him for, whether it was slippers in the hall, shaving brush in the sink, oversalting the dinner she'd slaved over, or staying late at work far too often. Leon had overheard his dad call her a "bitter little shrew" once and wondered why on earth they bothered putting up with each other.

"It takes two to screw up like they did."

"Men!" Grace grumbled.

Leon smiled. Grace tried to sound like a grown-up, but most of the time she sounded like one of those precocious child actors who talked about inner dialogue and character motivation.

Leon shook his head. "Jesus, Grace, why can't you just be like every other girl your age and just play with, I dunno...*dolls* or something?"

She sighed wearily. "*Play* is for children."

They walked on in silence for a while, weaving their way along the increasingly busy sidewalk that was filling up with early commuters and the tail end of kids going home from school.

"Anyway, it's *you* we're talking about."

"Yes, *Mom*."

She tossed her curly, dark hair and jutted her chin out. "You've got to make much more of an effort, Leon. Mom's stressed out enough as it is." *Mom.* Grace was hanging on to her accent as if it were a gift, whereas Leon had been doing his best to bury it.

"She doesn't need to be worrying about you being some weirdo loner as well."

"I've got friends, OK?"

"So, how come they never call or come around?"

Jeez. Gimme a break. "Because I value my personal space. That's not a frickin crime, is it?"

Grace looked up at him, smiling with pity. "Just try a little harder, OK?"

Pity? From a twelve-year-old!?

"I'm fine, Grace. Can we just leave my social life out of it?"

They walked past a convenience store, and she stopped suddenly. "OhmyGod!"

"What?"

"I need to buy a paper! They're printing coupons for free Maybelline samplers all this week." She headed for the open door. "I miss a coupon, I lose out. Wait here."

Leon nodded obediently, watching his sister stride inside—so small for her age, with drainpipe arms and legs and knobby knees, her long, dark curls held tidily back from her face by a headband... and so *annoyingly* precocious. Even as a baby she'd been protective of Leon, patting him affectionately on the nose as she sucked on a bottle of milk.

Among the halal meat hanging in the shop window, he saw handwritten ads taped to the glass. Beneath the awning, the afternoon edition of the *Evening Standard* sat on a rain-damp rack, a tall headline spread across the entire front page.

MYSTERY VIRUS IN WEST AFRICA

He took a couple of steps closer to the window to read the story underneath.

"...an as yet unidentified virus has turned up today in several other isolated villages in Nigeria, Cameroon, and Ghana. The World Health Organization has already dispatched a scramble team to the three locations where symptoms have been reported. We understand that personnel from the United States military's medical research division, USAMRIID, have also been sent. So far neither organization has commented on the nature of the virus, although some eyewitness accounts from within the affected villages have talked of extensive hemorrhaging and external bleeding, symptoms similar to those of Ebola."

Grace came out of the shop, leafing through the paper in search of her coupon page.

"You seen this?" asked Leon, pointing to the newspaper rack.

She momentarily cocked an eyebrow at the headline before returning to her own paper. "Oh, you worry way too much. It'll be another false alarm."

She led the way up the busy street. Leon cast one last glance back at the window before following her.

CHAPTER

6

Amoso, West Africa

DR. KENNETH JONES LEANED OVER IN HIS SEAT TO LOOK OUT of the window. Below, the small town of Amoso was barely visible in the night. There were no streetlamps on, although one or two buildings were showing lights, presumably powered by portable generators. He could see several oil-drum fires scattered across the area, but apart from that, it looked like a ghost town; there was nothing going on down there—no cars on the roads, no pedestrians.

"I can't see anything moving," he said into his throat mike.

The helicopter's beam played steadily across the narrow streets, picking out the flat, corrugated steel rooftops encrusted with antennas and satellite dishes.

Jones spotted something pale flicker into the intense beam of light and out of it again. And then in...

It was just…a plastic bag stirred up by the downdraft of the helicopter.

Dr. Gupta leaned forward to take a look. The helmet of his containment suit clunked awkwardly against the window.

Above the deafening drone of the helicopter, Jones heard Gupta's voice over his headphones. "Dammit. I can't see anything clearly in here. These UN-issue suits are too bulky."

Jones nodded. He hated them. They were incredibly cumbersome and stifling. He was just managing to hold in check a suffocating sense of claustrophobia. The sooner they were done getting a sample back to their hastily assembled UN ops center, then hosed down three separate times and out of these damn suits, the better.

"Are we safe to go down?"

"We clear the 'elicopter first, Doctor."

Jones looked at the five men sitting across the cabin from him: French Foreign Legion. Elite troops—Jones knew them by their reputation. "We establish a safe perimeter," the squad's sergeant continued. His accent was thick. "Then you come out. You understand me?"

Jones nodded quickly.

"Relax," added the sergeant. "We take good care of you two."

This wasn't Jones's first time. He had gone into Sierra Leone in 2014, at the first outbreak of Ebola, and last year there'd been the suspected outbreak of Marburg in Liberia. But this time there was the added danger of bullets, hence the legionnaires accompanying them. He and Dr. Gupta had been briefed that there might be a Boko Haram presence in the town; the government forces had cleared Amoso half a dozen times of those terrorists, and they kept creeping back in like a persistent cold.

Dr. Gupta turned to the other men in the helicopter's cabin. "We don't know if there are any survivors down there. If there are, we must keep them away from us. If this is an Ebola outbreak—"

Jones looked at Dr. Gupta. "It's *not* Ebola. This is too fast a spread pattern." He frowned. "We don't know anything yet. Hemorrhaging, that's what eyewitnesses have reported. Ebola, Marburg, Lassa—it *might* be a pathogen related to one of those. But..."

There'd been just nine seconds of footage from a cell phone. That's all. Nine grainy, hand-shaken seconds—the only visual information from which they had to work. Dr. Jones had seen bodies...dozens of them lying in the streets of this small town earlier this afternoon. Heard a woman's voice shrieking, terrified, the camera view whipping frantically from side to side.

Then it had ended abruptly.

Gupta was listening to a message coming in on another frequency. Jones saw him nod and reply, his words drowned out by the deafening roar of the helicopter's engine. And then his voice came clear and crisp over the headphones.

"The pilot is taking us down now."

The helicopter lurched forward, gliding across the town as its floodlight swept one way then the other, looking for a suitable place to land. It picked out a crossroads clear of any obstructing vehicles, then quickly began its descent.

Below, the town seemed to stir to life, dust and trash whipped up into a frenzy by the intensifying downdraft. Finally, gently, with a thud that Jones felt rather than heard, they were down on the ground.

The sergeant pulled the sliding cabin door open and let his four men exit first. They scrambled out of the cabin, clumsy and heavy footed in their biohazard suits, onto the potholed asphalt of the road, all of them dropping to a kneeling position and scanning the perimeter with quick, precise movements.

Jones watched the sergeant and his men, one by one, getting to their feet and securing covered positions around the helicopter. Whispered orders in French crackled over their earpieces, and finally the sergeant gave the doctors the all-clear to get out.

Gupta tapped Jones's leg. "You ready?"

Jones nodded. "A little scared to tell the truth."

"We'd be idiots *not* to be."

Gupta stepped out and Jones followed, awkwardly struggling to keep his balance. The air pack on his back was heavy, forcing him to lean forward like an old crone carrying firewood. He looked around him. To their left was one of the few buildings in the town that had lights on. A sign in Hausa and English—REPAIRS, FIXES, SALE OF CAR AND TRUCK—indicated that not so long ago it had been a garage. The sign was pitted with ragged bullet holes, as were the cinderblock walls either side of the raised shutter door.

Open for business.

By the flickering beam of his flashlight, he could see mounds of cloth dotted around the junction, fluttering in the downdraft as the helicopter's blades still spun and the whine of the engine slowly wound down.

Gupta walked cautiously toward one of the small mounds of cloth and knelt down beside it.

Jones heard his voice over the intercom. "What the hell is this?"

Dr. Gupta beckoned to him. "Jones...come and have a look here."

He hurried over and knelt down beside him.

There was no corpse, certainly nothing that could be described as a body. Instead, they were looking at a mess of darkly stained clothes, crumpled and blotchy, wrapped around a bundle of bones. A skull lay on the road beside the pile—mostly ivory-colored bone, with just a patch of dark scalp and a tuft of hair left where the victim's crown would have been.

Beneath the bones and clothes, a murky puddle of viscous liquid had pooled.

"My God. Complete liquefaction of all the soft tissue..." Gupta shook his head. "In just a few hours?"

"That's *impossible*," whispered Jones.

There were other lumps of cloth and bone on the road. "It kills quickly."

Jones nodded. He knew what Gupta was getting at. It had killed too quickly for these victims to make their way to some triage center. They'd literally dropped where they'd been standing.

"That's...an *encouraging* sign," said Gupta. The phrase felt poorly chosen. "At least it appears that there is no incubation period."

"Flash-fire infection," said Jones. Maybe this pathogen, whatever it was, was going to be too efficient for its own good—no hosts living long enough to quietly carry the infection to fresh pastures. Hopefully it would burn itself out before it could spread too far.

Gupta pulled out a small plastic container and a sample pipette. He set the container down and unscrewed the cap. He then picked up the pipette in his thick-gloved fingers. "I will get a sample of the fluid."

Carefully, he touched the tip of the pipette to the dark liquid. Jones thought he saw the surface quiver or ripple slightly. Gupta squeezed the rubber bulb and released. Air bubbled out, and the liquid, thick as syrup, began to climb up the inside of the narrow glass cylinder. Finally, he placed the pipette in the container and screwed the cap back on.

"We should look around... Try to see if there are any survivors."

Gupta shined his flashlight across the front of the garage. Through the half-raised shutter, the glow from a solitary, fizzing striplight spilled out.

They made their way across the uneven road, potholed with cracks and craters—decades-old asphalt that needed resurfacing. Gupta ducked under the raised shutter. Jones followed him inside.

The oil-stained concrete floor was littered with tattered blankets, discarded cans of food, clips of ammunition, and AK-47s.

"Oh shit," whispered Jones.

Gupta heard him and nodded.

The town was back in Boko Haram's possession. "They must have been holing up here," said Jones.

"I see no bodies though."

"Then they must have fled."

"That doesn't surprise me," said Gupta. Boko Haram

propaganda videos portrayed them as benevolent protectors and saviors of the people. In reality, they took what they needed, abducted whom they wanted, and moved on.

The sergeant ducked under the shutter and stood up beside them. "Everything is OK?"

They both nodded. "We're fine," said Jones. "Fine."

He nodded. "*D'accord.*" He looked around. "The militants were here."

"And left in a hurry."

The sergeant shook his head. "No. Not even in a hurry. They would not leave their guns behind." He quickly barked an order in French, and several seconds later, two of his men ducked under the shutter and joined them. "You two stay here," he said to the doctors. "We will check this place."

Gupta and Jones nodded.

Jones watched as the three soldiers worked together silently, two covering, one moving, probing every dark corner of the garage. Finally they disappeared as they went through a doorway at the back.

Gupta looked at him. "Terrified?"

"Very."

"Me too."

"This is not Ebola." Gupta's comment sounded halfway between a question and a statement.

Jones nodded. "No pathogen works this fast. It's not Marburg. It's not L21-N. I have no idea what it is."

"Maybe a chemical weapon?"

Jones shrugged.

Suddenly the sergeant's voice crackled over their earpieces. "Dr. Jones? Dr. Gupta! Come, please!"

They looked quickly at each other, then hurried over toward the doorway at the back of the garage. Jones stepped through first. He could see flashlight beams whipping back and forth across what looked like a small storeroom. It was difficult to understand what he was seeing by the stark, flickering beams. He turned to his right, saw a switch, and flicked it hopefully.

A striplight in the ceiling blinked reluctantly several times, then finally winked on.

"God!" Jones gasped. He looked down at the bundle of clothes and bones and the pool of dark brown *mulch* beneath it...then at the bizarre sight spread across the floor.

CHAPTER

7

LEON'S MOM ARRIVED HOME LATE FROM WORK, AS SHE ALWAYS did these days. Grace had made a start at preparing dinner. That was one of the new routines they'd gotten into the habit of over the last six months. Back in New Jersey, his mom had always been waiting for them at home at the end of the school day, all milk and cookies and "How was your day?"

She worked for an estate agent in Shepherd's Bush now. Her days were spent taking buses and subways around West London, meeting potential clients to show them around ridiculously overpriced and dingy town houses. Nowadays it was Leon and Grace waiting with the milk and cookies and asking her how her day had been.

"Rubbish," she responded when they asked her. She dropped her keys in the kitchen bowl. "Lots of standing around like an idiot and waiting." She kicked her work shoes off into the shoe basket and gave Grace a hug. "How are my two babies?"

Leon rolled his eyes.

"How's your arm?"

Grace was stirring the pan with her good arm. "Sore."

"Leo! Why are you making *her* do the cooking?"

"I'm not *making* her. Jeez. You know what she's like—she took over. She said I was doing it all wrong."

"You want some aspirin, honey?"

"I'm OK. Maybe at bedtime. Hey...by the way, I got a commendation for my short story," Grace crowed. "My English teacher is putting it up on the school website."

"Oh wowzers...clever girl!" She kissed the top of Grace's head and looked over at Leon. "And what about you? How was your football?"

"Soccer," he corrected her.

"No..." She wagged a finger and smiled. "Over here we call it *football.*"

Leon sighed. "It was OK."

"Did you score any goals, love?"

"Sure. One or two I guess."

"Did you put your dirties in the laundry basket?"

"Uh-huh."

"Good boy." She let Grace go, came around the breakfast bar, and put an arm around him. Leon let her squeeze him and made a halfhearted effort to squeeze her back. He knew it was her guilt reflex—another day spent focusing on rebuilding her life, her career, and all that she had left to offer her kids at the end of the day was a squeeze and a few token questions.

"I'm exhausted," she sighed. "Been on my feet all day." She

slumped on one of the breakfast stools. "So…what do you guys fancy doing this weekend? I heard there's a music festival in Hyde Park. We could go and—"

"I have Pony Club on Saturday," said Grace.

"You can't ride with your arm."

"They're showing us mucking out and grooming. I gotta go."

Leon's mom turned to him and raised her brows.

"Sorry, Mom… I got a Clash of Clans team meeting." Leon kept in touch with a few friends back home. Once a week they hooked up on Skype and mostly played dumbass first-person shooters that bored Leon, but at least it was some form of contact with his old life.

"We could go in the evening if you guys want?"

The prospect of pointlessly milling around a rock festival with his mom and kid sister was pretty grim. He could see her cajoling them to go see this and that, herding them like a sheepdog, all phony excitement and forced smiles, and then it would eventually end up with her moaning at them for being miserable when all she was trying to do was get them to spend some quality time together. The subway journey back home would be in silence… and Sunday would be one long sulk.

"Fine," she sighed. "It was just an idea."

"Maybe next time, Mom," offered Leon.

She nodded at that and almost looked relieved. "OK." They sat in silence for a minute. "Mmm! What's cooking?"

"Out-of-the-jar own-brand sauce," replied Grace. The microwave pinged in the corner. "And nuked pasta."

They ate off their laps in the small living room, Leon on the sofa with his mom, Grace sitting on the beanbag, a fork in one hand and the TV remote control right beside her. Another rerun episode of *The Big Bang Theory* was about to start.

"Grace, can we have something else on?" By that their mom meant *EastEnders* or some cooking show.

"How about the news?" Leon asked.

She looked at him. Surprised, possibly even impressed. "Yeah... the news. Why not?"

Grace rolled her eyes and huffed, then zapped the channel over to BBC1.

"Something caught your interest, Leo?"

"There's the African thing."

Leon's mom shrugged and looked at him. "What African thing?"

He pointed with his fork at the screen. "Over there? On the TV?"

She turned and watched. Currently the news was running through the tail end of the headlines recap: how the prime minister's son was coping with his first term at an inner-city academy; Betsy Boomalackah on the red carpet, promoting her new movie; then it cycled back to the headline story.

A senior cabinet member caught up in a sex scandal...

"What African thing?" asked Leon's mom after a couple of minutes.

Leon shrugged. "Maybe it's over... It was, like, on the TV news this afternoon."

The very next item was the African thing. A reporter was on

ALEX SCARROW

the ground in Abuja, Nigeria, wearing khakis, a flak jacket, and a blue helmet.

"...scenes of violence today as Boko Haram fighters pushed south into the city's northern suburbs..."

"*That* African thing?"

Leon shook his head. "Not those Boko guys... The *virus* thing. It was, like—"

The image on the screen changed to a press conference, flash photography, a panel of worried-looking faces behind a forest of microphones.

"...continuing mystery surrounding the news this morning of the outbreak of an as-yet-unidentified virus in Northern Nigeria, which now appears to have spread to the neighboring states of Ghana, Benin, and Cameroon.

"Dr. Ahmand Saliente, a spokesman for the World Health Organization, has already ruled out the possibility that this is an outbreak of Ebola, the frightening hemorrhagic disease that was brought to public attention several years ago. 'We know this is not Ebola or Marburg, and we wanted that message to get out quickly. We are dealing with something that has a very different and rapid spread pattern...'"

"Oh"—Leon's mom wound pasta on to her fork—"those poor people. It's one thing after another over there, isn't it?"

"...the as-yet-unidentified virus has spread remarkably quickly in just twenty-four hours, and the foreign office has issued an advisory travel warning to those considering trips to any of the West African nations..."

"That doesn't look good," said Leon.

34

"Are you worried about it?" his mom asked.

He hunched his shoulders. "Just saying..."

She narrowed her eyes at him. "Leo...don't get all worked up about it. I know what you're like. You'll obsess about it, just like your—"

He closed his eyes and stifled an urge to snap at her. She was going to say *Just like your dad...* She'd managed to stop herself though.

The news had moved on to a story about Amazon trying to buy out Walmart.

"Is that it?" said Grace. She picked up the remote. "Can I change it back now, please?"

Their mom nodded. "It depresses me—the news. One thing after another." She tried tacking on something humorous about the prime minister's son and whether his best mate in year seven was a midget bodyguard in disguise, but Leon's attention was elsewhere.

He pulled out his phone and logged on to DarkEye.com. It was his go-to website for conspiracy news. There were dozens of links to do with the story. He hit one that took him to a place called UnderTheWire.com. The banner proudly claimed they served up the world's *unfiltered* news, news that the likes of Fox, CNN, and even the BBC "Don't Want You to See!" The latest submitted story, right at the top of the page, was of "smoking-gun evidence" that NASA never landed on the moon. The next headline down was about Taylor Swift being a secret CIA operative.

The third article was what he was after.

There are unconfirmed reports that the mystery illness in Amoso and several other towns in Nigeria has turned up in a number of other locations outside of West Africa. The source of this UnderTheWire story is unknown, although it could well be tapped intelligence traffic or somebody within the WHO, or perhaps the U.S. military biological weapons division, USAMRIID. There is speculation that this may be a bioweapon being tested out by the U.S. on a number of radical Islamic strongholds, a small-scale field-testing of some sort. There are even rumors of a CIA mission currently investigating the outbreak sites to evaluate the weapon's effect...

"Leon?"

He looked up at his mother. "Huh?"

She tapped the side of his phone with her fork handle. "I don't want you sitting up all night fixating over this and giving yourself a headache for tomorrow."

"Just showing an interest in something...OK?"

"Come on. Phone away, please. Let's at least have dinner together before you disappear on to the internet."

Dinner together? Hardly. It was the three of them eating a microwaved meal off their laps while they gazed in silence at an old rerun.

"Fine." He tapped his phone off and tucked it back into his jeans.

CHAPTER

8

Amoso, West Africa

A SMALL TRIBUTARY OF DARK, VISCOUS LIQUID FLOWED across the concrete floor of the storage room toward an open door that led to a side alley. At several places, the liquid flow had branched.

"Jesus..." Dr. Jones whispered.

The branching looked like a photo of a river delta taken by satellite—fanning out, branches off branches, like a root system seeking nutrition.

He squatted down and dabbed at the liquid with a sample stick; then he dropped the stick into a plastic container and labeled it.

His eyes tracked a small tributary of liquid that had emerged from the bundle of clothes and bones on the floor.

That's not right.

He looked around for something and saw what he wanted: a

can of Coke stacked in a pile of other canned goods, no doubt commandeered from the townspeople. He popped the can's tab and poured its contents on to the floor. The liquid hissed and bubbled in a puddle, but what it *wasn't* doing was flowing in any particular direction. There was no slant to the floor.

The viscous fluid from the body, on the other hand, was somehow making its own decision about which way to flow.

Dr. Gupta looked up at him as he understood why Jones had poured the soda on the floor. "Impossible."

Jones got down on his hands and knees and peered closely at fine, threadlike tendrils feathering out from the main stream of liquid—the sort of quadratic branching you'd expect to see from a sample grown in a Petri dish.

"*Merde!*" a voice crackled loudly through Jones's earpiece. He looked up to see that the sergeant had stepped out through the open door into the back alley. "*Regardez!* You need to see this!"

Jones rose to his feet and crossed the floor, stepping through the open door into the alleyway. It was dark, no lighting down here where boxes and trash cans of spilled garbage were piled up against the walls on either side.

Gupta joined him in the middle of the narrow alley. A two-story building overlooked the garage. He was shining his flashlight on the cracked and flaking whitewashed plastered wall in front of him. In the stark brightness of the flashlight beam, Jones could see an almost ink-black fine line, rising up the wall, like a vine. It formed a familiar fanning-out pattern.

Gupta shined his flashlight across the alley floor and into the open doorway through which they'd both just stepped. "The liquid managed to find its way outside," he said. He looked at Jones and said it again. "The liquid *found its way* outside."

Jones followed the snaking, black line of viscous fluid across the littered floor.

"My God. It's not *flowing...*"

"It's growing."

"Like fungus mycelia."

Jones turned to him. "I really don't know how to begin to analyze this. I've never... This is something else—"

"We'll get more of an understanding of it if we can locate a body in early-stage infection."

"Yes...yes, of course."

Dr. Gupta aimed his flashlight up the plastered wall. The dark line had snaked all the way up toward a second-floor window, where a feeler had branched off and appeared to have *found* the opening. The main stream had doubled back down in a scribbled arc toward the window, where the feeler rejoined it. The vine flowed over the window frame, through the gap, and inside.

"We're going in," he said.

"Shouldn't we...uh...send the soldiers in first?"

"Oh...yes, absolutely."

———

On the second-floor landing, the sergeant and one of the other legionnaires, took up covering positions, weapons raised and ready, while Jones and Gupta went in. At the far end of the hallway was the open window they'd seen from the alleyway below, the faintest ambient glow of blue light from the garage's rear door spilling in from it.

The hallway was dark; several light sockets dangled from the ceiling minus bulbs. The walls, painted an unpleasant lime green, flaked paint onto a tired linoleum floor. Numbered doors lined both sides—apartments, cheap ones. In a poor town like Amoso, Jones suspected there'd be entire families living cheek by jowl in each. They were going to find bodies undoubtedly—lots of them.

Gupta shined his flashlight on the window at the end, picking out the distinct, dark line of liquid zigzagging down the wall beneath the ledge and across the linoleum floor, up the hallway toward them.

"There it is," he said.

The thin line snaked along the floor, several tributaries branching off on their own paths, almost as if consciously *dispatched*, like scouts. The line drifted toward the left-hand wall, running along its base, eventually disappearing under a door.

They advanced slowly, squatting down and examining the vine-like trail as they went.

"You took a sample from the storeroom?"

Jones nodded, his breathing getting heavy now, steaming up the Plexiglas plate in front of his face.

"It seems to be the same stuff. I'll take another sample anyway."

He turned to face the two soldiers holding position farther down the hallway. "Check in this apartment, please," he said, nodding at the door beside him. They moved forward quickly. Hesitating for only a few seconds, they kicked the door in and ducked inside.

Jones could hear their muffled voices coming from within,

verifying each room was clear before moving to the next. Heavy boots, the sound of doors being thrown open, then nothing as they made their way farther in.

Gupta and Jones looked at each other. They waited awhile and then finally Gupta called out, "Are you OK in there?"

Nothing.

"Is it safe for us to come in?"

Nothing. Then, finally, the sound of boots approaching, hurrying back. The sergeant emerged from the dark interior breathing heavily, his face damp with sweat.

"Sergeant? What is it?"

"There is a *live* one in there."

Both men quickly followed him back inside toward a back room, negotiating the cramped confines of the family home in their bulky containment suits. Light from a flickering candle sputtered a faint dancing glow across the sparse room. Jones noticed one of the other legionnaires, doubled over, apparently fighting an urge to vomit against his faceplate.

On the bedroom floor, across a threadbare rug, the black line weaved its way toward a large, dark puddle from which hundreds of other short feathered tributaries had branched out. As Jones took a step closer, he could see—amid the sticky dark-brown pool—what appeared to be a hand.

"It hasn't liquefied *all* of this person yet!" He hunkered down beside the hand and, closer now, could see why. "Ah…it's just a prosthetic."

The sergeant pointed toward a door leading off the room. "The live one…he is in there."

Gupta stepped toward the open doorway, hesitating momentarily before leaning in.

And then Jones heard his breath catch and a gurgling that sounded very much like gagging.

"Dr. Gupta?" asked Jones. "Someone in there? Alive still?"

Gupta took a moment to respond. "What's left of him." He stepped back out of the doorway, turned his back to Jones, and retched noisily.

Jesus. Jones stepped forward, grasped the doorframe, wary of what he was about to see. *If a veteran like Gupta can't handle it...*

He poked his head around the doorframe.

"Oh God..."

An old man was sitting on a toilet. But not sitting as such. Maybe he had been, once, but now all that was left of him was his torso from the hips upward. He was slumped back against the tank, one hand holding the edge of the toilet seat. His hips and legs—the bones—mimicked the seated position, but were now mostly stripped of tendons, skin, and muscle, as inert and lifeless as strap-on artificial limbs.

The old man was staring at him with wide, bloodshot eyes that were leaking tears down his dark, craggy cheeks.

"It's...OK... It's OK!" Dr. Jones found himself shouting. "We're here to help!"

The man opened his mouth and a pink froth began to bubble over his lips. He said nothing—just a hoarse rustling wheeze of breath came out.

The only other sound in the small bathroom was the

intermittent noise of internal soft tissue dropping from the gradually hollowing-out interior of the man into the toilet bowl.

CHAPTER

9

LEON LAY IN BED WITH HIS LAPTOP BALANCED ON HIS CHEST and a can of Coke within reach on his bedside table. He had a headache brewing and had already taken one of the two aspirin his mom had given him.

He'd spent the last hour surfing DarkEye and UnderTheWire. The forums there were beginning to buzz with excitement over the African plague story. The virus had picked up an informal name among the conspiracy-heads. They were calling it Ebola-Max. It made the outbreak sound like some kind of potent new energy drink.

The various forum posters were loving it, lapping up the unfolding story like it was a Christmas gift. Leon had caught himself beginning to latch on to their gleeful tone. There were posters who were already talking about their survival strategies, how they had "apocalypse bolt-holes" all sorted out and ready for something like this. How they had water and food stashes set aside and an arsenal of firearms ready to defend themselves.

Jeez, they're really getting off on this.

He moved on to Facebook. It seemed the discussion had already begun to spill from the dark underbelly of the internet to social media. There were several threads discussing where the "West African Plague" had sprung from. The opinion gaining most traction was that it was a genetically engineered pathogen. A bioweapon. The usual likely suspects were all being trotted out—the CIA, the North Koreans, Mossad, the Russians.

Another theory that was picking up likes was that it was of extraterrestrial origin. Sci-fi fanboys were quoting that movie from a few years ago, *Prometheus*, talking about "alien goo" designed to "reset" the planet's biomass with an alien-friendly "eco-matrix." The kind of pseudo-science garbage that gullible idiots with barely any scientific knowledge could grab hold of and quote easily, trying to sound smart.

A message popped up in the corner of his screen. It was his dad. Last time he'd tried getting in contact via Facebook Messenger had been months ago. It had been awkward, forced and, well...embarrassing. His dad had wanted to talk about what had happened, why he'd done it, trying to justify the whole thing. Leon didn't want to hear about it, really didn't want to know what "her" name was, and didn't care if they were history or not. It was just plain awkward.

He tried ignoring the message. Then the notification jingled again. Another one. Reluctantly, he opened the message box to see what his dad had written.

> Hey, Leo...big guy, you OK?

> You busy downloading pix of Latisha-X?

> Hey, buddy? MonkeyNuts? U out there?

Leon shook his head. Truly pitiful. He was trying every damned trick in the book: old between-him-and-Leon nicknames, text-spells, trash talk, trying the whole "We're just guys together, huh?" thing.

Leon's dad was a complete asshole; he'd cheated on his mom with some young woman at work. Sure, his mom might have been difficult sometimes, but she didn't deserve to be treated like that. Leon did feel a little sorry for his father. *They* were all here in London, and his dad was alone over there and, he guessed, feeling lonely.

> Why r u still up so late, buddy? Gaming?
Getting your ass kicked, huh? ;-)

Leon rolled his eyes at his dad's ham-fisted gamer lingo. There was something desperately sad about those few words sitting on the screen, trying to sound cool, fun, friendly. His dad, selfish though he was, was still his dad.

> Hi, Dad.

Leon tried resuming trawling the net, looking for breaking-news stories on the virus, but his attention was now on the task bar and, sure enough, a minute later the message icon flashed for his attention.

> Leon. Relieved you responded. You OK over
there in Britain?
> Fine. How's home?

As soon as he'd hit Send, he regretted using the word. Home was here, London—now.

Better get used to it.

> States are fine. Leo, look, I'm worried about
this virus in Africa. You know about that?
> Yes. I watch the news.
> The govt here is taking this thing VERY seriously.
They're talking about locking down borders,
points of entry. From what I can see, it doesn't
seem like the Brits are reacting as quickly.

Leon found himself sitting up in bed. He set his can of Coke down.

> It's all the way over in Africa, Dad.

He waited a full minute for his dad to reply. No longer multi-tasking and filling the wait time looking on some other page.

> Leon, you know with my job I have "high-up"
friends in the govt, right? Well, they're all acting
real funny about this. I think they're spooked.
Which means this is maybe a BIG deal. They're

47

getting ahead of the game. Making plans. I'm worried that you guys are going to be unprepared.

Leon felt the first tickle of fine hairs on his forearms stirring.

> So? What do you want me to do about it?
> I've texted Mom, tried calling her. She won't answer and I'm pretty sure she just deletes my texts without reading them. I want you guys to just be ready, ahead of everyone else, if this thing really does turn out to be serious. OK?
> Is it going to be serious?
> I don't know, Leo. But all the high-ups seem to be getting twitchy. Remember what I told you about herds and watchers?

Leon's dad's job had something to do with the commodities markets, something to do with watching out for early trend indicators. He'd once tried to explain to Leon that the money markets were as fickle and skittish as a herd of gazelles. That every herd had watchers, outliers, that kept a beady eye open for lions as the rest grazed...and that his job was effectively watching the watchers.

> Yeah, I remember.
> Good boy. Mom won't listen to me. But I know you will. I want you to be ready, just in case this thing IS a big deal. Tomorrow get in

some supplies, food and water. Get cans and bottles, OK? Nonperishables. Mom's parents live out in Norfolk. Why don't you suggest to her you guys go out there to see your grandparents this weekend?

Leon felt his head thumping. His migraine was coming back to have another swipe at him. He took the other aspirin and knocked it down with the last dregs of his Coke.

> Leon? Will you do that for me?

A small part of him wanted to tell his dad to just leave him alone. That he'd surrendered his rights as a father, to hand out advice, to be listened to, the day he'd decided that a little fun at work was more important than his family.

> OK.
> You know, I love you and Grace still. I miss the two of you so mu—

Leon shut down his browser and closed the screen of his laptop. He lay back on his bed in the dark, and watched the sodium glow of the streetlamps outside and the passing flare of car headlights play across the low ceiling.

His dad was full of crap. But…

…he did tend to be right about stuff.

CHAPTER

10

"Come on, wake up."

Grace was gone from Leon's room before he could groan in response. She left his bedroom door wide open, so he could hear her banging around noisily in the kitchen. He got dressed and came out.

She was at the breakfast table, a Pop-Tart half-eaten on the plate in front of her, flicking through a magazine. "That African plague of yours?" She nodded at the small television under the window. "They think someone in France might have it now."

"What?" Leon took a bowl from the cupboard and sat down at the table. At the bottom of the screen, a scrolling news update asked:

Has the African plague reached Europe?

The people on the *SKY Breakfast* sofa were talking about a

small town whose name they were all struggling to pronounce correctly. They had a government "expert" on—an epidemiologist—who was giving his take on whether the French thing and the African thing were linked. He looked as if he'd been yanked out of bed, thrown into a suit, and handed a script from which to read.

"...there's really no need for anyone to be unduly alarmed. To be honest, this is far more likely to be an outbreak of foot and mouth. We've had several in France earlier this year and I suspect..."

"Where's Mom?"

"She left already," replied Grace. "She's got an early house showing."

Leon picked up the remote and put on BBC1.

"Hey! I was watching that!" she protested.

"No you weren't."

"I was! There's a thing on Betsy Boomalackah's film coming up—"

"I want to watch some *real* news."

"...about ten o' clock last night. At this stage, there's no further news coming out of the quarantined area around the town. A spokesman for the ECDC said that while there's no reason to assume a direct link to the African virus, no chances are being taken. Michael Emmerson, the minister for transport, confirmed earlier this morning that scheduled flights going in and out of Nigeria will be canceled for the next few days. And recently arrived passengers from certain points of origin, particularly Nigeria, are being traced and may well be quarantined..."

"This is not looking good," Leon muttered.

Grace looked up at him. "You want to know why you get

migraines all the time? It's because you stress about literally everything."

"No I don't."

"You're like one of those little wind-up monkeys with clashing cymbals in their paws."

"Did Mom see the news?"

"I don't know." She shrugged. "She was in a real hurry to get ready."

"...no further details from the team sent into the town of Amoso. The illness remains unidentified, and there is no information yet on how many fatalities there are. Although experts analyzing the cell phone footage that came out of the town have said that while it appears there are images of bodies in the short video, these may well have been victims of the Boko Haram militia, currently pushing south..."

Leon recalled his brief exchange with his dad late last night. He pulled out his phone to see if he'd sent any more messages, but there were none. He wondered if he should tell Grace he'd been in touch with him last night. Probably not. She'd tell their mom, and then his mom would be crabby with him and spend the next few days telling them both how much of a shit their dad was. Not that he disagreed with all of that, but he'd heard enough of it over the last six months.

He poured out his Weetos and drenched them with milk, not realizing this was going to be one of the last "normal" breakfast times he was ever going to experience.

Soon, very soon, it was all going to start falling apart.

CHAPTER

11

Normandy, France

THE FIELD WAS LITTERED WITH THE BODIES OF SEVERAL dozen cows. Many of them half eaten away, as if a highly potent industrial acid had been liberally poured over their carcasses.

Dr. Danielle Menard stepped cautiously toward the nearest of them, trying to avoid the wet soil, soaked with dark liquid oozing from the large, prone form. As she knelt beside the carcass, she switched on her Dictaphone, holding it close to her mask and speaking as loudly and as clearly as she could through the thick rubber.

"We have dairy cows, about thirty of them. They're all dead. The bodies appear to be decaying—no... I'd say *dissolving*, rapidly. Not just soft tissue, but cartilage and hide."

She leaned closer to the body. "Fur, teeth, bones seem to be the only parts of the body that aren't being affected. Or maybe whatever process is occurring takes longer with those things."

She turned off the Dictaphone and stared at the sagging mush in front of her. "This is impossible," she muttered. No pathogen was capable of this kind of process. If someone had told her this field had been hosed down with fluorosulphuric acid half an hour ago, she could have willingly accepted that.

But a pathogen?

Dr. Menard stood up and wandered across the field, toward a barn at the far end. Several more of her team were standing in the open doorway, talking in muffled, unclear voices through their oxygen masks. She could only see their eyes through their plastic visors.

"Danielle, there's more inside," one of them called out. She couldn't tell which one of her coworkers it was, but she guessed from the voice it was Dr. Guillot.

"More cows?"

"It's hard to say. I think so."

She and Guillot were closer than the other team members. She leaned toward him, their eyes met, and she knew, right then, that he was thinking the exact same thing:

This is *the Nigerian bug.*

They'd been rushed out here to investigate. Been told to tell anyone who asked that this was a suspected foot-and-mouth infection site. They'd been told to inspect, to observe, and to get a sample. She could hear Guillot's breathing, the rubber membrane of his mask flapping, and the hiss of air being drawn and expelled with each breath. "Remy," she spoke quietly. "I'm absolutely bloody terrified. I've never seen anything like this."

"No one has," he replied. "There seems to be no species barrier whatsoever."

"This just doesn't happen."

He nodded. "I know."

"And, my God, the rate at which this thing is breaking down those carcasses."

"I know."

Their eyes remained locked, only the hiss and click of their breathing apparatuses breaking the silence.

Finally, Danielle stirred. She ducked inside the barn and began looking around. There were more cattle carcasses here; some of them had clearly still been hooked up to the milking machines when they'd succumbed to the virus, as the pumping machinery still whirred and chugged in the background.

At her feet, she noticed the smaller skeletal remains of what had clearly once been a dog. A red collar with a name tag on it lay among the organic mulch and fur and bones.

"It's liquidizing *every living thing* it comes into contact with."

Guillot nodded. "And it's fast."

Danielle looked down at the dirt floor. At the pools of dark, viscous liquid and the curious linking patterns as one pool trickled toward another. She had some of that gunk on her yellow boots. She couldn't help the urge to scrape it off on the dirt-like dog muck.

"Remy?"

"Yeah?"

"There's no way something like this can be contained." She realized her voice was trembling. She looked at him. "Do you think this is *it*?"

Guillot knew what she meant by that. Over glasses of

after-work wine, they had once discussed epidemiology, getting quite philosophical at times, considering that in the grand narrative of Life on Earth, it was the "little fellows" that told the big story. The subject of a viral extinction level event had cropped up, and they'd both casually agreed, maybe fueled by the bottle of Château Haut-Brion they'd nearly finished between them, that it was likely one day—by natural means or man-made—that mankind wasn't going to vanish with a bang, but with a dry cough and a sniffle.

He was about to say something, maybe agree with her, maybe tell her she was jumping to an overly pessimistic conclusion, when someone outside called her name. She stepped out of the barn into the daylight. Guillot followed her.

"Dr. Menard, Dr. Guillot?"

They both turned to look at the young man who had just come up from the far side of the field.

"What is it?"

He raised an arm and pointed with a gloved hand back at the field. "Look!"

They both turned around to look in the direction he was pointing. "At what?"

"Over there!"

Dr. Menard did as he said, not really sure what it was he had noticed. And then she saw it too—and in that moment she felt a dizzying realization that made her unsteady on her feet.

"Oh God," she gasped.

"What?" Guillot hadn't noticed it yet. "Look, over there...on the grass."

He turned to look where she was pointing. Then he saw it too. Their eyes met again.

"Shit!" he said. "In answer to your question…"

On the field, a cluster of crows lay stranded, flapping their wings spasmodically. Their dark feathers broke free and fluttered away on the breeze.

"…I think this time, we're screwed."

CHAPTER
12

Leon took Grace to school, dropping her off at the front gate. Almost as soon as she stepped inside the school grounds, several of her friends peeled away from various chattering groups and hurried over to offer to carry her shoulder bag.

Queen bee of the playground.

Leon sighed. *She always fits in so easily.* She always had. He envied that about her.

He watched her go, flanked by her two best friends, both babbling into one ear, each eager to outdo the other with whatever inane gossip they'd managed to scoop overnight.

She glanced back over her shoulder and offered him a tight, motherly smile that quite clearly said, *Try to make an effort today, OK?*

He waggled a hand at her and watched through the gate until she'd disappeared inside.

He had half a mind to skip school today. He was exhausted after last night's restlessness. His dad's few words over messenger had been playing on his mind. And, also, his head was thumping like crazy this morning. His mom was usually lenient when it came to his headaches. She knew they were nasty, made him feel nauseous sometimes. They'd been to the doctor; he'd had an eye test and even a scan. Apparently his eyes were fine, and there was nothing on the scan to worry about. Their doctor said more than likely it was simply stress. Probably caused by recent events: the split up, the move, the new school. He said he saw plenty of students with identical symptoms every year as the months rolled up to exam time. His mom had even taken him to a therapist, and she'd said pretty much the same thing, although she'd prescribed a diary, not pills.

"In your diary, I want you to write to your father. Talk to him. Tell him how you feel, what's bugging you. Write to him like you're talking to him, as if he's right there. Just a few sentences every day."

He'd bought one. Hadn't used it yet though.

Leon decided today was probably a day best spent at home under the duvet. Because this wasn't just another headache. This felt like the start of a cold; his throat felt rough and his neck ached. He wanted to go home and sleep, maybe down another couple of aspirin. He could crash on the couch and watch the news all day.

Hey, MonkeyNuts, is that it? Is that what this is all about? Skipping school so you can watch the news?

He wasn't entirely sure. Maybe he was trying to convince himself he was coming down with man flu, instead of admitting that he was doing exactly what Grace had said he was doing on the bus ride in.

You obsess about things, Leon. You do. Seriously, you're like a dog with a bone. I swear you're on the spectrum somewhere! Another phrase she'd picked up without really understanding it, but it sounded convincing when she said it.

"Jeez…get a grip," Leon muttered to himself. Every year, it seemed, there was an apocalyptic plague story. He could imagine news editors around the world holding a news story like this in reserve ready to whip it out on a slow news day. If it wasn't SARS, it was bird flu. If it wasn't bird flu, it was swine flu…or a resurgence of meningitis or HIV. The news thrived on scare stories, whether it was plagues or terrorist threats or "video games that'll turn your teenaged son into a gun-toting psychopath."

He shook his head as he walked back through the Kings Arcade. In contrast to the news he used to watch back in New Jersey, stations like FOX or CNN, the BBC news seemed to be a lot less foaming at the mouth and excitable. Almost laid-back, by comparison.

Maybe his dad's perception was colored by the way the news was reported over there, because, frankly, looking around, he wasn't seeing any signs of panic here; he was seeing business as usual.

He walked past the glass front of the mall's electronics store. In the window, a large tablet screen was streaming Sky News 24. There was bulletin tickertape scrolling beneath, the image of a reporter in the field.

> *WEST AFRICAN VIRUS: Several infection sites confirmed in Europe.*

He stopped where he was.

Infection sites also confirmed in India, South Africa, Egypt…

The list continued. "Shit," he said.

"It's getting a bit unsettling isn't it?" He turned to see a woman standing beside him, just like him, caught midstride by what was on the tickertape.

He nodded. "First I heard about this thing was, like, yesterday over breakfast."

"Me too. I heard someone on the tube saying it might be an ISIS thing…like a terrorist biological weapon or something."

He looked at her. "Really?"

She hunched her shoulders. "It's what I heard." She looked down at the two plastic shopping bags in her hands. "I know it's probably silly, an overreaction…but I thought I might get some extra bits and pieces in. Some extra milk and bread…just in case." The woman almost looked embarrassed as she admitted it. She shrugged. "Anyway…" Then she turned and continued walking up the mall.

Leon watched the screen for another minute. The tickertape was repeating the same things and the reporter had now been replaced by a return to the studio and some other news story. He set off, his pace just that little bit more urgent, keen to get back home, turn on his laptop and the TV.

Twenty minutes later, he was back home and on the couch, wrapped in a quilt with the laptop resting on his legs and the TV remote in his hand. He sipped at his steaming mug of Lemsip cold medicine, still trying to convince himself he was simply coming down with a cold rather than stressing himself into a storming headache.

He put CNN on—the *international* station. Unlike the let's-all-be-calm-and-not-get-excited-here BBC, they were all over the virus story. They were calling it Super-Ebola, because it seemed they didn't know what else to call it. He saw a map of the world being superimposed in the background with red dots marked up on it—there were thirty or forty of them, evenly spaced, not clustered around a particular country or city, just dotted evenly. And as he watched the graphic on-screen, several more dots appeared on the map like cartoon measles. If this wasn't so serious a story, he could imagine the sound-effect guys would have played a *boing-boing* sound as each new dot appeared.

He logged on to the DarkEye website.

The site's forum was buzzing about Super-Ebola. All the other usual topic threads had been bumped right off the landing page. The site's home page was one long list of headlines and links that wandered down off the screen, each one being commented on by hundreds...no, *thousands* of people.

There were reports of infection now coming in, it seemed, from pretty much every country in the world. And cell phone photos...lots of them.

He clicked on the images, many of them poor in quality, blurred, shaken, and pixelated—pictures taken quickly by frightened people. The images seemed to be largely the same: streets littered with piles of clothes. In the background, the car license plates changed, the languages on roadside signs changed, but in virtually every picture, the scene was essentially the same—humps of clothes, presumably bodies, lying in roads, half-in or half-out of cars, in the doorways of buildings.

In some of the less hastily taken, clearer images, he could just about make out other curious details. The bodies looked...old. Like they'd been dead for some time. They reminded him of some of the grisly images of exhumed bodies from mass graves in places like Syria or Bosnia: all bones and rotten, degraded material. In one picture, he could see the bodies of an entire family on a pale tile floor... They seemed to be linked together by dark, snaking lines of string, as if someone had drawn a spider web over the image in Photoshop.

"What is that?" he muttered.

He turned his attention to the comments, scrolling down to the most recent entries on the last added headline.

Posted 11:37 a.m.—xaanMan

It's global culling. This has government skunk-works written all over it. Those pics look like the Kurdistan gassing pictures from back in Saddam's time. This Ebola+ stuff is a stupid decoy name. No way it's biological. It's chemical frickin warfare.

Posted 11:38 a.m.—Lenny1234

You're a paranoid idiot. What? U think it's the big old evil military/industrial complex again? NeoCons out to destroy the world? Moron. It's hitting us here in the States just like every-where else.

Posted 11:38 a.m.—DarkHorse3

I'm getting scared. They not telling us anything on RTU news. All they saying is that situation is under control and not panic.

Posted 11:38 a.m.—Garpy-n-nan

I'm not seeing "new" bodies in those pictures. They all look old. Are they even real bodies? Whatsup? I think this is a big hoax.

Posted 11:39 a.m.—kilbofraggins

Those ARE REAL bodies, asshole. This virus is like Ebola but a thousand times worse! People are being turned into liquid within a few hours.

Posted 11:39 a.m.—XllnnGng

I'm a microbiology grad and I'm telling every-one here there's no way this is a natural pathogen. Nature just doesn't operate this fast. A successful virus doesn't kill its host in minutes, that's crazy, because it needs a host to act as both a transport unit and as a factory producing more of it. Any virus that can kill this quick wouldn't even end up getting going in the first place. It would become extinct with patient zero.

Posted 11:40 a.m.—GunProm

How come this shit is happening everywhere? Surely there should be some sort of spread pattern? You know, spreading via airplanes, airports, and so on. Unless it's airborne, but even then you'd get a pattern.

Posted 11:40 a.m.—JerryMcD

Anyone here stunned at how quickly this is happening? I mean this time yesterday we were all discussing the latest IOS Trojan, and now it feels like arma-frickin-geddon. You want my dollar's worth? It feels like this was a synchronized job. Terrorists, maybe those ISIS scumbags, placed around the world with vials of this nightmare, and then they all dropped their vials at the same frickin time.

Leon rubbed his eyes. He felt completely wasted—weary, tired. His joints ached, and even with his duvet wrapped around him like a poncho, he couldn't get warm enough. And, for a moment, a shudder of fear passed through him.

Oh, crap... Maybe I've got it?

He spent five panic-stricken minutes scanning through the forum, doing a search on "symptoms," "early symptoms," "Ebola+," and "flu-like symptoms."

And got nothing back.

Jeez, relax, MonkeyNuts... It's just a cold.

He was already feeling a little better than he had first thing this morning, with the Lemsip now inside him.

Seriously...if Lemsip's happily dealing with what you've got, then you're probably OK. No need to freak out, all right?

He still felt tired though, and his head was thumping. He finished the last of his hot drink, settled back on the cushion, and rested his heavy eyes.

He closed them for a moment, fully intending to just doze for five minutes and then read some more. But his dizzy mind reliably assured him that there wasn't a lot he could do right now. Reading a website and watching the news wasn't actually going to change anything. All it was doing was stressing him out and making his head worse. It might be a good idea to crash out for a while.

Get some perspective, moron.

He was pretty sure by the time this cold—if it *was* a cold—had come and gone and he was back at school, the world's news stations and conspiracy nerds would have moved on to some brand-new, shiny news story to get all worked up about.

Ain't that always the way, Leo? The world goes on...and on... and nothing ever really changes.

CHAPTER
13

Soho, Central London

IT FLUTTERED DOWN TO EARTH, AN ANONYMOUS DOT OF LIFE—
not even life yet. Something dormant, inert. A light breeze, the
upward warming gust of the city below, kept it dancing and airborne, a small flake just visible to the naked eye.

This particular dot had been in a slow descent over the last
few days, a protracted and leisurely free fall entirely at the whim
of the warm air currents that had carried it aloft from hotter,
more humid climates. A long and leisurely journey northward to
cooler places.

But since dawn of this particular day, the speck had been gradually descending toward the busy urban carpet below, drawing
close to the source of that noise—a hum of activity, traffic, the
occasional faint peal of a police siren.

Finally, as the morning sun peered over the city and flashed rays of light through the spokes of the London Eye, the speck's graceful descent came to an end, as a chance downward gust of wind pushed it horizontally, to settle on the plastic rim of a grimy window box, sitting high up on a soot-encrusted windowsill overlooking a relatively quiet backstreet in Soho.

The sound of life was all around now: the distant rumble of traffic on Tottenham Court Road reaching the far end of this quiet cul-de-sac, the cooing and flutter of pigeons on another ledge nearby, the tinny rattle of music drifting from the open window of a building opposite, and the echoing clang of scaffolding poles being tossed from the back of a flatbed truck farther up the street.

Amid all this, the small flake, the particle, remained lifeless. It had yet to be revived from its deep sleep.

But this was about to happen.

Another gentle gust nudged the particle along the plastic rim of the flower box—just a couple of inches, but that was far enough.

The particle met a solitary drop of rainwater.

It was finally time to wake up, to stir, to change from a dormant grain of genetic material, to something else—a living agent. *Life.*

The moisture permeated its husk, rehydrating the package inside. Biochemical machinery began to stir, to reboot, and the fragment of life began to listen to simple, ancient genetic commands to begin its work.

Others like it were out there, caught by the air currents in the upper troposphere and deposited in other countries and continents... Many would fail to awaken, because they hadn't encountered liquid water, or had been incinerated as the tiny micrometeorite on which they'd been hitching a lift had exploded in the upper atmosphere. But this one particle, like a few others, found a fertile foothold.

Home, for the moment, was on this lofty fifth-floor windowsill.

The awakening was gradual. The first single-cell life form it encountered within the microworld of the water droplet was an uneven battle of lightweights. The cell succumbed to the much larger dot of life and was absorbed and stripped of its resources—a veritable feast for this hungry organism. But simple genetic commands compelled it to do more than merely feed. Its primary objective at this stage was replication. A toehold was all it had in this droplet-of-water world. A larger microorganism with an appetite for upstart newcomers could easily have overwhelmed it. It needed help; it needed more copies of itself. Replication was the highest priority.

Very soon it had "fathered" a copy of itself, and now both of them were working hard on replicating again.

Twenty minutes passed. At this point, if someone had examined the droplet under a magnifying glass, they might have just detected the faintest dark smudge in the middle. Under a microscope, they would have seen the faint, feathered line of this growing community, now numbering tens of thousands, beginning to reach out and explore.

An hour later, the raindrop was a viscous little bubble as black as ink. Several threadlike strands had emerged from it and stretched along the plastic rim of the window box. Another precious raindrop had been encountered by one of these, and a chemical signal had been fed back along the thread to the "home world" that a nearby satellite, rich in resources, had just been encountered.

The thread thickened ever so slightly as thousands of cells reinforced it, eager to feast on the new droplet of water and the hapless cells of amoeba floating inside it.

By the time another full hour had passed, the plastic rim of the window box had been colonized, and a thicker, more adventurous thread had found its way down the plastic rim to the rich, fertile soil in which several stunted geraniums had done their best to flower.

The dark soil was a veritable buffet of cellular life. Like Victorian-era naturalists on safari, slaughtering the new species they came across, then carefully preserving, stuffing, and sketching the corpses, this colony of the curious encountered, absorbed, deconstructed, and stored the genetic information it was gathering in its growing chemical pool.

While the soil was becoming a soup, the geraniums remained unaffected. Their cellulose membrane was as impenetrable as the plastic of the window box.

The conquest of this tiny ecosystem, perched up on the grubby, soot-covered, fifth-floor windowsill, was coming along nicely... Then a much grander prize landed nearby.

A pigeon.

The bird studied the windowsill, looking for crumbs. It had learned from experience that ledges populated with clutter like this sometimes yielded interesting morsels. A keen, beady eye surveyed the stone of the sill but found nothing of interest.

It hopped up on to the green plastic of the window box and

looked curiously at the flowering geraniums, slowly drooping as their roots' hold on the soil softened. It stepped sideways along the box rim. One stunted foot stepped on that first colonized drop of rainwater, home of the founding fathers of this thriving community.

As the pigeon shuffled along another step, several thousand spores were carried away on the bottom of its claw.

The pigeon lost interest in this lonely window ledge and instinctively assumed there were richer pickings down in the busy, bustling world below. With a flutter of wings, it was gone, swooping down along the quiet backstreet, over the flatbed truck where half a dozen workmen were dismantling scaffolding poles, toward the hubbub of activity at the far end.

And, all the while, the several thousand passengers it carried on its foot had already, eagerly started their work.

CHAPTER
14

Grace woke him up when she got home. "And where were you?"

Leon jerked fully awake on the couch. One hand went up to his still throbbing forehead. "Oh no..."

"You were supposed to meet me at the school gate!" Grace stared down at him sternly, her good arm crossed with the one in the sling as she tapped a foot impatiently.

"Sorry, Grace... I just..."

She sighed, then flapped a hand his way. "Don't worry about it. I got some useful networking in. I got to walk home with Peter Durst. He's, like, *the* popular guy in the year...so, you're good." She disappeared into the kitchen to get something out of the fridge.

"Don't tell Mom, OK?"

Her head poked out of the doorway. "That all depends on how nice you are to me."

Leon nodded. She had leverage. His mom was paranoid about

letting Grace walk home alone through Hammersmith. Surely it was no worse here in London than New York. This place was all leafy alleys and busy streets and sweet old ladies with wheelie carts. Not exactly the projects.

"I need a favor!" Grace called from the kitchen.

He pulled himself wearily off the couch and joined her. She was standing at the counter with a bag of sliced white bread and a jar of peanut butter beside her. "Two handed job, bruv, innit?"

He winced at her mock London accent.

Sighing, he made her sandwich. He looked at her arm in its sling. "Don't get too used to me being your servant. That arm's going to heal one day."

She shrugged. "How's your head today?"

"Sore. I'm ready for another aspirin."

"How many have you had?"

"One at breakfast," he lied. "What about you?"

"Arm's really aching. Some kid bumped into me in the hallway. Practically knocked me on my ass." She fluttered her eyelids. "Then *Peter*, my knight in shining armor, sorted him out for me."

Leon shook his head. "Jeez…didn't take you long to get your claws into this school."

She blew a raspberry at him.

He pulled a glass from the dish drainer, filled it with tepid water, and popped a pill from the bottle.

"You know, Leon, you really just need to, like, stress less." She took a hearty bite of her peanut butter sandwich. "That's what all these headaches and nosebleeds are—it's you being totally neurotic and stuff."

"*Neurotic?* Where do you pick this stuff up?"

"Yeah, neurotic! I know...new word. Yay for me. But, seriously, you sulk and worry about, like, *everything*."

"Yeah, well..." He didn't have an answer better than that. He was saved by the ringtone of his phone. Pulling it out of his jeans, he stared at the screen.

"That Mom?" asked Grace. "Tell her—"

He shook his head. He let it ring another couple of times, reluctant to answer.

"Well? You gonna get it or not?" prompted Grace.

"Uh...it's Dad."

She tucked her sandwich into her sling, then flipped her middle finger at him. "Tell Dad *that's* from me."

He tapped the screen and held the phone to his ear. "So, what's up...Dad?"

"Leon, *don't* hang up on me!"

"I wasn't going to. I—"

"Leon, I need you to listen very carefully to me." The line was crackly. "This African virus is spreading fast. The media over here is being pressured to downplay the whole story, but I'm telling you the government is *rattled*. They're taking action...but they're doing it quietly."

"Uh-huh."

"Leon, I need more than a grunt from you."

"God, Dad...I'm listening!"

"What does *he* want?" sniffed Grace. She turned her back on him, grabbed her sandwich, and left the kitchen.

"Leon, I need you and Grace and Mom to get out of the city.

74

Go visit your grandparents and stay there! Do it before this thing hits the UK."

"Dad, we can't. Mom's got a job now. I've got school. Grace has to go to school. We can't just—"

"Screw that! This thing is already in Europe! Do you know about those migrant ships?"

"Uh...no. I've been at sch—"

"It was mentioned on the news over here this morning. Then they dropped the story like a goddamned brick. There are thousands of boats adrift on the Mediterranean, *fleets* of them...hundreds of thousands of people, *millions*, fleeing Africa. The media are doing their best to link it to an escalation of various conflicts over there—to terrorists, radicals—but they're not saying what this is *really* about."

"The virus?"

"For God's sake, yes!"

Leon wandered into the living room. Grace was on the couch, flicking through TV channels, texting, and attempting to eat, all one-handed.

"I don't know if the BBC or any Euro stations are making much of it yet, but the point is everyone I know over here who has contact with the government is grabbing their kids and heading out of town!"

"Dad...come on. Just, like, chill—"

"Leon, don't you think it's damned odd that twenty-four hours ago the news was jumping on another exciting virus story...and now they're hardly mentioning it?"

Leon silently nodded—not that his dad would see that. But maybe he had a point.

"Look, maybe I'm overreacting, but...I want you guys out of London as soon as possible."

Leon grabbed the remote control from Grace's hand—

"Hey!"

—and cycled through the stations until he hit BBC News 24. The volume was down low but on the screen was an armada of bobbing, overladen fishing vessels being circled by Italian navy speedboats.

"Well...it's on the news here," said Leon. He read the ticker-tape at the bottom. "'Sudden spike in migrant ships as African unrest escalates.'"

"OK, so they *are* reporting it. But *unrest*? God! Not using the word *virus* or *plague*?"

"No...not those words."

"That's it, Son. That's the big goddamn warning sign, right there! They're locking the story down. If they're doing that already, then this thing is bad, Leo. It's not good."

His dad was beginning to scare him. Leon wanted to hang up but couldn't bring himself to do it.

"What's going on over there, Leo? Are the Brits doing any-thing? Are they closing down borders yet? Are they turning them back? Are they taking this thing *seriously*?"

"Jeez, Dad..." His voice was cracking and beginning to sound shrill. "Calm down, will you?"

"Are they taking *any* action at all?"

"I don't know! Look, I just got back from school"—a small white lie—"and I really—"

"Leon, listen. When does Mom get back home?"

"About six, usually."

"Right...that's lunchtime for me. I'm calling you back then. I want you to tell Mom to *take my call* and not hang up on me, OK?"

"Sure. But she won't—"

"Make sure she talks to me!"

Leon shrugged. "I'll try..."

"Good...good boy." Leon thought for a moment that his dad had hung up. The line crackled and rustled.

"Dad? You still there?"

"Leon...I...I'm really sorry you guys are stuck over there and I'm stuck here."

"Well...you know, that's kinda all your doing."

"I know, I know. But that doesn't stop me loving you and Grace...and your mom."

Yeah...Mom...sure.

"Leon, remember that story I used to read you? The wheels on the wagon?"

It was an old picture book Leon's dad had grown up with about a wagon train crossing the Wild West. The repeated mantra of their grizzled trail guide had been, *Watch them bolts on them wheels, folks! They come off, you're stuck out here. The wagon train goes on without you...and you're as good as dead!*

"The wheel's going to come off, Leon...real soon. I just want to make sure you guys react before the rest... OK? You've got to make sure you're one step ahead... That's all. *Just one step.*"

The call disconnected. He looked down at Grace. Her brows were raised.

"Well...that sounded pretty intense."

"I told you! I'm not bloody well speaking to him!"

"He's calling back, Mom. He said you *have* to speak to him."

His mom shot a quick glance at Grace, then back at Leon. As far as she was concerned, the cheating bastard was history, someone else's life. She didn't care what he was doing, whoever he was with right now, whether he was alive or dead. Her name was no longer Jennifer Friedmann; it was Jennifer Button, the name she'd been born with and every piece of plastic in her handbag—credit cards, loyalty cards, discount cards—said the same thing.

"I'm not talking to him. You...go right ahead. I can't stop you. But I'm—"

"It's about that virus. The African virus."

She shrugged a what-the-hell look at him. "And what's *that* got to do with him...or me?"

Leon looked down at his phone. It was ten after six. Maybe his dad wasn't going to call after all. "He's just worried about us."

"*Worried!*" She barked out a humorless laugh. "Well, it would've been nice if he'd been *worrying* about us when he decided to sleep with—" She stopped herself abruptly.

Grace rolled her eyes and muttered. "I know what he did, Mom. You don't need to censor yourself for me."

"Mom, this thing is getting pretty serious. Dad said the news stations are playing it down...and, if they're doing that, then things might be worse than we think."

Leon's phone suddenly vibrated in his hand. He looked down at the screen. It was his dad. His mom shook her head. "Don't answer it. I'm not speaking to him!"

Leon swiped the screen. "Dad, it's me... Mom's right here."

"Leon!" She thumped the arm of the couch with her fist and shook her head. Leon held his phone out to her. "Mom!" he snapped. "Take it!"

She closed her eyes tightly, then after a moment's hesitation, snatched the phone from him. "What do you want, Tom?" she said icily.

Leon expected his mom to listen to his dad's opening few words, then either toss the phone back at him or launch into a shouting match. Instead...she was silent. He studied her face, locked perfectly still except for a frown slowly forming between her brows.

"When?" she said finally.

She was listening. Leon turned to look at Grace. She'd put her own phone down for once and was watching their mom's face too. For the first time in God knows how many months, his little sister actually looked...*concerned.*

Another long silence. Leon's mom's frown was deepening, and the color seemed to be draining from her face.

"Seriously?" She wandered out of the living room, into the kitchen, and out of earshot.

"I guess this must be pretty serious," said Grace. "They're actually, like, *talking* to each other."

Leon nodded slowly. "Dad sounded...real twitchy. *Scared.*"

"But...Dad doesn't do scared," said Grace. For the first time in a long time, Leon's younger sister's normally composed face, prematurely teenaged, all heavy lidded and confident and sooo certain, ever the congresswoman in waiting...began to soften into that of a twelve-year-old girl. "Leo...is this *really* bad?"

"I don't know."

They could hear the murmur of their mom's voice, lowered almost to a whisper. Leon got up off the couch and was about to take several light steps toward the kitchen when he heard the last few words of the phone call.

"...and you too, Tom...you too."

Their mom came out of the kitchen, looking as pale as a ghost. "Five minutes."

"Mom?"

"Both of you. You've got five minutes to pack some clothes... one bag each. Then we're leaving."

CHAPTER
15

THE EIGHT THIRTY OUT OF LIVERPOOL STREET TO NORWICH was one of the last of the rush-hour trains, busy with a mixture of frazzled-looking *I stay later than the next guy* types and sloppy *one or two drinks after work* types.

The train rocked and rattled out of the station. Their car was silent except for a couple of men several seats down noisily breaking down the results of some soccer match. Leon looked around. Pretty much everyone else was staring at a phone or tablet. He could see the red flash of the BBC banner in the reflection of the dark window beside him.

News...everyone's checking the news.

"Mom," whispered Grace. The same question again. The same one they'd both asked over and over on the subway. "Come on. What did Dad say?"

"Please...Grace, just give it a rest. I said I'll tell you when we get to Grandma and Grandad's."

"But I've got really important schoolwork to hand in tomorrow!"

"I'll call the school and tell them you're not feeling well. Now just…please, be quiet and let me think."

An old man was sitting across the table from them. He looked up from his phone. "Getting out of the city?" he said quietly.

Leon's mom flicked a polite, noncommittal smile at him and nodded.

"Because of…the news?" he added softly.

The news? Leon inwardly laughed at the term he'd used. No one seemed to want to say the *V* word, the *P* word. No one seemed eager to look like a panicking idiot.

Except us.

"Yes," she admitted.

He nodded approvingly. "One step ahead of the herd. Very sensible." He turned his phone around so she could see his screen. "I go to Reuters for my news. Things look a lot more worrying the way they're being reported there."

Leon leaned forward. "My dad's really worried."

The man cocked his head. "Is that an American accent I detect there?"

Leon nodded. "But actually I'm British."

"His father's an American," added Leon's mom. "He's in New York."

"I see they're not taking any chances over there. Martial law? Mobilizing the National Guard?"

"That's exactly what Dad said. But over here?" Leon shrugged. "It's, like, hey, no big deal."

The man smiled. "I know. *Don't panic. Don't panic. It'll all be fine. Just sit tight have a cup of tea and watch* EastEnders."

Leon's mom laughed politely. "What about you?" She looked around the car to check if anyone appeared to be listening in on their conversation. "Are you taking, you know, precautionary...steps?"

"I live in a quiet little village. I've got water and canned food and bottled gas central heating. I suppose we'll be fine to sit tight for a few weeks." He tapped the screen of his phone. "And I suspect tomorrow... I might just decide to call in sick." He winked at Leon. "I'd rather look the silly, old fool than be caught at work."

———————

"Oh, marvelous." Stewie Delaney spotted the red signal up ahead and sighed. He eased the pressure off the speed-control lever and gradually pulled on the brake handle.

They'd finally emerged from the stop-start snarl of train signals out of London and left the sickly nighttime glow of endless urban sprawl behind and were now entering the relative darkness of the countryside. An irritating buzz of radio traffic came from the speaker beside him: comments from other train drivers behind him about the tail-end-of-the-day train congestion, inappropriate quips about unlucky passengers racing and gasping to catch the train as it pulled out. (Commuter Bingo: one point for each passenger left stranded; five points if they raise a fist; ten if they hurl their bags to the platform in frustration as the train pulls out.) And there was somebody bitching about today's news of the vast flotilla of migrant ships: "Just what we need. Looks like they've *all* decided to come over!"

Stewie had been hoping it was going to be a straight run out to Norwich. Two more hours and then he was done for the day. The train finally lurched to a halt, and he picked up the radio controller. "Stewie on the nine from Liverpool Street. Dave, what's the red light for? I thought you said it was an all clear ahead for me?"

The speaker crackled beside him. "All right, Stew? Sorry, mate, I thought you were still back at Manningtree. I was just about to call you."

"Call me about what?"

"Obstruction on the tracks."

"Where?"

"Hold on..." The line was left open; Stewie could hear other voices in the background, somebody sneezing, then apologizing. "OK...you're waiting at signal N32, right?"

"Yeah."

"It's right up ahead of you, then."

Just up ahead was an overpass. Stewie closed his eyes and sat back. *Please...not another jumper.* He'd had one last year. Seen the mess on the tracks, then made the mistake of finding out about the woman...her story. Discovered what chain of events had led her to do such a pointless and tragic thing. Big mistake.

He'd ended up with a name, a face, enough to haunt him for years to come.

"Dave, please tell me it's not another jumper."

"Relax...someone just called it in. Looks like an animal."

He sucked in a deep breath. "Thank Christ for that. How long are we going to be waiting here?"

"Not good news. I've called section maintenance and they said it might take an hour to get someone down there to clear it off."

"Shit." Stewie tapped his fingers on the console for a moment. "Dave, how big is it? Are we talking *cow* big?"

"The caller said it might be a dog or sheep or something."

"Well for Christ's sake. I'll just kick it off the tracks."

"Uh…Stew, come on, mate. You know you can't do that. Union rules. Health and safe—"

Stewie switched channels. "Ladies and gents, this is the driver. Sorry about the temporary stoppage. We've got a red signal up ahead. Apparently there's an animal on the tracks. I've been advised we should be on our way soon."

He unclipped his seat harness…

Damn health and safety.

…and opened the door to step down onto the gravel bed.

Stewie's dad had been a driver back in the good ol' days of British Rail. How many times had he booted a dead dog or deer off the tracks…and *survived* to tell the tale?

Flippin' ridiculous health-'n'-safety managers these days.

The train's headlights illuminated the rails and steel ties clearly for a hundred yards. His shadow stretched out ahead of him in extended sharp relief. He started down the apron of track, gravel crunching noisily beneath his boots.

Health 'n' bloody safety. Stewie was amazed anybody got anything done these days. Just a small dose of common sense was all that was needed. They could sit here like a bunch of Muppets for an hour waiting for some "qualified" external contractor to kick it aside. Or he could just get off his arse and do it himself.

He could see it already—a small, pale carcass. It looked like a lamb or a sheep.

Small enough to grab by its hooves or trotters, or whatever damned thing you called its feet, and swing it aside. He closed the last few dozen yards and then squatted down in front of it.

Stewie curled his lips in disgust. It looked like the train before his had gone over it already and pulverized it. Turned it into raw kebab meat.

"Lovely," he grunted. He pulled the cuffs of his high-visibility jacket down to cover his hands, then grabbed the animal's hind legs. They came away from the carcass with a sucking sound, like loose drumsticks pulled from a well-cooked roast-in-a-bag Sunday chicken.

"Ugh."

He swung the legs and tossed them away into a clump of nettles beside the tracks. The rest of the body looked like a mess of minced meat and fluff. Its head was caved in like a deflated balloon.

He stood up. "Right. Good enough."

The carcass wasn't an obstruction, certainly no danger of derailing him. He turned around and headed back up the tracks toward his waiting train. A minute later, he pulled himself back up into his compartment. He clipped his safety belt back on and picked up the mike.

"Ladies and gents, the obstruction on the tracks is clear now... just waiting on a green signal to go."

He switched channels. "Dave, it's Stewie. I just kicked the thing off. I'm good to go."

There was no response from Dave. Unusual. "Helloo? It's

Stewie again, mate. The obstruction's been cleared. You can cancel the maintenance lads. Can I have a green, please?"

Another minute waiting, then the speaker finally crackled. "Sorry, Stew, did you say you cleared it?"

"Yup. What's going on there? Did I catch you having a dump?"

"No...we...uh...we're getting a lot of traffic from *above.*" The young lad sounded harried. Distracted. Stewie had never met Dave. Just knew the voice from five years of running Norwich to London. He had a mental picture of some gawky, pale bloke with a pronounced Adam's apple and thick glasses.

"Problems?"

"I don't know... Something about terrorist action in London, maybe? I dunno... It's all mixed messages coming down from the controllers."

"Terrorists? What, like a bomb or something?"

"I dunno. Looks like they want to shut down all the London stations *immediately.*"

"Well I'm *out* of London, thank God, so any chance I can have my green light?"

"You said you cleared the obstruction?"

Stewie nodded. He caught sight of his face reflected in the dark windshield. "Yeah, it was just a bunch of mush. Decomposed sheep, I think. Must have been there for days."

He could see a small, dark spot on his left cheek. He swiped at it and looked at his finger. A smear of blood. *Oh, lovely.* He picked up the napkin that had come with his Starbucks coffee and vigorously rubbed his cheek clean. He looked at the pink-stained paper for a moment, then tossed it out of the window.

"Dave? Come on, mate. Just flip that switch for me."

"Yup, sorry. There you go, Stew. Green light. You'll have a good run back. Looks like you're going to be the last train up to Norwich tonight."

The light up ahead changed to green. "Cheers, mate. Catch you again on Monday."

CHAPTER
16

As the train began to roll forward, clanking and clattering over bolted joints, Leon's phone vibrated. He looked at the screen. "It's Dad." He looked at his mom.

She nodded. "Might as well."

He swiped his phone. "You OK, Dad?"

"That you, Leon?" He mustn't have heard him answering. The line was rustling with interference.

"Dad? What's goin—"

"It's *here*, Leo! *It's right here in the city!*"

"What? In...New York?"

"Yes! There are people dying in the goddamn streets!"

Leon's mom grabbed his arm. "What's he saying?"

Leon ignored her. "Dad...where are you? Are you safe?"

"Leo...listen to me, Son! Listen! Stay inside! Do *not* go outside! It's in the—"

"Dad, you said we should try and get out of London!"

"Listen to me! This thing is airborne! They're saying it's like flakes. Stay inside! Stay at home. Tape up your windows and doors and *stay inside!*"

"But we're on a train, Dad. You said get out of London. You told us to—"

"I know. Shit...shit..."

Leon could hear voices in the background, the familiar echoing wail of a NYPD siren.

"Are you close to Mom's family? Are you near to Norwich?"

"I don't know. Train's about halfway, I guess."

"OK, soon as you get there, you tell Mom, you tell Mom's parents, they gotta stay inside. Do you understand me?! Stay inside, close the windows. Don't go out again!"

"OK, Dad." He could hear his father's labored breathing on the end of the line. There were other voices in the background, car horns beeping, more sirens joining in the chorus. "Dad? Are...are *you* outside?"

"Yuh...I'm just... Shit... Gimme a second..."

Grace reached out for the phone. Leon shook her hand off.

"Is Dad OK?" she asked. "What's happening?"

He answered her question by pulling the phone away from his ear and putting it on speakerphone. They all listened to the crackle and rustle of the call, their father's panting breath, distant screaming voices. A gunshot.

Grace's eyes rounded. "What's happening?"

"Dad?" shouted Leon. "Dad! Was that a gun?"

"Listen to me." The noises were suddenly muted. He must have stepped inside somewhere and closed a door behind him. He was panting heavily. "Listen... This thing's in the air. You can *see* it, like...like *flakes*. It's fast! It's killing people everywhere...touching their skin then they're dying and melting..."

The phone signal began to break up.

"—on't let it *touch* you...the flakes! Don't—"

"Dad, your signal's going out. We can't hear what you're saying!"

"...liquid... There's lines of it all over the... Do not let it...you... Do...understand? *Do not*..."

"Dad?"

"...love you...love...both... God...I... Hey! Get out of my goddamn way—"

The call disconnected. Leon looked up from his phone, at his sister, at his mom, at the old man sharing the table with them, at the three commuters sitting around the table across the narrow aisle. All of them staring at him, wide-eyed, as if he were the messenger delivering news of the apocalypse.

"That call... Your call just then? That was from New York?" asked a woman sitting at the opposite table.

Leon nodded.

"Oh God. My daughter lives..." She didn't finish her words. Instead, she reached into her bag for her phone.

"Was that about that West African virus thing?" asked one of the two men sitting across the table from her.

Leon nodded again as he quickly tried callback, but there was nothing but a flat digital tone. He tried again and got the same thing.

"Miriam?" The old man sitting opposite Leon was already on

his phone. "It's Ben. What? I know... It's getting rather worrying, isn't it? Look, call the children!...What?...I know! Call them anyway and tell them..."

A minute ago, their car had been silent, save for the ticking of a heater, a few murmured conversations, the hiss of a young woman's headphones, and the occasional irritated sigh from the woman sitting next to her trying to read on her Kindle. Even the three drunk young men farther up the car had finally managed to settle down and were sleeping off the alcohol. Now, all of a sudden, the car was filled with the gabble of one-sided conversations. A ripple effect rolled down either side of the aisle: a murmured question from one commuter to another, a whispered answer, the answer evolving, mutating, as it passed from mouth to ear to mouth again. Unrest turning into concern, concern turning into alarm, phones coming out, and calls being made home.

"Mom," whispered Grace. "Dad's in real trouble, isn't he?"

"I don't know, love." She was on her phone, dialing her parents. "It sounds like we might *all* be in a bit of trouble." Leon stared out into the dark night as the clattering train picked up speed. It all looked so normal out there. The railway embankment had sloped down now, to give him a view of small office complexes, tidy rows of businesses with trucks parked in the back of each, and asphalt bathed in the ever-present, fizzing, sodium-orange blanket of urban lighting. In contrast to this, his imagination was filling in details of downtown New York. It would be midafternoon over there. Leon knew what it would normally be like—Manhattan, tourist-busy right now; a couple more hours and it would be commuter-busy. How many times had he taken the train under the Hudson River to Manhattan after high school for a couple of hours to hang out with his friends? Coffee in a Dunkin' Donuts, talking gamer stuff, grabbing free Wi-Fi and a view across Times Square.

What he was imagining right now was all that normality replaced with a Roland Emmerich disaster movie: burning cars, rampaging crowds, police roadblocks, cops firing their guns into the air to keep order, and some action-movie hero hustling his kids through all that chaos.

And Dad's stuck in that movie...somewhere.

He wanted his dad over here with them. They needed him. He noticed Grace was crying beside him. Quietly, privately. He actually hadn't seen her cry for a long time. Not even when the big bust up happened. She kept that kind of stuff under wraps, probably because she thought it made her look childish. He could hear her breath hitching, saw wet streams of tears rolling down her cheeks, past her curved lips, and onto her dimpled chin.

He felt an instinct to do the whole big-brother thing, to tell her it was going to be fine, that a week from now the news would be all about how social media fueled an overnight global panic. How easy it was for hysteria to spread—a virus far more quick acting and communicable than any real pathogen.

He was about to give her a whole load of bull like that to think about when the clattering of the tracks beneath the train suddenly changed to a deafening metallic scream.

Leon jerked forward, the hard edge of the table slamming

painfully against his sternum. His phone flew across the table into the old man's lap. Someone farther down the car yelped, briefcases and laptop bags skated along overhead storage racks and began to pile up and spill out onto passengers below.

The shrill metallic scream increased in volume and pitch, and everyone in the car was pulled forward in unison by the braking force—those facing forward bent over their tables, those facing opposite pushed back into their seats. Everyone's faces were stretched and crinkled into the same expectant grimace, awaiting the sudden and catastrophic impact.

Instead, the braking force began to tail off—the screaming of brakes died down to a dull whine, and, finally, the train lurched to a halt. Everyone in the car lurched with it.

For a moment, the entire car was completely silent, except for the sound of someone's can of soda rolling all the way down the center aisle and the continued soft ticking of a heater.

"Good God!" gasped the man opposite Leon. "What was that about?"

Leon looked at his mother. She shook her head. She had no idea. "Maybe something else is on the tracks?" Her voice had a tremble in it that she was trying to hide for Grace's sake.

He looked around at the other passengers nearby—the two men and the woman at the table opposite, the three younger men farther down, the young woman wearing the hissing headphones, the older woman beside her who'd been trying to read on her Kindle—all of them now looking at each other wide-eyed and waiting for some kind of an announcement over the intercom.

Finally, the car's speakers crackled. They heard the rasp and rustle of heavy breathing. Then the train driver's voice:

"*Help...me...*"

CHAPTER
17

"MOM, IT'S GOTTA BE THE VIRUS!" SAID LEON. "MAYBE HE'S got it? Maybe he's sick?"

"Leon!" she snapped at him. "For God's sake, just calm down. We don't know what's happened yet—"

One of the passengers sitting across from them stirred. "That poor sod sounded like he was having a heart attack or something." He was in his midthirties Leon guessed, smartly dressed in a way ex-soldiers looked. He peered down at his phone, shifted in his seat, shuffled across the empty one next to him, and stood up in the aisle. "Does anyone here have a phone signal?"

"I do," said a woman farther down.

"Dial 999, then. Call an ambulance!" He headed up the aisle toward the car door. It hissed and clattered open for him.

"Where are you going?" Leon's mom called out.

"I'm an ex-medic." The door hissed and clattered shut behind him.

"What do we do now?" asked Grace.

"We just sit tight for the moment, love."

"What about Dad?"

"He can look after himself, Grace. He only needs to take care of himself."

Leon shot her a look. That sounded like an unnecessary dig.

"Your father..." said the old man. "I'm sure I heard him say, on your phone, something about this virus breaking out in New York?"

"Yeah."

"Uh-huh...and I heard that too!" A head popped up over the top of the old man's seat. A black woman with long turquoise nails. She stared at Leon. "Was that your phone, love?"

Leon nodded.

"Sounded scary. Like loads of people rioting."

"Panic," said the old man. "Nothing quite like a good old-fashioned medieval plague to get people running for the mountains and screaming blue—"

The woman tapped the top of his head with a nail to shush him. He turned and looked up at her irritably.

"That your husband who called, love?" She didn't wait for Leon's mom to nod. "Is he right, do you think? Do we all need to be worrying about this?"

Leon's mom bit her lip.

Leon noticed there were a dozen faces looking their way. The sound of that phone call had carried. They were all looking at his mother for an answer.

"Tom... He... Well, he doesn't normally panic easily," she

replied. "Something's definitely happening over there." A complete nonanswer. Heads ducked back out of view.

The woman with the nails rolled her tongue over her teeth beneath her closed lips. "Your hubby sounded terrified."

"*Something's* happening over here too!"

Leon craned his neck into the aisle. It was the woman who was calling for an ambulance. She was waving her phone around. "There're no ambulances! None! They're all out! I'm in a call-waiting line!"

Her words hung heavily in the air.

"OK, and now there's this," said the other man on the table opposite. He tapped on the screen of his phone. "I've got a BBC News notification. There's some kind of terror alert in London that's just been announced. All mainline rail stations have just been closed."

"Mom...I'm scared," whispered Grace.

"I know...just...just..." Leon could hear the heel of his mom's shoe edgily tapping the floor beneath the table. "Just sit tight, lovely."

Mom's beginning to panic. He decided to help her out. He reached for Grace's hand. "It's OK, kiddo." Normally she would have rolled her eyes at Leon playing the role of big brother. Instead, she clasped his hand tightly and gratefully.

"Including Norwich station!" A young man with a thick, dark beard and shoulder-length hair popped up like a meerkat beside the lady with the nails. "BigTravelGenieDotCom," he continued. "They're saying *every single* mainline station in the UK has just been closed. It's not just London."

"Hey! Does that mean we're stuck here?" called one of the hungover city lads. "You saying we're stuck, mate?"

The bearded guy shrugged. "I dunno. I guess so."

"Ah, that's just bloody great!" The city boy smacked a hand on his table, loosened his tie, and swore.

The old man opposite Leon leaned out into the aisle and craned his neck. "Can you mind your language back there, please? Swearing isn't going to help anyone."

"Piss off."

The old man shook his head and said, "There's a frightened little girl up here. Just keep it to yourself, all right?"

The city lad ignored him, picked up his phone, and checked again for a signal.

"Uh...look," started the bearded guy. "I work for a news website. We collect and package news..."

Leon wasn't sure who he was speaking to. It sounded as if he wanted everyone in the car to hear him.

"Excuse me...everyone? Down at the end, can you hear me?"

This far end of the car quietened down for him.

"OK, so...I work for a news website. We had this weird email go around just before I left work this evening. It was something to do with that African virus, a heads-up that we weren't to post any stories relating to it without getting approval from our senior online editors." He shrugged—that's all he had. "I don't know if that means anything, but...I thought I'd share it anyway."

"Panic management," said the old man. "They're smothering the news."

"Right." The bearded guy looked down at Leon. "Mate, was it *your* phone we all heard?"

Leon nodded. "Yeah."

"And your dad was calling from America?"

"Yeah."

"He said something about the virus being *airborne* or something, right?"

Leon struggled to remember exactly what his dad had said minutes ago. He could only remember that he'd sounded really scared, that it had sounded like movie dialogue. *Airborne* though… yeah, he'd definitely used that word.

"Yes…I think so."

"Then, it's got to be over here too now. That's what this station lockdown is all about. It's infection containment." He looked around at everyone. He grinned, looking sheepish and unsettled both at the same time. "Or am I just sounding like a paranoid idiot?"

It was quiet. No one seemed to want to answer that. Leon could faintly hear conversations leaking through from the next car down. Possibly with the exact same exchanges going on here; strangers, overcoming their natural instinct to exist in a private bubble, were turning to each other and pooling information.

"I wonder how that train driver is?" said the lady with the long turquoise nails.

That's when they heard the first sounds of a commotion coming from the car up ahead of them.

The old man leaned out into the aisle and looked forward. Their door into the foyer between cars was open, but the door beyond that, into the next one, was closed.

"There's something going on up there."

Leon squished over Grace's legs to get into the aisle.

"Leon, please...stay put!"

He ignored his mother. "I'm just gonna have a look." He stumbled into the aisle, standing in front of the old man. The noises coming from the car ahead were growing louder. Voices. Raised over each other. The commotion sounded to Leon like the start of a fight. He could imagine that. The atmosphere was charged and tense. There were tired people, stressed people, drunk people, all crammed into these cars all the way down, and none of them were getting a shred of information about what was going on outside in the big, wide world. He could well imagine some hapless conductor being confronted by an angry mob, maybe given a hard time, pushed around.

He stepped forward, toward the door. It was open, whirring and clattering softly, trying to close itself, but held back by a kink in the rubber floor runner.

"Leon, please come and sit down!" snapped his mom.

The voices up ahead in the next car were getting noisier, but it didn't sound like a fight to Leon now. The voices weren't raised in anger...

That's panic.

Through the small, scuffed, window of the closed door leading to the next car, he could see people getting out of their seats quickly, clogging the aisle. Coming this way.

"What's going on?" asked the bearded guy who said he worked for a news site. He was young; his beard was neatly clipped—the kind of trendy-looking hipster that seemed to populate every lifestyle ad.

"Uh...it looks like *everyone's* coming this way!"

The bearded guy was suddenly beside Leon. He leaned around him to get a look. "Looks like a bloody stampede!"

Leon caught sight of an old woman in the next car tangling with someone and falling down into the aisle, and a younger woman trying to step over her and falling down too as someone from behind her pushed hard to get past.

"Shit! Something's going on! They're *running from* something!"

The old man at their table turned to Leon's mom and Grace. "Come on, ladies, get up!" He stood up and turned to face down the car. "Everyone! Get up and head back! *Head back!*"

His voice seemed to carry some authority. Leon imagined he might work in a courtroom, maybe as a clerk, maybe a lawyer or something. The aisle quickly filled with people not stopping to ask why they were moving, but instinctively reaching for coats, briefcases, laptops.

"Go!" bellowed the old man. "All of you! Leave your things and...GO!"

Leon looked back through the window of the closed car door beyond the joining foyer. Someone, a thickset man with cropped hair and tattoos up the side of his neck, had managed to pull himself from the logjam of tangled limbs in the aisle. The door, sensing his proximity clattered open for him.

Now the sounds weren't muffled anymore.

There was screaming coming out of there: desperate, high-pitched *get me out of here* screaming. The man staggered through the open doorway into the space between the cars. He caught sight of Leon staring at him.

"*Someone's got it!*" he bellowed.

Leon spun around. "Mom! Grace! Move!" he barked. He yanked on Grace's arm and pulled her up out of her seat. His mom followed suit.

Meanwhile, the hipster quickly squeezed past Leon, toward the clattering, whirring door, and grabbed the handle of it.

"What are you doing?" said the old man.

The bearded guy braced his shoulder against the frame and pushed the door across the opening. It resisted stubbornly. It might not be able to rattle fully closed, but having sensed a passenger, it was damned if it was going to be prevented from opening up. The whirring motor complained as the hipster wrestled to close it.

Over his shoulder, Leon could see the man in the foyer beyond staggering toward them.

"Shit, we can't let them in!" hissed the hipster. With a savage jerk, he pulled. The motor gave up resisting him and the door rattled closed just as the tattooed man reached them.

"*Hey!*" He thumped on the scuffed window with his fist. "Open the bloody door!"

The bearded guy had his hands wrapped around the handle, holding it firmly upward in the latched position and against the frame. The motor whined and clicked persistently. "Someone help me hold this!"

Leon was the closest.

"Leon!"

He turned at the sound of Grace's shrill voice.

"Come on!" she squealed.

"No! Help me here, mate!" yelled the bearded guy. "Help me!"

Leon flapped his hand at his mother and sister. "Just go! Go! I'll catch up!"

"*Leon!*" snapped his mom. "*You come right now!*"

"Shit!" grunted the bearded man as the door rattled and shook under the impact of shoulder barging coming from the other side. "I can't hold this thing on my own. Help!"

"Mom! Just go!" said Leon. He turned back toward the young man doing his best to keep the door firmly in place.

"We've got to tie this thing closed! You have any string? Rope? Cable? Something?"

Leon shook his head. The old man who had been sitting opposite Leon joined them both. He loosened, then pulled the tie up from his collar and handed it to the bearded guy. "Use this!"

"I'll keep holding this. You tie it!" said the young man.

Leon nodded. He threaded the tie through the handle, then around an emergency brake handle beside the frame.

"*Let me in!*" screamed the tattooed man from beyond the window. His eyes were locked on Leon's. They were wide, round, terrified...and completely bloodshot. "*Open the bloody door!*"

"Sorry!" replied Leon. "I'm sorry, I'm sorry...I'm sorry!"

Others were now stumbling into the space beyond the tattooed man. They joined him, slapping desperately against the window.

"Look at their eyes!" said the bearded guy. "Do you see that? Jesus, they're bloodshot! They're hemorrhaging!"

The old man snatched the end of his tie from Leon. "You need to tie it off with a proper knot, lad." His big, clumsy, pale, desk-job hands worked quickly, while the door rattled under the impact of fists and palms and shoulders.

"*Pl-e-ease!*" someone screamed behind the window. "Please let us through!"

The window was smearing with something. Sweat? Palm grease? Spit?

"Done," gasped the old man. With a final firm tug, he cinched the knot tight. "That should hold for a bit!"

The bearded guy tentatively loosened his hold on the door handle. Immediately it flipped down, unlatched, and the door tried to slide open a couple of inches. The tie went taut, the knot tightened, and the door held there. Fingers immediately protruded through the narrow gap, curling around the rubber lip, trying to pull the door wider.

Leon heard the chorus of voices, a wide-ranging ensemble from shrill and feminine to deep and threatening, all begging, pleading, snarling.

"Please...please!" Leon found himself staring into the bloodshot eyes of the tattooed man, their faces just a couple of palms' width apart. The man's nose protruded through the narrow gap, his lips squished by the gap into a puckered kiss. "Come on, mate...please!" he rasped. "We're all goin' to *die in here.*"

"I can't!" cried Leon. "I...j-just...just go back! Please!"

The man's fingers waggled through the gap just beneath his chin, like a spider emerging from its hunting hole. They squeezed through between the rubber and the doorframe, then his palm, then the whole hand suddenly thrust forward as a fist and caught the bearded man on the side of the head, knocking his glasses askew. "Shit!" He took a step backward. "Everyone get back!" shouted the old man.

Leon did as he said...and now no one was holding the door. Just the tie.

"Back up some more," said the old man. He pulled on the bearded guy's shoulder. "Don't let them touch you."

Leon stared at the window. So many different hands were slapping it, thumping it, punching it. Male and female. A flurry of rings, bracelets, gold watches, varnished nails. The window was becoming foggier and foggier, smeared with spirals of hand grease, like the touch screen of some phone played with by a grubby-handed toddler.

"Oh my God..." The bearded guy shook his head. "The poor bastards..."

"Come on," said the old man. "You too, lad!"

Leon felt the old man's hand on his shoulder.

The chorus of wailing, crying, screaming... If Hell was a real thing, he imagined it would sound like this. It must. Through the foggy window, Leon could just about make out rough hand shapes. The smearing now seemed to have acquired a color. Pink—like some cheap hotel shower gel—smeared in artsy circles, like some primary school finger painting.

"Leon! *Leon!*" He heard the voice above the din. He turned to look down their car, now almost completely empty—his mom and Grace, waiting for him at the far end. Both of them crying and frantically waving at him to come join them.

"Come on," said the old man. "Standing around here won't help those poor sods."

The bearded man nodded and stepped dizzily backward, bracing himself against a head rest. He shook his head and winced.

"You OK?" asked Leon.

"Yeah...yeah." He rubbed his temple. "Just...took a punch."

The old man waved his arms at the two of them to get moving, and they began to jog down the center aisle, stepping over abandoned briefcases and handbags as they went. Leon turned to look back and saw one last glimpse that he knew was going to haunt him for the rest of his life, however long that was going to be...

Faces. One above the other, pressed up against the tiny gap between the door and the frame, from the floor, almost all the way to the top. Young and old, male and female, white, brown, black—all of them with the same gaping mouths...baring teeth and bleeding gums. And eyes spilling tears that were tinted pink like rosewater.

CHAPTER
18

LEON HURRIED DOWN THE EMPTY CAR WITH THE OLD MAN to join the others. The compartment at the far end was log-jammed as the passengers from what Leon now considered to be *their* train car, C, poured into train car D.

His mom and Grace were waiting for him just beside the door to the compartment, and now they both reached out toward him and snatched at him as if worried he was about to turn around and head back into danger.

"Leo!" snapped his mom, using a voice that hovered indecisively between anger and relief. "I told you to come with us!"

"You OK?" asked Grace.

"I...I... Yeah, fine."

"Your boy's all right," said the old man. "But it has got to be that virus on the news. That's what's going on. Somebody in the car ahead must have had it."

The young, bearded man was panting and sweating from the

last couple of minutes of exertion. "It's so fast...it's insane." He turned to Leon. "Thanks for helping me... What's your name?"

"Leon."

He puffed air. "I'm James."

The old man looked back over his shoulder at the far end door. "Ben."

"Guys," said James, "can we get off the train? Maybe we should get out?"

Leon's mom nodded. She ducked into the foyer and tried the car door. An orange light glowed to the left of it.

Locked.

"The doors are all locked!"

"They always are between stations," said Ben. "The driver needs to flick an emergency override or maybe someone needs to pull the emergency handle."

"Jesus! Just pull the window down," said James. "We can climb out—"

"No!" said Leon.

"What? Why?"

"Dad said it's airborne. Like snowflakes or something, floating in the air." He pointed out of the window. It was pitch-black outside. Not a single light to be seen. "It's right out there."

James jabbed a finger down the car. "It's in here too!"

They all glanced at the door at the far end of their car. The noise of crying and wailing, the banging on the window, had subsided. Through the smeared window, there was no longer any sign of movement.

"But at least it's contained beyond that door," said Ben. "For now."

"It's bloody airborne!" said James. "I heard his dad's call too! Airborne means we could be breathing the virus in right now!"

"He said *flakes*," said Leon.

Ben nodded. "That's right... He did, which means we can *see it*. And if we can see it we can *avoid it*."

They all glanced again at the dark windows, and all came to the same conclusion at the same time. "First light, then," said Ben. "If no rescue services come for us during the night, then tomorrow morning when we can see, we'll walk. How does that sound?"

James nodded. "Sensible."

"We don't know how it's spread," said Leon's mom. She had her arms wrapped tightly around Grace. "It could be passed by touch."

Ben ran a hand through his thinning gray hair. "Yes, that's a possibility." He looked at James and Leon. "Did that man with the tattoo touch either of you?"

Leon shook his head.

Ben looked at James. "You?"

"No...I... No, I don't think so."

"Think? Or *know*?"

James scratched at his beard, then adjusted his glasses unnecessarily. His eyes darted from Ben to Leon. "I... Well, he threw a punch at me. I mean...it was only a glancing blow. Hit the arm of my glasses rather than me."

Leon felt his arm being tugged. It was his mom, pulling him back from the young man. "You need to step away!" she said sharply. "Right now!"

James looked incredulously at her. "What the—?"

"You can't come into the next car with us." She softened her voice. "I'm sorry."

He snorted humorlessly, shot a glance over his shoulder down the empty car. "I'm not staying in there!"

"Actually, she's right," said Ben. "Just to be on the safe side, James." He nodded at the young man's glasses. "I'd remove those as well."

James instinctively reached up with his hand to remove them, but Ben intercepted.

He grasped his arm. "Don't touch them... Just shake them off."

James nodded. He took a few steps back into the car and shook his head like a wet Labrador shaking its coat. His spectacles flew off and landed softly on one of the seats. He turned back to face them, blinking. "There, is that better?"

No one said it was.

"Now what?"

"Just stay where you are," replied Ben.

"I'm not staying here!" James looked at Leon for support. "Mate?" He stepped forward and reached out a hand to him.

Leon recoiled.

James stared at them all. "So? What? I-I'm, like, *quarantined*?"

"We'll go into the next car," said Leon's mom. "You stay here... just for a bit. And we'll see."

"*We'll see?* What does that mean?"

"She's right," said Ben. "Whatever happened in the other car... it happened quickly. Just wait and see...for a bit."

A bead of sweat rolled down the side of James's face and into the bristles of his beard. "How long? Five minutes? Ten?"

"Just for a bit," said Ben. He gestured at James to back up a step or two. "Just sit tight, catch your breath. I'll take this lady and her children through to the next car. Then I'll come right back, OK?"

James looked hurt. "Come on! For God's sake! I *saved* us! It was my idea to block the door!"

"I know. And we'd all now be like those poor sods back there if you hadn't," replied Ben. "We're grateful. It was quick thinking." He smiled. "Just sit tight. I'll be back in a minute."

"We're not abandoning you," said Leon's mom. "It's just a—"

"Yeah, yeah… I get it," interrupted James. "Just a precaution. Fine. OK." He glanced once again down the length of the car. It was entirely still and quiet down there, the door still held closed by Ben's office tie. James wiped his eyes with the back of his hand, then slumped down on to the nearest seat, letting his head roll back on the headrest. He closed his eyes and stretched his long legs out into the aisle. He looked like an ad for first class.

"That's it, James. Make yourself comfortable." Ben smiled.

The rest of them stepped back into the compartment until the door's sensor decided it was clear and it quickly rolled shut, thumping against the rubber stopper. James stirred and opened his eyes, then settled again as he realized the door was going to do that anyway.

"We should probably tie off this door as well?" said Leon's mom very quietly. She looked at the old man.

He nodded.

She looked at Leon. "Leon? Have you got a belt or something?"

He shrugged. "No."

"I have," said Ben. He reached around his belly and pulled off a long leather belt. He quickly glanced through the scuffed and scratched door and saw that James was watching them warily.

"I know what you're doing," they heard him say. "Go on, then, if you're going to do it."

Ben nodded at him through the window. "This is just going to be for an hour or so, all right? Just to be on the—"

"On the safe side, I know."

He looped his belt through the handle of the door, then around the horizontal bar of a luggage rack. "I'm going to have nothing left to wear by the time we're done."

Leon peered through the window at James.

James nodded back at him and smiled. "I'm all right, mate," he said. "I'll see you in a while."

The old man cinched the belt tight and tugged it for certainty. "That's good."

"Right," said Leon's mom, "I'm taking my kids into the next car." She pushed Grace and Leon ahead of her and turned to go. Ben remained where he was. "You coming?"

"I'm just going to keep an eye on the lad for a bit."

"You should come," she replied. "You'll need to explain to the people in the next car what's been going on."

"I'm sure they know already."

She nodded.

Grace was tugging her hand. "Come on, Mom!"

Leon shot one last glance back through the window at James. He was sitting down now. At the last table in the car, he picked up

ALEX SCARROW

a discarded copy of the *Metro* and made an effort to start flicking through it casually.

"Do you think he's got it?"

Ben shrugged. "God help us all, lad, if it's *that* easy to catch it."

Leon turned and followed his mother and sister as they stepped past the bathrooms and approached the next car. The door swish-thumped open, and it was suddenly noisy with voices, everyone talking over the top of each other, no one getting heard. As they stepped into the car, the exchanges abruptly ceased.

The woman with the long turquoise nails took advantage of the pause to make an announcement to everyone in the car.

"Listen up, everyone. That African virus is over here now!" Her voice carried loud and clear down the length of the car. "It's here in Britain. It's proper official now; the BBC has announced it an' everything." She held her phone up for all to see.

The car was perfectly silent.

"And they said we've all got to stay indoors." She turned to Leon's mom. "Just like your hubby said on the phone. There's, like, poison snowflakes in the air coming down, and if they touch you, then you get it."

"And if somebody who's got it touches you, *you* get it!" added somebody else.

"'S'right," said the lady.

"Is that door to car B still tied shut?" shouted someone. Leon saw it was one of the three drunk lads. Only they all looked stone-cold sober now.

Leon's mom nodded. "It's secure, but I think they might all be dead now anyway."

A gasp rolled down to the end of the car.

"Oh my God! Dead already?" uttered someone.

"Where's the old man who was with you?" asked the woman with the nails.

"He's watching James," said Leon. "The guy who tied the door shut," he explained.

The lady's eyes widened. "He's not got it too, has he?"

"Is he infected? We don't know yet," replied Leon's mom. "He thinks he might have been touched by one of the others. It's OK. We've contained him."

The car filled with voices again, the sound of panic building up an unstoppable momentum. The lady with the turquoise nails, the loudest voice in the car it seemed, raised her hands.

"Everyone, shut up! Shut up! SHUT UP!"

She had them all at that. She had silence.

She turned to Leon's mom. "So what do we do now, love?"

Leon looked at his mother. *They're all turning to her?* For a moment, he expected his mother to recoil from that kind of pressure, to throw the question back at the lady...to let her, or anyone else who wanted to, assume the role as crisis leader.

Leon's mom cleared her throat. "We have to sit tight. We have to close any windows that are open, and we have to wait."

"Until when?"

She looked out of the nearest window at the perfectly black night. "Until the morning, when we can see where we're going. When we can see if those flakes are coming down."

She nodded down the car. She could see more people moving around, craning necks curiously to see what was going on.

"Meanwhile...I guess some of us better head down into the other cars and explain what's going on to them."

CHAPTER
19

THE LIGHTS ABOARD THE TRAIN FLICKERED AND DIMMED AT about half past eleven. They finally winked out and left them in complete darkness at midnight. Grace gave a small whimper of alarm when that happened.

"It's OK, honey," said Leon's mom. "I guess the train's batteries finally ran out."

Someone overheard her in the dark. "It's worse than that—that's the power grid failing. The electricity's gone."

Leon looked out of the window at the darkness. A few moments ago, there'd been a faint glow up in the sky, the bottom of a low cloud stained a sickly amber—light pollution from a town somewhere nearby.

But that was gone now. He looked up, hoping to glimpse the reassuring blink of distant airplane lights. He saw nothing. It was just an ominous pitch-black now. Not even the glow of moonlight or the faint twinkling of stars; it was overcast, a thick blanket of what his dad liked to call "British Tupperware sky."

Several pale squares of light had winked on inside the car, casting dancing shadows across the ceiling—just enough ambient light for his dark-adjusted eyes to pick out silhouettes. Leon was tempted to turn his own phone on for Grace's benefit, so that they'd have their own light, but he decided to preserve what little charge he had left. "Mom, I'm frightened," Grace whispered.

"Me too, hon."

"I wish Dad was here."

Leon turned to look at his mom. He could just about see her face by the faint light of someone's phone. He expected an icy response to that.

Instead she nodded. "Me too."

"Do you think he's OK?" asked Grace.

"You know what he's like, a real boy scout. Always prepared. I'm sure he's OK," she replied. "Try to get some sleep, Grace."

"OK."

Leon watched his sister's small outline huddle up against his mom. In half a dozen hours, she'd gone from Miss Queen Bee to frightened child. No longer Miss Playground Princess or Miss Congresswoman to Be or Little Miss Big Mouth. Just a kid, scared and missing her dad. Five minutes later, he could hear the soft purr of her snoring. He looked at his mom and thought he could see her watching him.

"You too, Leo. Get some sleep."

"OK, Mom." He closed his own eyes and huddled down against the armrest.

Leon woke a while later and checked the time on his glow-in-the-dark watch. Quarter past four. Outside, the night had been replaced with a dim blue gray, and he could faintly see a steep bank covered in nettles.

"Mom?" he said softly. Little more than a whisper.

"Uh-huh?" She was still awake.

"You OK?"

"I'm fine, love."

"You get any sleep?"

"Uh-huh," she whispered a little too quickly.

No, she hasn't. He figured she'd kept a lonely, silent vigil. Wide awake, looking out for her kids. Meanwhile he'd been slumped across the table, his hoodie bunched up over his arms, forming a crude pillow. He reached out a hand toward hers and squeezed it. "I love you, Mom."

"You should get some sleep too, Leo."

"I can't… My head's pounding."

"Did you bring some aspirin?"

"In my backpack."

"Well, take a couple."

"Can't. I've got nothing to drink."

She looked around. Across the aisle, the black lady was sitting hunched over a table. She was awake too. She'd heard them talking. She raised her own water bottle and waggled it. "I'm sorry, darling. Mine's all gone."

His mother made a face. "I think everyone's out."

Leon dug into his backpack and took out a couple of pills.

"You going to try dry swallowing them?"

He shook his head, shuffled out of his seat, and stood up.

"Where are you going?"

"Bathroom. Might try the sink in there."

"You can't drink that water, Leo."

It was probably going to taste horrible and was quite probably laced with stomach-churning germs. "Just a sip, Mom. It's not going to kill me."

His mom made another face, then finally nodded. "OK."

"I'll go check in on Ben and James again."

Last time, Leon's mom had done it. Just before midnight, she'd looked in on them and spoken briefly to Ben. Ben said James appeared to be sleeping.

"Just be—"

Leon nodded. "I know—be careful."

"And don't go waking up Ben if he's sleeping. He's just an old—"

"OK, OK," he sighed.

He pushed past the half-open, now unpowered and useless door into the compartment beyond. The toilet was to his immediate right. He pushed the door open and was instantly struck by the appalling stench.

No power...*no flush.*

The toilet had been used quite a few times by the smell of it. He pulled his phone out and used its dull glow to get his bearings. The toilet was almost overflowing with a stew of urine, feces, and balled-up toilet paper. He swiped his phone back off again, popped two aspirin into his mouth, ducked down to the tap, and pressed the foot pump. There was no whine of a motor, but the trickle of water still in the pipe dribbled out and on to his tongue.

Enough. He gulped it down.

He quickly stepped back out of the bathroom and breathed through his nose again, relieved to be out of that rancid space. He stepped across rubber-matted joining between the two cars and into the area beyond.

By the dim light of predawn, he could just about make out the outline of the old man.

"Ben?" He whispered softly. "You awake?"

"Wide awake."

Leon swiped his phone on again and saw the old man sitting on the floor, his suit jacket rolled up as an improvised cushion. Leon slid down the compartment wall until he was squatting beside him. "You OK?"

"You better turn your phone off," said Ben. "Save your battery."

Leon nodded and switched it off, leaving them in a faint pool of gray light.

"How's James?"

"Last time I checked he looked like he was sleeping."

"You think he's OK?"

"I really don't know. Those others?" Leon heard the old man's voice hitch. "Good God...those poor sods. They were affected so damned quickly, weren't they?"

Leon nodded. Those people in coach B had gone quiet within ten minutes. Maybe even less. Leon found it hard to judge how long they'd been bracing themselves against that door hoping that Ben's tie would hold.

It could easily have been just a few seconds.

"That poor man's eyes... You saw, didn't you, lad? The man who was reaching through the gap?"

"Bleeding. Yeah."

"I got a good look at his face, Leon. I really wish to God I hadn't. His eyes—they weren't just hemorrhaging. They looked like..." He stopped himself.

"What?"

"Leon?"

"Yes, Ben?"

The old man let out a wheezy laugh. "Normally I insist the boys call me Mr. Mareham. I'm a headmaster, by the way."

"Oh, right." Leon had figured he was someone used to being in a position of authority. For some reason, he'd imagined him as a judge or something. A headmaster? Now he felt vaguely guilty for casually using his first name.

"How old are you, Leon? I'm guessing fifteen?"

"Nearly seventeen. I go to a sixth-form school in Hammer-smith." Leon shrugged. "I know. I get that all the time. I look way younger than I am. Which sucks."

"Look, I'm no expert. Anyway, I used to teach physics before running a school. But before that, long ago, I actually used to be in the army."

"Did you, like, fight in Iraq or something?"

"Iraq?" Ben laughed dryly again. "I suppose that must be ancient history for you. No. Long before then, back in the seventies, my boy. We were in Rhodesia. It's called Zimbabwe now."

"Uh, OK."

"We were called in to a village to provide medical assistance. They had a hemorrhagic fever...horrible, horrible thing. Vomiting blood, diarrhea. I saw a dying child literally spill her guts out on one of the cots. It was very infectious. Contact, Leon, contact with any secreted liquids, and you were in trouble. And it was fast. Very fast. In the morning, you might have a headache. The next day, a fever. Forty-eight hours later, you were dead."

"You think this is the same thing?"

"Oh good God, no. This...whatever *this* is, is far worse. That's what I'm trying to tell you. *Then*, we were dealing with a fever that was called *Marburg*. Quite honestly, the most evil thing Mother Nature, or God, if you're of that persuasion, could have come up with. But this?" He shook his head. "This is something else altogether. This is—from what little I know of microbiology—well, frankly impossible."

Leon could hear the fear in his voice. "We're in big trouble, aren't we?"

He sighed. "That's why I asked your age, lad. You're old enough to know it. Yes, I rather suspect we are."

The words hit Leon like a slap on the cheek. "What are we gonna do?"

"I really don't know. I...really don't know." Leon could hear Ben's breath whistling through his nose. "Well, for starters, when it's light enough, we need to get off this train."

"That's what Mom said we should do."

"Good girl. That's what we'll do, then."

"What about James?"

Ben shrugged. "If he's OK and he wants to, he can come along with us. That all right with you?"

Leon nodded.

The old man was quiet for a while. Then finally, he stirred. "So, your father...does he work in America?"

"Yeah."

"What does he do?"

"Shares and markets an' stuff. He works on Wall Street."

"And you, your mother, and sister came over here for a holiday?"

"No, we live here now. Mom and Dad split up, like, eight months ago."

"That's not very long ago. How's your mother been coping with all of that?"

"She keeps real busy. That's pretty much how she copes." Leon didn't want to give him any more than that. Ben Mareham seemed like a nice old guy, but they were all just strangers in a crisis, and his mom was always telling him and Grace that if friends asked what the deal was, they could just say it was "complicated" and leave it at that. She was like that, tight-lipped.

Leon changed the subject. "Do you think anyone's gonna come looking for us?"

"I don't know. The power's down. It looks like the telephone system is down as well. It's not looking very encouraging, is it?"

"No." Leon shook his head. "I...I'm pretty scared, Mr. Mareham."

"Me too. But that's a perfectly sensible thing, to be scared. It means you're keeping your wits about you."

"We're not going to survive, are we?"

"I have no idea what's going to happen, Leon. Whether this is some horrific crisis that's going to be cleared up in a month, like they always inevitably seem to be, or whether this is the viral outbreak that doomsayers have been warning us all about for God knows how long. But you, Leon, have more than yourself to think about. Your little sister? Your mother?"

"Mom? She's OK. She—"

"I suspect your mother is *brittle*."

Leon looked at him. "What's that supposed to mean?"

"She's the *brittle* type—"

"You don't even know my mom. You just spoke a few words with her earlier."

"I'm not *criticizing* her! In fact, she reminds me of my daughter, Margot. Strong. *Very* strong. You can throw the world at a person like that and they can take everything you hurl at them. They can take it." Mr. Mareham looked away. "Until one day they...*can't*."

Leon understood that. He'd had that feeling about her for a while. Like that old kid's game Buckaroo!, where you piled up a spring-loaded plastic mule with a load of junk until that spring finally clicked and the mule buckaroo-ed. All her false cheeriness, all her bravado, all that positive spin on everything... Part of him had been waiting for a monumental crash, a nervous breakdown.

Now this.

"I'm just saying, Leon, that you need to help her. Just keep an eye on her."

"We're staying together, right? You, me, Mom, Grace?"

"Of course. We all want to get to Norwich. Like everyone else on the train."

"But we can keep together afterward? Right?"

The old man sighed again. "Let's get to Norwich first, lad."

They sat in silence for a while.

"Tomorrow morning," Leon started. "What about James?" Leon wanted him to be OK. He seemed smart and proactive. He'd been the first one to react. He'd basically saved everyone on the rest of the train by acting decisively. They needed him.

"We'll have a look in on him and see how he is. You should go get some rest, Leon."

"You coming back to get some sleep too?" Leon asked.

"I'm not going to get any sleep wherever I am. But you should try. When it's light enough, I'll come back and wake you."

"Then we're definitely heading outside?"

"We really can't stay here...so, yes, that's what I suggest. We can walk to Norwich."

"OK."

CHAPTER

20

Leon opened heavy-lidded eyes and stared stupidly at the smudged window his head had been leaning against; the natural grease in his hair had produced a spiral pattern. Beyond the glass his eyes slowly focused on the steep bank carpeted with thick, dark-green nettles that swayed gently in the breeze.

It took him a full minute for his sleepy mind to realize it was much lighter now. It was time to make a move. He looked around the car. One or two others were beginning to stir and stretch, aching from a night of uncomfortable sleeping.

Leon's mom was asleep, her neck cocked at an angle that was going to make it stiff and sore when she came to. Grace was still fast asleep on her lap.

"Morning." The lady with the long nails gave him a warm smile across the aisle. "You OK, love?"

For a moment he struggled to remember her name; then it came back to him. "Yes, thanks, Eva."

He rubbed his temples. His head throbbed dully with fatigue... and stress, predictably. On the Richter scale of his usual headaches, it was just a minor tremor though.

"Yeah..." He craned his neck. "Where's Mr. Mareham?"

"The old man?"

"Yeah. He said he'd wake us up when it got light."

Eva shrugged. "I only just woke up myself."

Leon pulled himself up out of his seat, stood, and stretched the stiffness out of his limbs, then looked down both sides of the aisle for any sign of Ben.

Pretty much every seat was taken. Ben must have decided to remain in the compartment, then. Sleeping on the cold hard floor, if that was even possible.

"I'm gonna go wake Ben. He said we should get out of here when it was lighter."

Eva nodded eagerly. "No way I want to stay cooped in 'ere another day."

Leon pushed past the half-open door into the space beyond. It was still gloomy. The small windows in the car doors let in only a small amount of the dull, gray light from outside.

Jeez. It stank in here. The smell from the toilet compartment had had the night to stew and fester and was now producing a heady, eye-wateringly bad odor.

He stepped across the segmented rubber matting. "Mr. Mareham?"

No answer.

"It's Leon. You said we should make a move when it got..." He squeezed past the luggage rack into the other half of the linking foyer and stopped dead in his tracks. His eyes struggled to assemble what he was seeing into something that made any kind of sense.

The first thing that he *did* recognize was Ben's polished black shoes, on their side, one on top of the other, like twins in a bunk-bed. Above them, the light-gray flannel cuffs of Mr. Mareham's trouser legs had risen up an inch to reveal a playful pair of lime-green socks. It was the next part that didn't make sense. At the knees, the material was dark and spots of moisture had soaked through, becoming a solid stain of dark brown as the material approached Ben's waist. The last thing that Leon could make sense of was the waistband of his trousers and the bottom of his shirt, which, once, had been a crisp, freshly laundered white, but was now a mottled-sepia color.

The shirt disappeared into a tangled mass of quivering, dark jelly that reminded him of the drippings Leon's mom used to set aside in a tray on the counter when making roasts on Sundays. In among the jelly, he thought he could make out the uniform curve of ribs and the distinct disc segments of a spinal column.

He fought the urge to retch as he finally comprehended what he was seeing.

The skeleton of Mr. Mareham, poking through the jelly here and there, was unaffected, un-liquidized, and told an instant story. Ben had died as he slept. The bones indicated he'd been lying on his side, knees drawn up, hands balled beneath his rolled-up jacket, propping up his bloody, tufted-scalp skull.

Leon retched and vomit spattered the floor in front of his tennis shoes. He reached out and steadied himself.

Oh shit... Oh God.

His eyes were getting used to the pale gloom and picking out more details. The dark jelly that used to be Ben Mareham seemed to have spread in a peculiar way: thin filament lines snaked and weaved in all directions across the rubber-mat floor.

He quickly looked down at his shoes to check if he'd stepped on any.

No.

He traced the lines, picking up on one tributary that seemed thicker and more established than the others around it, thin lines that fanned out and came to feathery dead ends. He followed this line, increasing in thickness until it started to look like a length of electrical cord, then thicker, like tarred rope. It squeezed through the narrow gap beneath the door and disappeared into the next car.

He stepped carefully up to the door and peered through the scuffed window.

"God, *no!*" he gasped and took an involuntary step backward.

There was even less of James left...

The dark tributary that had sneaked under the door in the last couple of hours had...

Oh God.

...had been a part of James reaching out for a part of Ben.

...James...

...reaching out for Ben...

...making contact with him as he slept...

Right behind him, Eva screamed. "*OhmyGod he's dead!*" Her hand grabbed his shoulder, her long nails digging in. "*OhmyGod!*

OhmyGod! OhmyGod!" She pulled him roughly backward by the arm. *"It's got inside!"*

Leon wanted to shake her off. Wanted to take another few seconds to make sure he fully comprehended what he was seeing—not with ghoulish fascination, but with a desperate need to understand *how* they were all eventually going to end up.

He also wanted to run.

She dragged him back into train car D. *"Everyone!"* she bellowed.

Those few who were still fast asleep jerked wide awake; the rest all spun to look in her direction.

"Get out now! Get out now!"

Leon caught his mother's eyes. They were wide, round, and questioning. He nodded at her and then looked at all the other eyes locked on him and Eva. "She's right. We... W-we have to get off this train. Now."

One of the lads who'd been drunk earlier stood up. "Hold on. The warnings 'ave been that we got to stay *inside*, not go out and—"

"It's inside now!" yelled Eva. "It's in our car!"

"What?"

"It got under the door...got Mr. Mareham while he was sleeping...and it's growing this way!"

A wave of voices and gasps rippled down train car D. Leon saw faces crammed into the doorway at the far end, and over their shoulders, other faces appeared, trying to listen to the commotion going on this end.

"Growing... What the hell does that mean?" asked the man. He looked much less like a smart city trader this morning, with his disheveled hair and untucked pink office shirt.

Leon's mom stood up protectively in front of her son. "Leon? What's happened to Ben?"

"The virus...it's grown, Mom. It came right under the door, like a fungus or something," he started quietly. For the benefit of everyone else listening, he raised his voice. "This thing is grow-ing...*feelers, tentacles*...or something, across the floor, like it's... like it's looking for us!"

"*It found that old man,*" added Eva loudly. Her shrill voice car-ried down the car like a police siren. "Turned him to...*mush*!"

Leon's mom stepped past both Leon and Eva, pushing through the half-open door into the gloomy compartment beyond. The car went quiet, awaiting her return. Seconds later, she reappeared ashen faced. She looked ready to faint or vomit.

"We...we can't stay here any longer," she said quietly to Leon. She looked down at Grace. "Come on, honey, get your things. We're getting off."

"Mom? But...what if—"

"*Now!*" she screamed.

"Where are you going?" asked the young man.

"It's light," she replied. "The warning mentioned flakes, like snowflakes. We can see them coming down now."

Every pair of eyes in the car was on her.

"And I don't think anyone's going to come for us."

———

Leon jumped down onto the gravel beside the tracks with a heavy crunch.

The noise startled some birds roosting on the electric cables

PLAGUE LAND

above, and they scattered into the cheerless, gray sky with the sound of beating wings.

The sight of them was vaguely encouraging. *Birds...are they immune?*

He held out his hand for Grace and guided her down, then his mother. He heard the impact of other feet landing to his left. Word appeared to be spreading quickly down the train that outside might be a safer bet than staying on the train. Doors were swinging open, and other passengers were hastily joining the exodus.

He held out his hands for Eva. By some unspoken arrangement, Eva had become part of their group.

Leon's mom turned toward the front of the train. Ahead of them was C, the car they'd started in, then B, the car that had first been infected. Beyond that was A and the driver's cabin at the very end. Then it was a straight, empty track flanked by raised banks as far as she could see.

"Norwich has to be that way, then," said Leon.

Leon's mom stared warily at the cars ahead of them.

"Mom?"

She stirred. "Yes...yes...I know. We have to go that way."

Leon stepped slowly forward, loose stones clattering beneath his feet. He veered to the right, off the gravel bed and up the lower slope of the embankment, as far as he could get to the right before nettles and brambles stopped him, giving the cars as wide a berth as possible.

He led the way forward, past C, toward B, the first of the two first class cars. Behind him he could hear his mom's footsteps,

133

Grace's, and Eva's. Morbid curiosity compelled him to look to his left to try to snatch a glimpse of what was inside the first class cars.

He found a break in the nettles and brambles and clambered several steps up the steep bank until he was high enough to look down and into the front part of the train.

He heard his mom telling Grace to keep walking, to not copy Leon. *Just keep walking and looking forward, hon.* They passed by below him as Leon slowly scanned the length of coach A. Every window appeared to have a delicate pink lace curtain drawn across it for modesty, as if each one were a dear old lady's dressing room.

But they're NOT curtains, are they?

They were sheets of fine, semi-opaque membranes revealing vein-like threads within, and hinting at the slaughterhouse horror beyond.

Shutter-click images of Ben and James flashed into Leon's head: the soft tissue of their bodies melting, leaving behind raw bones that dangled unwanted or unneeded shreds of cartilage; their clothes stained dark, hanging on empty frames, like poorly stuffed scarecrows.

You don't *think about Ben, OK, Son?* Leon's dad's firm voice, scolding him. *You* do not *replay what you saw. He's gone. James is gone. All those poor bastards in there are gone. They're in a better place now.*

OK, Dad.

That's my boy, MonkeyNuts. Now...you just think about walking to Norwich.

Leon took several staggered steps back down the embankment and hurried to catch up with the others.

"I don't want to know what you saw," his mom said quickly.

Leon nodded.

They were in front of the train now and swerved back onto the train tracks, preferring the wide-open way ahead, the gravel, the ties, the rails, rather than the steep bank, with its nettles and brambles and the stunted overhanging trees at the top that cast forbidding shadows.

He turned around and saw that they were at the head of a long trail of bedraggled commuters picking their way slowly between the train tracks.

You listen to what that old guy said, Son. You help Mom where you can. She's strong, but she's not Wonder Woman.

He trudged in silence beside Grace and his mom. He reached out and put a protective arm across his sister's shoulders. Forty-eight hours ago she would have gone *ewww* and shrugged him off. Forty-eight hours ago, she was giving her lame older brother advice columnist tips.

She let go of their mom's hand and squeezed his gratefully.

CHAPTER
21

ABOUT TEN O' CLOCK IN THE MORNING, THE SOUND OF crunching gravel and weary footsteps was broken by someone calling out for everyone to stop. Leon turned to see a young woman waving her phone around like a rallying flag.

"Hey!" she shouted. "I've got a signal! I've got 3G!"

The news caused everyone to stop trudging along the tracks and turn to converge around her. Most people's phones had been dead this morning. There were just a few people with a trickle of battery power left. There was a hope—everyone was thinking it even if they weren't saying it—that the world was still out there, phone networks still operating, internet still alive and well, power stations running, law and order...somebody still making decisions. And the only reason they were getting nothing on their phones was that the train had dumped them in a signal black hole.

Leon, Leon's mom, Eva, and Grace joined the crowd gathering around the woman.

"BBC website!" said someone quickly. "Don't mess about, love! Get the news website!"

"OK, OK." She sounded hassled as she tapped at the screen. "What is it...BBC dot com? Or—"

"Here..." Someone snatched her phone off her and directed her browser. Faces pooled around the dull screen, brightness turned down to preserve what was left of her charge. They waited for the page to load.

"Shit. I've only got five percent," said the girl apologetically.

Leon shuffled around until he could see the screen. The red BBC logo was up, but the page was just a blank gray placeholder. He looked at the expectant, anxious expressions around the phone.

Finally the page loaded. One picture, one headline. The picture was of the British prime minister. He looked haggard, pale, and terrified.

West African Virus in UK: Emergency Measures in Full Force.

"For God's sake...someone read it out loud!"

The young woman nodded. "'The prime minister declared a state of emergency late last night. All airports, ports, stations, and motorways are closed with immediate effect. Everyone is instructed to stay in their homes, to only drink bottled water, *not* tap water, and to wait for further announcements.'"

"Is that it?"

She shook her head. "'COBRA, the emergency authority mobilized in times of extreme crisis, has declared a number of martial laws with immediate effect. One: full home quarantine—no one is to remain outside. Two: army and police have full authority to shoot on sight anyone breaking home quarantine...'" She looked up from the screen. "OhmyGod."

"Is there any more?"

She looked back down at the screen. "'Three: COBRA, military personnel, and police have full authority to requisition any supplies and resources required to remain operational.'"

"That's crazy!" someone barked out.

She shook her head. "There's another article... 'Cases of infection have been reported in most if not ALL countries. Media services, internet services, and phone services have gone down in many places...'"

"This has got to be some kind of reality-TV joke, right?" said one of the beered-up lads from train car C. He looked around hopefully.

"'...the virus is able to cross all animal species barriers without exception and is lethal in all cases, although the rate at which it kills seems to vary. The etiology as yet is unknown.'"

"This isn't happening," insisted the young man. "Come on. It's clearly a joke."

"'The origin is suspected to be either an artificial, genetically engineered pathogen, or, as some experts have suggested, quite possibly something extraterrestrial in origin...'"

The man laughed, relieved. "There you go, then! Alien invaders! OK. This *definitely is* a jo—"

"Shut up, mate," said his friend. "Just shut the hell up."

"'...possibly an organism carried in dormant form on a

meteorite and revived on contact with liquid-form water...'" The young woman stopped. She swiped at the screen.

"Is there more?"

She shook her head. "It's buffering again. Hold on..." They waited in silence for a full minute, listening to the breeze stirring the stunted branches of the trees planted along the top of the bank. Leon looked up and noticed there were no birds singing. It was ominously quiet. No distant hiss of traffic, no buzzing of insects. Just the breeze herding the heavy, low, gray clouds along above them.

"It's... The article's gone!" she said. She looked up at everyone, her eyes wide and moist with tears, her mouth hanging open. She turned the phone around to show everyone.

Leon leaned forward to see what was on the dim screen.

BBC news service suspended: 7:43 a.m.

"That was posted over two hours ago!" cried someone.

Leon turned and looked for his mother. He found her staring at him, mouthing his name. *Leon?*

"Mom, it's gone. The BBC's *gone!*"

It suddenly became very noisy. The young woman wanted to use whatever charge she had left in her phone to try to call her parents while she had a signal. The young man was still insisting this was some extreme reality-TV-show stunt and was being told to shut up by his friends. A woman who'd been repeating what the girl had been reading out for the benefit of those out of earshot started to cry. Eva's loud voice was booming, imploring them all to stay calm.

Leon pushed himself out of the knot of people toward his mom. "What're we gonna do now?" he asked.

She held out her hand, grabbed his, and pulled him toward her. "I don't know, Leo, I just don't know... I...I..."

She's the brittle type, Leon. Ben's words were there in the back of his mind.

"It's cool, Mom. It's fine. We're just going to keep going toward Norwich, right?"

She nodded, distracted. "Yes...yes, Norwich. That's..."

"Mom?" He looked around. "Where's Grace?"

"She said she needed to go to the bathroom."

Leon shook his head as though to say, *You just let her wander off like that?* He was going to say more when he caught sight of Grace standing up from behind a tall cluster of nettles at the top of the bank. She was starting to pick her way down the slope toward them when she stopped where she was, craned her neck curiously, and scrunched up her eyes.

She's seen something.

"Mom!" she called out.

Their mom turned toward Grace's voice, relieved.

Grace said something else, but it was lost beneath all the other raised voices. She pointed a finger.

Leon and his mom turned to look in the direction she was now pointing: back down the tracks. It looked like a blizzard of feathers billowing up the long, straight track toward them, carried along on the fresh breeze, swirling in lazy, unpredictable circles. Feathers, as if some children's pillow fight had gotten out of hand or a flock of pigeons had smacked into the windshield of a truck on a highway.

It was almost pretty, like cherry blossoms rolling along an

abandoned train track beneath a dark foreboding sky. It was a movie poster. A piece of hotel lobby art.

He looked at his mother. "Mom?"

"Is that...is that...?" Her mouth hung open, unable to finish her question.

The flakes. Dad's flakes.

"Mom...that's the virus! It's got to be!"

She was just staring at it, rooted to the spot, mouth hanging open...entranced by it, or too stupefied or terrified to snap out of it.

"Mom!" He grabbed her shoulder roughly. "*Mom! We gotta go!*"

It looked like it was coming slowly, idly. A jog across flat ground could easily have outpaced it, but they weren't on flat ground. They were in a long, straight gulley, flanked by steep banks covered in thick tangles of weeds. Trapped in its path, unless they made a start at climbing out of the way...right now.

Leon's mom nodded. "Eva!" The woman was just a few feet away, talking animatedly with a woman from another train car.

"Eva!" Leon echoed. He headed over and grabbed her arm. "Look!" he said and pointed down the tracks at the approaching cloud of particles.

It was much closer now. A slight updraft was carrying the white flecks up into the sky, while the banks on either side channeled it toward them. Leon wondered if there was any way of avoiding it, whatever they did.

"Ohmydays!" she gasped, confused for a moment by what she was looking at, but sensing immediately it wasn't a good thing.

"It...it's the virus," said Leon. "I think—"

"The virus!" she screamed. All heads turned to look in the direction her long fingernail was pointing. *"Look! Iiit's comin'!"*

The effect was instant. Panic. There was none of that stiff-upper-lip reserve anymore, that uniquely British incapacitating fear of looking like an idiot...of embarrassment. Leon pulled on Eva's arm and pointed up to Grace, still standing at the top of the small slope.

They scrambled off the tracks and ties, off the gravel, and up to the bottom of the steeply ascending bank.

Leon's mom joined them. She grabbed Eva's other arm. "Come on!"

The woman was large and struggling in her impractical work heels. She kicked them off and bent down to pick them up. "Ow! There's prickles an' stuff!"

Leon looked over his shoulder—the cloud was now only about a hundred feet from them. The banks on either side of the tracks were dotted with people following their lead, scrambling uphill through waist-high weeds.

"Keep moving," said Leon's mom, tugging Eva's arm.

One of the beer lads from train car C joined them—not the one who thought he was on some reality show, but the one who'd told that idiot to shut up.

"Come on, mate," he said to Leon. "I'll give you a hand." He planted his hands against the small of Eva's back and pushed.

Eva yelped as bristles and nettles and sharp twigs stabbed at her bare feet.

The man managed a grin. "We'll look like idiots if that's just the stuffing from some kid's teddy bear."

Leon turned to look again and wondered whether the man was right. It actually looked just like that. Not feathers, but soft-toy stuffing.

He turned to watch the dozen or so people who'd chosen to remain on the tracks, either because they too thought it was the stuffing from a toy or pillow, or maybe because they were too tired to react, too bemused by the sight, or too afraid of looking foolish...or, like that young man down there, still utterly convinced that this whole thing was some elaborate reality-TV stunt.

As the cloud began to engulf them, Leon saw the man who was convinced he was being filmed by secret cameras stare at something on the back of his hand. He flapped his hand vigorously as if he were trying to shake off a horsefly.

The feathers are sticky?

The fluff was settling as the light breeze abated and the particles began to seesaw lazily down.

Leon turned back to the task at hand and pushed Eva from behind more insistently. She was puffing and wheezing as the incline steepened. "I can't go any faster, love," she gasped.

Grace was hopping up and down at the top, screaming and pointing. "Oh my God! Look! *Look!*"

Leon's mom glanced back over her shoulder. Leon looked again. Others down on the tracks were now beginning to do the same thing as the disbelieving city lad: frantically rubbing at their hands, their cheeks, their arms.

Leon met his mother's eyes.

She nodded. "Come on! For God's sake, move it!"

"I'm...trying... I'm..." panted Eva.

They were two-thirds of the way up, the incline now at its steepest, and the nettles and brambles thickening.

We're not going to escape it.

As if to confirm his suspicion, Leon spotted a solitary particle of white fluff lightly settling on the topmost leaf of a tall stinging nettle just ahead of him.

"Shit!"

Leon turned in time to see the man beside him flick his hand. Their eyes met. "It's nothing," he said quickly. "Nettle sting."

They were nearing the top now. Grace was shifting from foot to foot anxiously. "Over there!" she shouted, pointing to something beyond the bank. With a last team effort and a cry of exhaustion from Eva, they emerged from the brambles on to the ridge of the embankment.

"Over there!" said Grace again. "There's a barn!" Leon looked across a field striped with deep plow lanes and rows of dark-green florets of broccoli, toward a rusty-looking corrugated-iron barn where several tractors were parked.

"OK," said Leon's mom. "Let's head there."

The others began to make their way slowly across the field. But Leon hesitated. He turned to take one last look down the bank at the people still on the tracks. No one seemed to be sick...yet. But they did all seem to be preoccupied with rubbing furiously at their skin.

He saw the young man, star of his own reality show, sitting down heavily on one of the rails, no longer rubbing or scratching the back of his hand, but instead dipping his head to one side as he closely inspected his hand. The stupid, bemused, *Hey, I'll play along* grin was beginning to vanish from his face.

CHAPTER
22

THEY WERE NOW WELL AWAY FROM THE CURIOUS CLOUD OF fluff as they crossed the field. All the same, they hurried, looking furtively up at the sky as they stepped from plowed rut to plowed rut, winding their way diagonally across the field toward the tractor barn.

Five minutes later, they made it under the corrugated-iron roof, just as a few drops of rain started to patter lightly against it. Eva sat down heavily on a low stack of wooden pallets, her bare feet so caked in mud that they looked like a new pair of misshapen ankle boots.

All of them were struggling to catch their breath. "OhmyGod, ohmyGod," wheezed Eva over and over again.

"Do you think... Just a sec..." started the young man. He sucked in a breath a couple more times to recover his voice. "Do you think *that* was it...the virus? Or did we just run from, I dunno, a bunch of pollinating dandelions?"

Leon was slumped against the large, ridged tire of one of the tractors. "I saw it settling on them and sticking to them, like..." He tried to think what it was like. But he couldn't come up with anything. It was like nothing he'd ever seen.

"I saw that too," said Grace. She shook her head as if she didn't want to agree with her brother but couldn't deny it either. "Those people on the track were rubbing and scratching...like it was starting to hurt or itch them or something."

The light tapping of raindrops on the corrugated roof increased in tempo and insistency.

"Maybe it was some kind of industrial pollutant," said Leon's mom. She looked at her kids hopefully. "A truck carrying something could have rolled over on a highway nearby, or it—"

"Oh...it's the virus." Eva spoke with such certainty that everyone turned to look at her. She held out her right arm and twisted her hand palm upward to reveal the slightly paler skin near her wrist. There was a mottled dark patch. "Flake went an' touched me right there." She bit her lip. "I was hoping maybe the stinging was a nettle." She shook her head. "I've got it now...haven't I?"

Leon's mom instinctively tugged at Grace's hand and pulled her back a few steps. "I don't know, Eva." Leon could see it on Leon's mom's face—she *did* know.

"Have we got it too?" asked Grace. "We were touching her!"

She shook her head firmly. "No. You're OK, Grace. I'm OK."

Leon looked at the young man standing beside him. He had one hand tucked behind his back.

"I...look, sorry...but something happened to you too. I saw you shaking your hand back there."

The man shook his head. "It's nothing, mate. Really."

"Show us," said Leon's mom.

He wheezed a laugh. "Nothing. A scratch." His hand remained behind his back.

"Show us," said Leon's mom more sharply. She softened her tone quickly. "Please...you have to."

The young man's face flickered with shame or pain. He held his hand out. The back of it was mottled red and glistened wetly where a weeping sore was beginning to develop. "Shit," he hissed angrily. "I've got this thing too, right?"

Leon's mom shook her head. "I don't know. But...please stay back."

He raised his hands in mock surrender. "Don't worry. I'm not going to touch anyone." He stepped slowly past Leon, crossed the muddy floor and sat down next to Eva. "I think you and me, we're out of the gang now, love," he huffed. "Which is bloody typical of my luck."

He looked up at Leon's mom and rattled out a humorless laugh. "Figures...I got top six-month salesperson yesterday. That's what me and my mates were drinking to. My big win."

Eva was staring at her arm. The mottled pattern on her skin was spreading. The skin itself was glistening and blistering like a burn. She probed it lightly with her finger and the skin gave way and tore open like wet tissue paper, spilling a thin rivulet of blood down toward her palm. At the sight of her own blood, her shoulders began to shake and she started sobbing. "This isn't happening to me."

"Looks like we're going to be melting buddies, love," said the man. He grinned drunkenly and offered her his uninfected hand. "I'm Greg, by the way."

Bemused, in shock, Eva squeezed his hand in response, then dipped her head down, cradling her face in her arms.

"I'm sorry," whispered Leon's mom. "I'm so sorry. I wish we could do something to help."

"Don't think there's much you can do," said Greg. "It looks like we're both screwed."

He sat back and smiled. A pink-stained tear rolled down his cheek. "Actually, do you have anything to drink? My mouth's dry as shit."

She shook her head, but then Grace said, "Sure." She dug into her shoulder bag and pulled out a bottle of grape-flavored water.

"Grace! No!"

She stepped forward and was handing it to him before Leon's mom could intervene. Greg reached out for the bottle, careful to make sure there was no skin contact. "You know...I can't give this back to you, love?"

She nodded, smiled. "It's OK. You can keep it."

"Thanks." He pulled the lid off and took a deep swig, swilling it around in his mouth before swallowing it. He held the bottle out to Eva. She took a sip, then handed it back.

"How are you feeling?" asked Leon.

Greg frowned and grinned at the same time. "Weird. Dizzy. Kind of like being drunk. Like, first-pint-at-lunchtime drunk, if you know what I mean?"

"Eva?" asked Leon's mom. "How about you?"

She sat up straight, her eyes firmly closed. "I feel tired. Very tired...like it's my time. My time...to go."

She eased herself back on the pallet, so that she was lying down, comfortable, looking up at the corrugated-iron roof and the shards of gray light spearing through its rusted holes. She half smiled. "I think...I think that's the Lord reaching down for me."

Greg chuckled at that and lay down beside her. "More like being stoned on a good joint."

"Are either of you in any pain? Discomfort?" asked Leon's mom.

Neither of them seemed to hear her. The rain drumming on the roof was getting louder and more insistent, and heavy drips were beginning to splash down through the holes, onto the ground.

"Greg?" said Leon. "Eva?"

Eva had started singing something softly. It sounded like a gospel hymn of some kind.

"Hey, that's really nice, Eva," said Greg dreamily. "Don't stop."

Leon watched as a trail of blood thickened with mucus, rolled out of Greg's left nostril, down his cheek, and soaked into the hair around his ear. He lifted his infected hand up to his face and stared up at it. A long ribbon of pink gel dangled down from it in a loop, swinging inches above him.

"Wow. I've never seen the inside of my hand," he said drunkenly. "I can see the bones...the tendons...the muscles... Fascinating."

Leon turned to look at his sister. Her face was white, her eyes round with horror.

"Mom," said Leon quietly. He nodded at his sister.

Don't let her watch this.

She nodded, got up, and tugged Grace after her. "Let's take a look around, honey, see if we can find supplies, anything useful."

149

They disappeared between the tractors, and Leon turned and resumed watching over Eva and Greg. Eva's arm was stretched out above her head now, like she didn't have a care in the world, was just some dreamer lying among the hay bales. Leon could see the process was accelerating. The infection seemed to be spreading quickly; her skin was mottled all the way up to the elbow now and faint lines showed the infection snaking ahead like scouts before an advancing army. The flesh along her forearm and around her wrist was drooping like melted wax, exposing glimpses of bone and tendon.

"Can either of you hear me?" asked Leon.

"Yeah..." whispered Greg after a while. "I hear you, mate."

"I have to go now... Is there anything I can do for you?"

"Thirsty," Greg replied, smacking his dry lips. "Thirsty work... this...melting business..."

Leon looked at the plastic bottle of grape-flavored water. He wanted to help them any way he could—hold the bottle to their lips—but he couldn't touch it now.

"The water's right there... It's right beside you, Greg."

The man's bloodshot eyes swiveled to the right. "My sight... Shit... It's going... I can't see... All blurry... Just light...glowing light."

"It's the Lord!" whispered Eva. "Coming down for us." Blood bubbled out of the side of her mouth. She started to gag and cough and turned her face to the side. Pink froth spilled out of her mouth onto the ground, accompanied by several loose teeth.

Leon wanted to leave, and yet felt he had to stay. To bear witness. On the one hand, he was storing up images in his head that were going to torment him with nightmares, but on the other, he needed to know what it was going to be like when they *inevitably* got this infection. He was certain it was going to happen to them sooner rather than later. They were going to die—he was going to witness his mom, Grace, himself...dying just like this.

He needed to know what it was going to be like. How it was going to feel.

Greg's left leg began to twitch and kick, almost in defiance, like it was the last part of his body putting up a fight. He started to moan and a deep gurgling came from the back of his throat, like he was now experiencing some sort of discomfort.

"Greg? Can you hear me? Is it...hurting?"

The moan became a whimpering cry, no longer the voice of a young man but the tearless mewling of a small boy.

"I...don't wan'...to go clothes shops, Mom... I don't want to..." Greg muttered. The rest of his words became an incoherent, childlike jumble. He was silent for a few moments, then suddenly began to shriek. The shrill sound lasted just a couple of seconds before it turned into a guttural click as something within his throat collapsed or snapped or gave way.

Enough! God, enough! You've seen enough.

Eva's upper arm was now beginning to slide off the bone like slow-cooked meat. The pooling liquid beneath seemed to be organizing itself, several small threads emerging from the pool like feelers, snaking inch by inch across the ground—explorers charting a new continent.

"Leon! Come on!" His mom's voice. "*Now!*"

He stood up and backed several steps away from the two bodies.

"I...I've got to go," he said softly. Neither of them seemed to hear him.

Eva resumed humming her hymn, while Greg just gurgled and whimpered.

CHAPTER
23

LEON FIGURED IT WAS JUST ABOUT MIDDAY WHEN HIS MOM finally did what Mr. Mareham predicted she would do.

She cracked.

They'd left the barn, Leon's mom not wanting to risk staying near the infection a moment longer than they had to. There was no way of knowing if there would be more of those lethal floating particles. They'd made their way across field after field, hoping to find a farmhouse, a gas station, an out-of-town strip mall, a main road…even hoping to find a police roadblock, despite the fact they might be shot on sight if they did.

"I thought Britain was supposed to be, like, overcrowded," said Grace.

Leon smiled encouragingly. Good to hear her have a go at trying to be funny.

She had a point. It seemed as if they'd made their escape from the train into the one unspoiled wilderness left in the country.

After an hour of cutting across plowed ruts of mud, they finally headed toward a nearby woods in the hope that it was concealing some sort of safe haven.

Leon spotted the corpses of dozens of animals—cows or bulls, by the look of them—in the far corner of the field they were crossing, sagging, black-and-white hides that had torn open to reveal rows of curved bones like the gnarled clawlike fingers of upturned hands. They were a safe enough distance away to pause for a moment, but then a gust of wind swooped across the field and scooped a cloud of particles from each carcass up into the air.

They scrambled toward the cover of the nearby tree line and skirted the edge for a while, looking for something else more promising to head for than the deep, dark woods.

Finally, exhausted and thirsty, they came to a halt beneath the low boughs of an elm tree. Leon's mom excused herself to go for a pee, ducking beneath a loop of barbed wire and disappearing into the woods.

Grace shucked the straps of her backpack off her shoulders, let it drop to the ground, then slumped down to sit on it. She inspected her mud-caked tennis shoes. "I wonder if school's closed today," she wondered absently. A stupid question, but it was something to break the silence.

"Of course it is," Leon replied. "Everything's closed, Grace."

"Like, forever and ever...the end?"

He shrugged.

She snorted humorlessly. "That's your dream, isn't it? Schools closed forever. The end of the world. Just like those stupid Xbox zombie games?" The way she said that, it sounded as if she was blaming him for wishing this on the world.

She was right about one thing though. How many times had he imagined how *cool* it would be to be the lone survivor in a postapocalyptic landscape as he hacked his way through legions of undead, risen demons and Slendermen? Brutal onscreen survival...from the comfort and convenience of his bedroom, with a mug of coffee and a warm Pop-Tart beside him.

"Just shut up" was all he managed to come up with.

"Great idea leaving town, Leo." Her voice had lost that croaky, sarcastic drawl she used for playground put-downs. "We should have stayed at home."

Home? Did she mean London? Or was she talking about the U.S.?

"Dad's a complete, total idiot...telling us to get out of—"

"Dad was totally right," he replied. "If we'd stayed, we would have been trapped."

"I hope he and his girlfriend are dead."

He spun around. "Why don't you just shut up?"

"No, *you* shut up! You always take his side."

"What? No I don't."

"Yeah, you do. You've done nothing but sulk like a baby since we moved. Making things even harder on Mom. And she's had enough to—"

"Jeez, Grace! Just stop trying to big-sister me! You don't know shit. You don't know anything."

"I made an effort to fit in here. Which is more than you've—"

"Mom didn't *have* to drag us to England! She could've worked

155

it out with Dad. She could've kept going... She just didn't like it there. This was just an excuse to leave—"

"Hey! Hey! Hey!" Leon's mom emerged from the woods. "Just knock it off, both of you!" She stumbled out of the undergrowth toward them.

"Grace said she wished Dad were dead!"

"Yeah, so what? And all you do is blame Mom just because you can't make any new friends over here."

"You're so full of it, Grace. You—"

Leon's mom ducked down quickly through the barbed wire— "The two of you just stop it! Please!"—catching her scalp on a rusty barb. As she stood up, it scraped deeply, tugging roughly at her hair and making her yelp with pain.

Grace and Leon shut up. They watched her straighten up, clutching the top of her head and grimacing. She lifted her hand away from her messed-up hair and stared at the smear of blood across her palm. Then, without warning, her legs buckled beneath her and she slumped down heavily, ending up kneeling in the mud, her face buried in her hands, sobbing and rocking backward and forward.

Just like Ben had said.

One thing too many...buckaroo.

Grace dropped down beside her. "Mom? Mom? Hey! Please! Don't cry!"

But Leon's mom continued wailing into her hands and then Grace started crying too.

Leon watched them both huddled together on the wet mud, with a sky threatening more rain and a silent woods beside them that should have been alive with birds singing but instead sighed mournfully in the breeze.

The three of them were stuck in the middle of nowhere... The other passengers? He had no idea if they were still alive. Still people. They were marooned here, with no food, no water, nowhere to go, and no one left alive to help them, so it seemed.

Time to step up to the plate, MonkeyNuts.

He closed his eyes and massaged his temple. Another bastard of a headache was announcing its timely arrival.

CHAPTER
24

Suffolk

AS THE RAIN PATTERED RELENTLESSLY ON THE CORRUGATED-iron barn roof, beneath it, on a low stack of abandoned wooden pallets, several trillion cells that had once formed the architecture of a being called Eva now began to work as a giant collective.

Nearby was another cooperative that used to be known as Greg. Both these colonies now served new masters—masters, or, more accurately, liberators: like a crusading army, advancing from city to city, freeing slaves from their shackles and recruiting them to the cause.

The virally infected cells—simple automatons with no real understanding of kingdoms or cities or slaves—now worked on a new basic chemical incentive: to find cells unlike themselves, non-brethren identified by their DNA, and store those sequences of nucleotides for later, while converting them just enough to enlist them in the process of hunting down the other non-brethren that remained.

Within five hours of very first contact, as the light faded from the gray sky and the afternoon became twilight, the last soft-tissue components of the former kingdoms of Eva and Greg had been absorbed and recruited as single-cell citizens of a far greater combined nation. What remained of those old kingdoms were the crumbling ruins, the defeated battlements and strongholds: bones, hair, teeth, and nails.

The indigestible and the unnecessary.

Between those brittle, forgotten remnants, the cells merged into a single big pool rich in stores of nutrition, a gathering place where cells swirled around each other and exchanged the tiny packets of DNA data they each carried like market square gossip, like mercenaries comparing their stolen goods.

They exchanged, compared, and every now and then, when pieces of DNA accidentally fit together, like jigsaw puzzle pieces stirred around in a box, they...*reconstructed.*

Somewhere, in the middle of the dark, glutinous puddle, a tiny part of Eva was remade; just a few hundred fragments of data that under the old regime would together have formed a single, solitary, not particularly important gene—a gene that decided the configuration of taste buds, a gene that used to have the tiniest say in the type of food Eva once favored.

She used to have a thing for banana smoothies. That insignificant gene was the reason for that. A tiny part of Eva, in that moment, had been recovered. The short DNA sequence was reproduced in the genome of several cells that were now promoted to a more important role: specialized cells with a particular purpose, guardians of a microscopic fragment of genetic knowledge.

Tiny little librarians, tasked with keeping that part of Eva alive for posterity.

Forever.

CHAPTER
25

THEY CAME ACROSS IT THE NEXT MORNING, AFTER A NIGHT huddled together beneath the plastic roof of a rural bus stop. Leon, Grace, and their mom...quite possibly the last three people left alive in Britain, perhaps the world.

Leon had spent the entire night looking wistfully down the long, straight country road, overhung by leafy branches that creaked and groaned, hoping to spot the distant pinprick of someone's approaching headlights.

As soon as the sky started to lighten to a dispiriting gray and they could see where they were going, they got to their feet and continued down the road, hoping to find a small town, maybe a gas station with a vending machine selling something they could safely drink. Leon's head thumped with every step, his headache compounded further by the ache of dehydration and exhaustion.

They passed a stream and considered for a moment dipping

their cupped hands into it. But Leon and his mom looked at each other and shook their heads. Not worth it. Not yet at any rate.

The gray sky gradually became a featureless white—it was midmorning, Leon guessed, when they finally came across the entrance to *something*: an old road of cracked, unmaintained asphalt leading up to a wire-mesh fence. There was an old Ministry of Defense sign above which a newer sign had been attached.

Grace read the sign. "Redevelopment of site: Hewitt and Hughes Contractors. This site is supervised twenty-four hours."

"Maybe there's someone here," said Leon. He could imagine finding a bowlegged, old security guard with a German shepherd called Saxon, stoically doing his job despite the coming of the end of the world. A cranky man who might at first try to gruffly shoo them away, but who would take pity and let them in. He would provide shelter and food, and in return, they'd show him how to open his stone-cold heart and learn to love again.

Just like some crummy TV movie.

The cracked road led up a gentle slope, past a cluster of saplings that looked as if they hadn't been deliberately planted but were the random scatterings of Mother Nature staking her claim.

At the top of the slope, they came to a halt.

"What are those?" asked Grace.

They were looking across a couple of fenced acres of weed-covered ground, punctuated at regular intervals by artificial-looking mounds of grass: uniformly round, with flat tops. Leon counted them—twenty-seven...three orderly rows of nine. There were several boarded-up concrete structures and a single prefabricated shed.

"Maybe there's someone in the cabin?"

They made their way toward it, up an overgrown pathway, between two of the rows of mounds. Leon noticed each one had a short flight of concrete steps that led down into the ground and a heavy iron door. They reminded him of the ruins of the Nazi fortifications along the Normandy beaches. Each mound's iron door appeared to be firmly sealed with heavy-duty padlocks.

The shed was also locked. They knocked on the door and waited a minute. Then, finally, Leon decided no one was home and aimed a kick at its flimsy door. It caved inward. Inside, they found several plastic chairs set around a table cluttered with copies of *The Sun*, the *Mirror*, and the *Daily Express* from three days ago. The headlines were all about some soccer player who'd been arrested for assaulting a referee, a former *Britain's Got Talent* star who'd been discovered living homeless on the streets, and an article on the recent spike in the number of African migrants "swarming toward Britain." There was an ashtray full of cigarette butts, several mugs that held the congealed dregs of coffee, and a long-handled night watchman's flashlight.

There was an empty kettle and a small fridge. Leon's mom hurried over to it and pulled it open. Inside there was a bottle of milk that was so old it had separated into three clearly distinct layers of gunk. There was, however, a plastic liter bottle of water. She pulled it out and opened it.

"Here," she said, holding it out to them.

Leon took it from her and sipped it. "It's pretty stale, but it's OK."

He handed it to his sister. She tested it and made a face, but then thirst overcame her and she eagerly tossed back several hasty slugs. Leon followed her, then handed his mom the bottle. She upended it and gulped a few mouthfuls. It was stale water that had been sitting there for a while with God knows whose backwash floating around in it, but they quickly finished it off between them.

There was nothing else to drink and little of use except the flashlight. Leon picked it up and tried it. It was working.

They stepped out of the cabin and made their way back down the path. It was then that Leon noticed that one of the many grassy mounds' doors *wasn't* padlocked.

"Mom, look!"

He took the half a dozen steps down and pushed against it gently. It creaked inward.

She shook her head. "Leave it, Leon. There could be anything, anyone—*druggies*—down there." She obviously didn't share Leon's hope of finding some friendly creaky-kneed old security guard, but instead feared bumping into some drug-crazed hermit.

He ignored her and peered into the gloom beyond. Directly ahead of him there was a curving wall, and to his left, concrete steps followed the curve and descended into darkness.

He snapped the flashlight on.

"Leon, please," said his mom.

"Let me just take a look. There might be something we can use." He took the first half a dozen steps down and out of sight.

"Leon!" snapped Grace after him. "Listen to Mom for once!"

He ignored her and slowly made his way down, circling clockwise and descending until the last of the meager daylight was gone and it was just the stark beam of the flashlight ahead of him. Finally the steps came to an end. He shined his flashlight around.

He was in what looked like a sleeping room for workers. There were four metal-framed beds, a filing cabinet, several folding chairs, and a small table. The concrete walls were painted a mint green and were marked with scuffs and scrapes. On one wall was a cork bulletin board with a number of yellowing paper notes tacked to it, a *Playboy* calendar with curling pages, a small poster of some ridiculous-looking, puffy-haired rock band called Bon Jovi, and a bunch of baseball cards.

"*Leon?*" His mom's voice echoed down the stairs. "You OK?"

"Yeah," he replied. He crossed the small bunk room and shined his flashlight on the calendar.

Jeez. 1986. It was over thirty years old. The place was a time capsule.

He shined his flashlight around some more. There were two doors. He tried one, which led to a small bathroom. The toilet was bone dry and feathered with spiderwebs. He tried the other door and discovered there was a splintered, ragged hole where a handle had once been. Somebody must have forced it, smashed their way in sometime in the past, as they had the padlocked door at the top of the steps. He pushed the door and aimed his flashlight inside the room beyond.

"Oh...you've got to be kidding me," he whispered. "Bazinga."

———

By candlelight, they drank greedily from the cans of orange juice; then, their thirst finally quenched, they turned to the other cans for something to eat. Each can was clearly marked with plain, no-nonsense text on a pale military-gray label.

BEANS IN TOMATO SAUCE: 400GMS, 2 SERVINGS. CALORIES: 400

MINCED PORK: 100GMS, 1 SERVING. CALORIES: 130

SKINNED POTATOES: 250GMS, 2 SERVINGS. CALORIES: 160

Leon talked with his mouth full. "This must be some kind of old nuclear bunker or something."

His mom nodded, her mouth bulging with food. "Missile silo." She finished chewing and swallowed. "Your grandad once told me they're dotted all over East Anglia from the Cold War."

Leon looked up at her and watched her hungrily digging into a can of peaches with her finger, trying to scoop one out. He was reassured by the tone of her voice. For the first time in twenty-four hours, it sounded more like her normal self, not clipped and fragile...not the vocal equivalent of a glass pitcher perched precariously on the edge of a table.

She sounded like Leon's mom again. Which was a relief. Leon had listened to his dad and stepped up...and hated every second of it. He was far happier tagging along than leading.

Now they had food and juice in their bellies, and somewhere safe and hidden away to sleep. For the first time in forty-eight hours of not knowing if life was going to be measured in minutes or months, it looked as if they were going to be OK for a little while. The storeroom was stacked with cardboard boxes of canned food and drinks. It was as good a place as any to ride out the apocalypse.

"Missiles?" said Grace. "You mean, like...*nuke-u-lar* ones?"

"Nuclear." Leon's mom nodded. "Uh-huh. But they're not here anymore, love. They closed these sorts of places down back in the late eighties, I think."

"Isn't there, like, radiation or something to worry about?" asked Leon.

"I don't think so."

Leon put down his can of corned beef and rummaged through some of the boxes nearest him. "They've got, literally, everything here. Not just food, but medicine and stuff."

"Good."

"Any aspirin?" asked Grace. She patted her sling gently. "My arm's been killing me for ages."

"I'll look... Ahh." He pulled out a carton of pills. Like the food, it was labeled clearly and blandly.

"Oh, now you both need to be careful. Medicines have a shelf life," said Leon's mom. "They may not be safe to—"

"Mom?" Leon looked at her. "Relax, OK? They're aspirin. Nothing more."

She nodded, returning his smile. "Yes, I suppose you're right."

Leon opened the packet and popped a couple out of the foil for Grace and a couple for himself. "The worst that happens with aspirin is they get less effective with age."

"You know that, or you're just guessing?" asked Grace. She was also sounding more like her old self now.

"I read it online...somewhere. Once." He tossed the pills into his mouth and knocked them back with a slug of orange juice.

Grace cocked her brow at his casual attitude but finally followed his lead. "If I end up getting poisoned, it's *your* fault."

"You can sue me, kiddo."

They resumed eating in silence, the concrete walls echoing with the sound of scraping cans and fingers being licked.

"Leo," said Grace after a while, "I...I'm sorry about what I said. I really don't wish Dad were dead." She pressed her lips together. "I hope he's OK."

He nodded. "Me too."

"Your dad's a natural survivor," said his mom. "I imagine you'd be far safer with him looking after you than me."

"You're doing fine, Mom." Leon stretched out a foot and tapped one of hers. "You got us out in time...just before they locked London down. That was really close."

"Do you think we're better off out of London than in?" asked Grace.

Leon thought she was asking their mom that, but he realized the question was directed at him.

"Maybe." He shrugged. He had no idea at all. Just a guess. "Probably," he added. "There're millions living in London, right? Even if the virus hasn't gotten in there, I guess there won't be enough food and water for everyone."

Crisis aftermath...that's when most people die, MonkeyNuts. It's not the earthquake that kills 'em—it's the mess afterward.

Leon recalled news stories from postdisaster shantytowns, people dying of hunger and from drinking polluted water.

You know, Son, a wise man once said that modern civilization is just three square meals and an internet connection away from total anarchy.

"We're much better off waiting this thing out sitting here, Grace. Far better than being stuck in Hammersmith."

Grace nodded. Then a thought occurred to her. "Remember when Dad took us camping in the Rockies?"

"This"—he gestured at the concrete walls—"reminds you of that?"

"No, *this*," she replied, holding out the can of baked beans she was pawing her way through. "Remember Dad's totally lame camp stew?"

Leon's mom laughed. "God it was awful, wasn't it?" He'd insisted on making dinner over a campfire in an old pot. He'd basically emptied a random selection of canned goods into the pot filled with river water and boiled the whole thing into a thick porridge-like paste. They'd gone camping with a colleague of their dad's and his family. Grace had, of course, gotten on really well with the other kids, while Leon had kept them at a cool distance. But the one thing that had pulled Leon into the circle was the universal disgust at his dad's "Survival Soup." It had ended up being tossed into the bushes, no doubt attracting some giant grizzly bear, and they'd all driven into the nearby town for McDonald's.

"Even your dad admitted it tasted disgusting," said Leon's mom. She smiled at the memory. Good times...there had been one or two.

They heard a heavy metallic clang. It came from above. Leon recognized it for what it was: the heavy door right at the top of the bunker banging closed.

Shit.

Was that the wind outside blowing it shut? The possibility that they might just have very stupidly entombed themselves down here forever hit him like a hard slap.

Shit. Shit. Shit.

Then he heard something far more disconcerting: the heavy *clunk* of a pair of boots descending the concrete steps toward them. Leon's mom reached over to snuff out the candle sitting between them.

Leon grabbed her hand to prevent her. He shook his head. "Better to not be a *surprise*," he whispered. There was nowhere for them to hide. It was better if they weren't a complete shock to whoever it was, especially if they were carrying a gun and had a finger resting on the trigger.

She nodded. They listened to the footsteps descending. "Hello?" Leon's mom called out.

The footsteps suddenly stopped.

"Hello?" she said again, doing her best to keep her voice sounding confident and steady.

Silence.

"You might as well come down. We *all* heard you slam the door!"

Another moment of silence, then they heard the scraping of a boot. A step...then another and another. Slowly getting closer and louder until with a scrape of rubber soles on the gritty floor, a dark figure loomed in the doorway at the bottom of the stairwell.

"That is *my* food you're eating."

"What? Oh..." Leon's mom set the can of fruit salad she was holding down on the ground. "I'm really...sorry... We just—"

"Go ahead and eat it. There is much, much more of it." The figure, a man, took several steps into the small room. He was holding a cardboard box, which he set on the ground, cans rattling inside it. Closer to the candle, they could see him more clearly. He was dark skinned, with a thick, black beard covering the lower half of his face.

"There's food like this in every one of these bunkers," he said. His brown eyes settled on each of them in turn. "If it is just the three of you, then, *inshallah*, there will be enough food for all."

CHAPTER
26

5/11

Dad, we're alive and we're safe and we've got food and water. I don't want to think about what would have happened (or if we'd even still be alive) if Mom hadn't gotten us out on pretty much the last train from London. I know you're alive too. Like Mom said, you're a born survivor. An alpha male, right? Unlike me. I'm more your knuckle-dragger type. But I guess I did my part by looking after Grace. Anyway, the point is we're OK. We're with this guy called Mohammed. We call him "Mo" for short. Yeah, I know...before you ask...he is. He prays and stuff but he's OK with us not doing the same. He's this big Bangladeshi guy, kinda gentle, and he speaks really softly like he's constantly trying not to wake up someone who's sleeping nearby.

We came across this old Cold War missile silo stocked with supplies that date back to, I kid you not, the eighties! I guess if there'd been a nuclear war, these supplies were supposed to last the missile crew until radiation was low enough to come out again. How long's that supposed to be— years, decades? So, none of the tin cans actually have "use by" dates on them. I guess the food was zapped to hell before it was canned. We've got no radios, no working phones, nothing. No power. So right now we've got no idea whether the rest of the country or the world has been affected. It's been two weeks, I think. And the farthest I've been from our bunker is a few dozen yards. I spent some time yesterday standing on top of one of the bunker mounds, looking across some fields for any signs of life. I didn't see anything.

For all I know we could be the last four people in the world. (Five, counting you.) It's weird. Every time I've stepped outside it's been so quiet. No planes in the sky, no sound of distant traffic, obviously. But also no birds in the trees. No buzzing insects. The trees, grass, weeds—the plants—aren't affected, but everything that isn't a plant seems to be.

What does that mean for the planet? Can plants get by without animals around? I know some plants need bees to pollinate, right? And other plants need animals to eat their seeds and poop them out, so doesn't that mean an unsustainable ecosystem? No animals means eventually no plants? And if no plants... eventually that means no breathable air, right? Or maybe I'm overthinking this. I guess that kind of process takes decades, so we're OK for now. If it really is just us left, there's probably enough preserved food out there in stores and supermarkets to last us for the rest of our lives. Only if it's safe to go out and forage though.

Mo says there's a high chance we might be immune to the infection. That's why the four of us are still alive. Some kind of inherited, genetic immunity. Which I guess suggests it must be from Mom's genes, and not yours, if that's the case. I've been trying to rack my brains to remember if anyone who was infected on that train touched me, or whether any of that pollen stuff landed on me. I don't remember. I don't think so. So...Mo's theory so far remains to be proven. Maybe we were just very, very lucky.

5/12
Why am I even writing this stuff to you? You're never going to read it.

5/14
Dad, is it totally weird of me to kind of know you're still alive even if the odds are against that? It's just that I keep hearing you butt into my head. If that's you somewhere using Jedi mind powers...don't stop. It's mostly good advice you're giving. So don't, you know, stop. OK? So, by the way, I guess with your super mind powers you must be able to hear me too? (That would be great, wouldn't it?)

I guess you want to know how Grace is doing. Better than you'd expect, I think. She's cried a few times. Mainly because she's missing her old life, her phone, her friends, Facebook, all that kind of meaningless stuff. She's OK enough to have bitched at me a few times about being a wimp. So I guess she's generally OK. Her arm's still hurting her though. I think it may have gotten banged up, knocked or broken or something during our escape. Mo thinks it might even be infected, although he's not sure.

And Mom? I think she's doing her best to stay strong for us. I know she's called you an asshole a number of times since we left New York, but deep down I know she still misses you. Maybe even still loves you. And I know she wishes you were here right now. Mo seems all right. But Mom never lets Grace out of her sight when he's around. I get that. We don't know anything about him really. I know she wishes you were here, taking charge of things. Because that's what you're used to, isn't it? Being "the Guy" when the shit hits the fan. Taking charge under fire, leading your men into combat. You never did tell me much about your time in Iraq. All I remember you saying was that it wasn't anything like Call of Duty. I wish I were more like you. I wish I hadn't been such a disappointment to you. Been Marine material, instead of a... What was it you called me once? Oh yeah, I remember...a "whiny little thumb-sucker." Nice.

5/25
Dad, I am trying to be better than that. I think I've done some growing up.

"It has gone septic, I think," said Mohammed. He studied the inflamed, red skin of Grace's forearm, scratched his thick beard, and frowned deep folds on his forehead. "This is not good."

"We've got antibiotics," said Leon's mom. She turned around and picked up several plainly marked boxes of medicine. "See? Look? Netromycin. Streptomycin."

Mohammed shook his head and wagged a finger. "Those are over thirty years old, Mrs. Button. Bacterial resistance has moved on a very long way since those pills were made. They will do nothing to help her."

"So?" She looked at Leon then back to Mohammed. "We have to go find some more modern antibiotics, then?"

He nodded. "Indeed. Yes."

"Where?"

"Little Buntingham."

She shook her head. The name meant nothing to her.

"It is nearby. It is where I was working. Just seven or eight miles from here."

Leon put down the old Marvel comic books he was reading. He'd found a stash of them beneath one of the bunks. "Walk eight miles? What about the virus?"

"Leon?" His mother stared at him sternly. "You do understand if we don't get some viable antibiotics for Grace she could get *really* sick?" She glanced quickly at Grace, then back at him.

Leon understood. "Really sick" meant far worse, but Grace was right there, listening to her. Really sick meant septicemia—or worse.

"We haven't seen any of those pollen clouds for nearly a week now. I think whatever stage of the plague that was… Well, it's happened. It's all done." She looked to Mohammed to back her up.

He stroked his beard thoughtfully. "We will have to go outside eventually."

Leon nodded slowly. It wasn't as if he'd said they *shouldn't* go out; he just wanted to be clear that they all understood this meant more than a casual trip around the corner to the local pharmacy.

"Maybe we'll find an abandoned car," he said hopefully.

"I cannot drive," said Mohammed.

"None of us can," added Leon's mom.

"I can," said Leon. "Not, like, legally, but I know how it's done… kind of."

"It's not like playing *Big Theft Auto*, Leo. You can't just—"

"*Grand Theft Auto*, Mom. And, anyway, jeez, it's not like there's going to be anything else on the road for me to hit. Or even any cops to pull us over."

Grace nodded, on his side for once. "Mom, just let Leon drive if we find a car. I don't think we should be walking around *outside* if we don't have to be."

Leon's mom stared at her rebellious kids, united on this particular issue, and found herself unable to put together a convincing counterargument. "Well, if we find one…you take it *very* slow, Leo. I mean it. Slow!"

CHAPTER
27

THEY FOUND A WHITE VAN THAT HAD SKIDDED TO A HALT AT the side of the very same road they'd been walking along two weeks ago. The driver's side door was open, and a dozen yards away, Leon saw a pair of Doc Martens boots and the frayed cuffs of a pair of jeans protruding from the bushes beneath a tree.

Mohammed wandered over and ducked under the tree to get a closer look.

"Don't get too near it," said Leon's mom.

He nodded, pulled a branch to one side, and made a face at what he could see. "Just bones and clothes left."

The driver presumably. It looked as if he'd been infected, come to a halt before he crashed into something, and then... What did he hope to find by getting out? Help? Leon wondered why the driver had even bothered to unbuckle himself. Maybe he hadn't seen up close what Leon had seen—the inevitability of death.

This must have happened after they'd walked this way. He

wondered how long after. Carefully, he pulled open the passenger's side door and peered inside, expecting to see the ghastly, stringy remains of some other poor soul. But the interior appeared to be clean, and the key was still in the ignition.

"It looks OK."

Grace remained several feet away on the other side of the narrow country lane. She stared uncertainly at the van. "What if there's still...bits of him inside?"

Leon cautiously climbed up on to the passenger's side.

"Please...be careful, Leo," his mom called out.

He looked around. "I can't see any...gooey stuff. It looks totally clean."

"I'm not sure it's worth the risk," she added. "It just takes one touch from one of those flakes or tendrils, and we'll get it."

"Unless we are immune," Mohammed reminded her.

Leon backed out and stepped down on to the asphalt. "Mom, we're going into a village and looking around for stuff. We're gonna end up touching lots of things. And on the way, if we come across one of those spore clouds, we're going to want something to shield us from it."

Grace bit her lip, remembering their escape from the cloud on the railway track. She nodded eagerly. "Leon's right."

"Then let's be sure...a hundred percent sure." Leon's mom went to the back of the van and gingerly pulled the rear doors open. Something dislodged inside as she slowly opened it. A can of paint rolled out and thunked on to the road. The back of the van was cluttered with cans, brushes, and paint-spattered dust sheets.

Ten minutes later, the rear of the van was completely empty, its contents tossed out onto the road. Leon's mom nodded, satisfied there weren't any hidden sticky strands of the plague lurking inside.

Leon settled into the driver's seat, his mom the passenger's seat, and Mohammed and Grace crouched in the back.

"OK," said Leon, turning the ignition key. The van started, grunted, lurched forward a couple feet, and then stalled.

"Neutral," said his mom. "Is it in neutral?"

Leon mentally smacked his forehead. He knew about gears and clutches. The basic theory of it all anyway. He pulled the gear column into neutral and turned the ignition again. The van's engine purred with begrudging approval this time. He glanced down at his feet and tried to identify the three pedals from memory.

Brake, clutch, accelerator.

He pressed down on the left-most pedal and then pushed the gear stick into first. A grinding, rattling whine came from the engine.

Oh yeah. Clutch...brake...accelerator.

He tried the correct pedal and waggled the stick into first, this time without the van complaining. He eased his foot off the clutch and the van lurched forward once again, kangaroo-hopping nearly into the tree and the bones beneath it. He spun the steering wheel and the van swung sharply back onto the narrow road and ended up thumping gently against a tree on the far side and stalling.

"For God's sake, Leon," cried Grace from the back, "you're going to kill us all."

Half an hour later, the van finally crawled into Little

Buntingham, the engine grinding and whining at Leon for his heavy-handed and heavy-footed treatment.

An improvised barricade had been set up across the road, nothing they couldn't knock aside: just some wooden packing crates, an old sofa, and a hastily painted warning on the back of a real estate agent's sign:

WE HAVE THE PLAGUE HERE

"This will have to do," said Mohammed.

Leon brought the van to a staggered halt and turned the engine off. He imagined this rural village was exactly the type of country setting for which American tourists came to the UK: a village green, a duck pond with a weeping willow dipping leaves into the water. No ducks now, of course. There was a pub, and next to it a post office and a convenience store. A church spire loomed over the top of thatched roofs. Real *wish you were here* picture-postcard stuff. But it was deserted and silent except for the gentle, soothing whisper of the willow stirring in the breeze.

"Maybe it's been evacuated?" said Leon's mom hopefully.

"No," replied Mohammed. "You saw the sign. It reached this place too."

Leon spotted a couple of small piles of clothing, one on the green, another across the flower beds just outside the post office. He pointed them out to his mom and she nodded sadly. "I guess nowhere escaped it, then."

"The pharmacy is just a bit farther along this street," said Mohammed. He climbed out of the back of the van.

Leon's mom opened the passenger's side door. "You kids stay right here. We don't all need to go looking."

Leon ignored that and reached for the door handle.

"No." She grabbed at his arm. "I said *stay!*"

"Mom, for God's sake, I'm just—"

"Leon," she snapped at him. "For once can you please just do as I say?"

He stared at her—a challenge. He wanted to make the point that maybe it was time for him to stand up and be an adult. OK, he wasn't eager...but it was probably time. She needed to know, the conversation needed to happen, but maybe not just now. She had her stress face on and was doing the voice-rising thing. Clearly, she wasn't going to take any shit from him this morning.

"You stay right here and you *watch your sister*. All right?" Her voice was sharp. The next notch up would be the mom screech, the one that went right through him like nails across a blackboard.

He nodded resentfully. "Make sure you get me some aspirin or Tylenol."

"Don't worry... We'll get a little of everything." She squeezed his arm gently before letting go. "Back in five, OK?"

She stepped down out of the van, closed the door, and followed Mohammed around the barricade and down the pretty little main street.

Grace stirred in the back. "Why do you always do that?"

He watched them until they disappeared around a bend in the road. "Do what?"

"Get her worked up like that."

183

He turned in his seat and looked back at his sister. She was slumped against the side of the van, cradling her throbbing arm. Eyes closed and skin pale.

"I'm nearly seventeen. She still treats me like a little kid."

"Yeah, well...you behave like one still."

He mentally counted to five. His sister irritated the hell out of him sometimes. That whole *little girl all grown up* voice she did. Like *she* was the older sibling here—sometimes it *really* grated.

———

"So you really think we might actually be immune to this thing?"

Mohammed nodded. "It is a distinct possibility. You told me you were on that train. Well, I was in the village hall here. The same thing happened to me. We were woken up by local police. All taken to the hall. The policeman was telling us what he'd been told, about all the emergency measures. Then somebody came into the hall, sick. We all ran, panicked, outside, and that floating white pollen was coming down on us like snow."

He shook his head. "There was so much of it. Some of it *must* have touched me—I am sure of it."

"And you didn't get ill?"

He shook his head. "No. Nothing. If...*if*...we have immunity, it is not like normal where you take on the virus, you survive, and now your body knows how to fight the infection, I think. If it is that we are immune, then the virus must have no effect at all. It cannot get established."

"Or we've been very, very lucky so far."

Mohammed nodded. "That is also possible."

They passed the village's one and only pub and its quaint, little beer garden. Just ahead of them on the other side of the narrow road was a church and, next to it, a single-story community center. Along its short gravel path, flanked by beautifully maintained flower beds, lay small bundles of clothes from which bones protruded, tufts of tangled and matted hair still attached to the tops of skulls. Leon's mom spotted a mottled brown skull emerging from the neckline of a blue bathrobe right beside her and, on the path, a pair of bright-pink dentures.

Her eyes flicked away from them quickly. It was just too much. She looked at the only safe place: the sky.

"Oh God, I feel like I need to throw up."

"Do not look so closely then," he replied.

She sucked in a deep breath. "That was where they rounded you up?"

Mohammed nodded. "I ran from there, then out of the village."

"What about family? Was there anybody else…?"

"I am lucky, I think. I have no family." He touched her arm lightly. "This is the village medical center. The pharmacy is inside."

———

Leon opened the driver's side door.

"And just where do you think you're going?" Grace clucked imperiously.

"Just going to take a look."

"Mom said you had to stay right here with me!"

"You stay here. I'm not going far." He climbed out.

"Leon!"

"Hey! Relax! I'm just going to go take a look at the pond."

"Why?" Her voice lost its scolding tone. "Leon, please don't!"

"I'm not going to touch anything! Just stay there. You'll be fine."

He left the door open, like a bank robber anticipating the need for a quick getaway, and made his way across the overgrown lawn toward the pond. He detoured slightly to get a closer look at a pile of clothing nearby.

It appeared to be the remains of someone young: sneakers, jeans...a soccer shirt that was once canary yellow, now mostly mottled with dark patches, and a mop of wavy, brown, shoulder-length hair. It could have been either a girl or a boy with Harry Styles hair. All he had to go on was clothes, bones, and hair.

Where's all the rest of him...her?

He'd witnessed Mr. Mareham's body reduced to a pool. He'd watched Eva and that guy, Greg, beginning to break down into that same liquid. Where did all that thick liquid go? He wondered if it had somehow dried out and become those white flakes, like dandelions turning from flowers to white puffs of seed? But not all that liquid, right? He wondered if it had just soaked into the ground, but there seemed to be no residue or anything else on the grass. It seemed that everything from this body that could be digested had been—perfectly efficiently—and then apparently vanished...leaving behind nothing but bones.

It can't have just evaporated, MonkeyNuts. It's there... somewhere.

Leon nodded. He'd seen it up close. It wasn't just a "dumb" liquid. He was certain he'd witnessed it trickle with some kind of purpose, not simply following the grooves of wood or the pull of gravity, but small rivulets of it moving deliberately toward other ones, reaching out for each other. Making connections.

It's not evaporated or soaked away. It's gone somewhere. He stood up and looked around, suddenly feeling vulnerable and exposed.

It's hiding.

CHAPTER
28

THERE WERE BODIES IN THE OFFICE'S WAITING ROOM. NOT that Leon's mom felt she could call them *bodies*; they were just clumps of clothes, almost like the small piles of laundry Leon left lying around for her in his bedroom like cow pie in a field. In the corner, she glimpsed a stroller and a pink snuggle suit; she was too slow when she looked away to not see the little skull and its two dark orbital sockets staring back at her. Much of the floor of the waiting room was dotted with clothes and scarecrow bones. She stepped warily clear of each pile, examining the floor for the weblike tendrils of fluid.

"Mohammed...where's all that stuff gone?"

He nodded. Clearly he'd noticed that too. There was little to suggest these bodies had ever been anything more than bones and rags, except for a network of faint stains on the office's knitted carpet, snaking pencil-thin lines that radiated out from each body like old, disused country roads, marking where the liquid had once been.

They made their way around the receptionist's desk to a back room lined from floor to ceiling with partitioned shelves and pigeonhole compartments stuffed with small, white packs and cartons of pills, many labeled with patient names.

"We should get several kinds of antibiotics for your daughter," he said as he pulled the cartons out one by one, reading the contents of each. "And also we should gather a selection of general-purpose antibiotics. Also analgesics of whichever kind you prefer. The brand is not important; it is the same whichever you choose."

Leon's mom started sorting through the boxes in the pigeon-holes. "You seem to know a lot about medicines."

"I used to be a practicing pharmacist," he replied.

"Here?"

"No, back in Syria."

She looked at him. "I thought you said you came from Bangladesh?"

He shrugged. "Originally."

"Then you traveled there?" She let the question be open and nonspecific, but he nodded.

He knew exactly what she was asking. "I went to help my brothers and sisters." He nodded solemnly. "Yes. I was there."

"Did you fight over there?"

He ignored her. Pulled out a cardboard box and emptied the contents on the floor. "Put what you find in here."

"Did you fight?" The question came out sounding like a courtroom accusation.

"No. I was just a medic."

She narrowed her eyes. "Healing wounded terrorists?"

"Healing wounded *people.*" He turned to look at her. "It is all ancient history now, Mrs. Button. Irrelevant. Now it is just the few of us who have survived that matter."

"Yes." She offered him a conciliatory smile. "You're right."

Leon squatted down at the edge of the duck pond and examined the water. Lily pads and a carpet of what looked like green algae rested on the still surface. He'd sat beside ponds before, the ones in Central Park, for instance. The water's surface there had rippled with activity, the wakes from radio-controlled boats, the ripples caused by ducks and geese paddling around and squabbling for hunks of tossed-in bread.

The water here was as flat and still as a mirror. Even the breeze stirring the willow was not a cat's-paw to the surface. There were not even the faint expanding circles caused by dipping daddy-long-legs or paddling water boatmen.

Silent. Still. Utterly lifeless.

He heard the van's rear door slam shut and turned to see Grace making her way across the lawn toward him, steering widely around that one body.

"Leon!" she called out. "What are you *doing*?"

She pulled up a few feet short of the pond, wary of it, wary of the floating algae.

"I thought there might be something left alive in the water," he sighed. "Fish or, you know, *something.*"

She was angry with him, but she was also curious. "Is there anything?"

He shook his head. "Nothing. I guess that means the seas have all been infected too." Made sense. Didn't something like ninety percent of the world's living things hang out in water? The virus would have probably had a great time wreaking havoc in there.

"You know what that means, don't you, Grace?"

She nodded.

"It's gotten everywhere."

"Uh-huh." He'd been holding on to a fading hope that someday soon a UN relief force was going to appear out of the sky like a host of angels, squadrons of helicopters kicking up dead leaves and dust, and spilling army boots onto the ground. But, if this virus was as effective at sea as it was on land, then not even a remote, far-flung island nation was going to have a chance of surviving. Not Tonga, not Hawaii, not Easter Island, maybe not even those dotted-around research stations in the Antarctic.

"We're alone. Not even ocean-bound places like New Zealand will be left."

"Except for other people like us," she said.

"Like us?"

"Maybe, I don't know, maybe…we really are immune to it?"

"You, me, Mom, and Mohammed?" He settled down on his bottom and looked across at the willow tree.

"There could be others too." She scratched at an itch at the end of her cast. "If we're immune to the plague, then there have to be others too, right? It can't just be us left." They heard the pond stir. The gentlest ripple of water lapping a few inches up the dry mud beside his feet. He looked out across the pond and saw a second concentric ripple following the first—gentler but distinctly there. He turned around to look at her.

"Did you just throw something in?"

"No."

He looked up at the tree again. Maybe the breeze had shaken a leaf or a seedpod loose. Then another ripple expanded in a circle from somewhere farther along, near the pond's edge.

"Shit," he uttered. He got off his butt and onto his feet, but stayed squatting at the pond's edge. "Maybe something's still alive in there?"

Grace took a couple of steps closer, until she was standing just behind him. "I can't see anything."

He stood up to get a higher point of view. The water that he could see between the pads and algae was green and cloudy. He stared at it for a minute, willing another expanding circle of movement to help him pinpoint where he should be looking.

Then he saw it. The faintest flash of something pale near the surface. Just a glimpse, then it was gone again.

"It's a fish!" said Grace, excited. She'd spotted it too—the pale underbelly of some pond fish or similar. The sight of it pleased them both, and they shared a grin.

"Maybe the sea is safe!" said Leon.

"Maybe we're not alone, then?" said Grace hopefully.

They heard their mom's voice and turned. She was approaching the van with Mohammed, each of them holding a large cardboard box in their arms. "I told you two to stay in the van!" she bellowed at them from across the green.

"Mom!" Leon waved his hand. "Come over here! You gotta see this!"

The two adults set their boxes down, hurried over, and joined them standing by the edge of the village pond.

"What is it?" panted Mohammed, his face creased with concern.

"It's OK. Nothing bad!" Leon pointed down at the still surface of the pond. "Look!"

"Leon…for God's sake! And you as well, Grace!" She shook her head angrily at her children. "I told you both to stay in the—"

"Mom! The fish are still alive in there!" said Grace. That shut her up.

"Alive?" said Mohammed. "Are you sure?"

Just then, another series of concentric circles rippled across the surface, and they all saw it, just for a fleeting second: the flutter of a dorsal fin, and then it was gone again down into the murky depths.

"Oh my God," gasped Leon's mom. "Was that a carp?"

"This…is very encouraging," said Mohammed slowly. "It means there is other life left. Certain species that could be unaffected."

"Exactly!" said Leon.

They waited and watched for several minutes, but it seemed the carp had developed a sudden bout of stage fright and wasn't going to make another appearance today.

"That's really great," said Leon's mom. She rested a hand on both her children's shoulders. "Sorry I shouted."

"That's OK, Mom," said Grace. "We got some good news." She managed a wry smile. "Finally."

"We should head back," said Mohammed.

They turned away and went over to the van, Grace elaborating on Leon's theory as if it were all her own, that maybe the virus didn't like water and maybe that meant the virus was being kept at bay by the various seas and oceans around the world. That maybe other island nations, like New Zealand and Hawaii, were just fine.

They climbed back in the van, and with a grinding of gears and a lurching motion, the van did a painfully slow five-point turn, bumping up over a curb before heading back down the way it had come, engine whining in low-gear distress, and Little Buntingham was left once more to its tranquil peace.

The breeze gently stirred the willow tree, and it swished in response. Scudding clouds allowed a break in their relentless gray lid. Blue sky appeared, and sunlight fleetingly dappled this peaceful rural setting. Picture perfect, if unnaturally quiet. No birds singing, no buzzing of dozy bees, no distant church bells or the humming of a groundskeeper's lawnmower. There was just the rustle of a breeze and the stirring of the willow.

Several beams of cloudy sunlight, filtered green by the algae, sliced down into the depths of the murky pond and rested momentarily on the back of the stage-shy carp.

Only it wasn't a carp. At best, it was a clumsy, malformed approximation of one: a fish scrawled by some untalented child with a crayon.

A best guess at a fish.

It was an attempt by a coalition of several billion cells to assemble the DNA fragments they'd gathered from the various creatures that had been absorbed from this cloudy, little universe into a working model. An ambitious project by their microcosmic standards. Lesser projects had been attempted with various degrees of success—floating single-cell life forms, various invertebrates...DNA templates that were modest by comparison.

Seven hours ago—decades by the timescale of entities as microscopic as these—an almost believable facsimile of a pond snail had been remade. Simple in structure, simple in locomotion, simple in thought. The successful assembly of an almost-complete species genome from the fragments stolen as the virus had rampaged and looted its way across the pond microcosmic centuries ago.

Baby steps, microcosm milestones.

Scaling up to the level of humankind, the almost-convincing pond snail was like mankind's first successful flying machine, a fragile construction of balsa wood and bicycle parts; the misshapen carp, the first successful satellite in orbit.

If microscopic intelligence could have cheered, popped champagne corks, and lit cigars as it regarded the fish, it would have. Instead it just stored at a chemical level the data as sequences of DNA, a record of the successful expression of the genome—another one to add to this colony's small but growing library of viable species templates.

And started again.

CHAPTER
29

5/28

Dad, where are you now? Have you found a survival shelter like us? Are you sitting safely at the top of some New England lighthouse with crates of food and bottles of water and a shortwave radio? I know you're alive. You're probably doing the whole I Am Legend thing, right? You think you're Will Smith. Ha ha.

6/1

So this is what we think. We *think* the virus is dead already. We think that it's a victim of its own efficiency. It was so frickin good at spreading that it hit everything it could affect within a couple of weeks and then had nothing left to infect after that. Maybe it was consuming what it infected as a food source, and now that's all gone, it has withered, dried up, blown away...or something. I don't know. But all I do know is that we haven't seen any sign of it for weeks now. The last sign of it I saw was one of those pollen clouds, I guess over a month ago.

Mo thinks it must have been an engineered virus, totally man-made. Because it makes no sense, in, like, an evolutionary way, to be so damn quick and efficient and not make some attempt to preserve its hosts. He said it's like the way a farmer preserves a proportion of his crops for the winter. It might have been a bioweapon? Or a research project, a cure for cancer, ,maybe, that just got to be a little too effective and saw everyone as a cancer cell? Whatever...the greedy, stupid bastard of a plague has left itself nothing to chew on. And now it's dead and gone too.

So, whether we were/are immune or not, we've decided that it's probably safe enough to go look around, see if there are any other survivors. Because the alternative is to stay in this dark dungeon until the food eventually runs out. We're going to Norwich.

That's where we were heading anyway.
Maybe Grandma and Grandad made it
through? I guess we'll find out if one of them
has got that immunity gene too.

THERE WAS A LOGJAM OF VEHICLES ON THE SIDE ROAD LEADING
to the A14 just outside of Ipswich. They had to spend several hours
picking their way through the cars and trucks. Several times, Leon
and Mohammed had to brush aside the dried bones and rags
(some still strapped in place by their seat belts) to sit in the driver's seats, turn over the engines, and steer vehicles to the side to
make way for their van. In most cases the engines all started perfectly. Leon assumed that wouldn't be the case six months from
now. Batteries would finally be completely drained, the elements
would have started to corrode the more vulnerable engine parts,
the tires would be flat. He imagined ten, twenty years from now,
this logjam would be a rusting, decaying mass, gradually merging
into a soup of flaking oxidized metal, leaving behind only the plastic components just as the virus only left behind bones.

Beyond the jam, the A14 was empty and Leon soon got the
hang of riding the gears smoothly all the way to the top, despite
his mother's frequent, insistent nagging to keep the speed down.

"It's not a race, Leo."

Twenty-five miles southwest of Norwich, near a place called
Stowmarket, they spotted a road sign for a service station. The
van's tank was showing less than a third full and needed gas.

Leon steered them onto the exit and up toward an empty
roundabout.

"Why don't we have these back in America?" said Grace.

Their mom shrugged. "They had intersections instead of roundabouts. I think they were starting to install them in California before—"

"They're cool," pronounced Grace as Leon swerved around the overgrown grassy island in the middle, then took the exit into the service station's parking lot. They'd expected to find an empty acre of asphalt. Instead, it was almost completely full of cars, in some places vehicles parked in orderly rows between the white lines; in others, cars were parked erratically, as if the final spaces had been fought for.

Leon looked for a sign that would lead them to the gas pumps. "Where's the gas station?"

"Stop over there first," said his mom, pointing. "We might as well take a look inside and see if we can pick up some more supplies."

Leon parked the van near the entrance to the glass-fronted service station store, and they climbed out.

There were the usual humps of clothing dotted here and there. It was a sight that had become so common they barely noticed it anymore; certainly, they no longer bothered to give the piles a wide berth for fear of infection. They were just harmless relics to be ignored...except where they converged in groups and told a story. Here their story was quite clear. Bodies were piled up along the glass front, packed more deeply around the wide double doors.

They wanted to get in. But someone inside wasn't letting them.

Leon could see the grease of palm prints, scuff marks and

scrapes, and in several places, hairline cracks in the thick plate glass. In his mind's eye, he could see the crowd clamoring to be let in, begging for compassion from those lucky enough to already be on the inside. Parents holding their little children up above their heads like green cards. Curses and threats hurled through the glass as, behind them, a billowing cloud of white flakes slowly drifted across the parking lot like an advancing bank of fog.

Leon shaded his eyes and pressed his nose close to the plate glass. It was gloomy-dark inside. The August sunlight was playing peekaboo from behind scudding clouds. Its light made short, momentary advances across the floor inside, and as it did, he caught glimpses farther in of more deflated humps of material and bone.

The virus still managed to find a way in.

Despite the locking of doors, despite the efforts of those within—maybe the service station's staff—it had all been futile. He imagined the horror not just for those standing out here, but maybe more so for those cowering inside. They would have had a perfect ringside seat. The perfect panoramic observation window to watch at leisure as the virus did its work on those outside. To see each grisly stage of breakdown and liquefaction, to see people dropping to their knees, flopping to the ground, cries of panic turning to keening whimpers of grief. To witness through scuffed glass a mother watching her baby cough blobs of blood onto its bib, to see another holding her dying children in her arms, to watch those forms glisten wetly and merge like wax figures held too close to a roaring fire—merging, a return to the mother's womb in a horribly different way. To see husband and wife, mother and father, embracing and dying...to watch a Greek chorus of figures slump to the ground, slowly withering and merging into one wet mass.

Those inside would have seen all that play out against the smeared glass. They would have witnessed in close-up detail the process, and they'd have known that was inevitably going to happen to them too.

Leon felt his scalp prickle and the skin along his arms began to goose bump.

Jeez. "Leon!"

He turned at his own mother's voice. "Whuh! What's—?" She'd been saying something to him.

She was standing a dozen yards back from the front of the service station, holding Grace's hand. "I *said*...you need to stand back. Mohammed's going to try to get us in." She nodded toward the sound of an engine being revved nearby.

Leon backed up a few feet, then watched as a white Ford Fiesta lurched forward from one of the parking bays, bounced over a curb, knocked a trash can and a wooden picnic table to one side, and then finally smashed heavily into the plate glass. It shattered, and a blizzard of glass granules cascaded and rattled on the hood and roof of the car.

Mohammed waited until the last fragments of glass had finished dropping, then emerged from the car rubbing at a smear of blood on the bridge of his nose.

"You OK?" asked Leon's mom.

"*Ach.* Banged my nose on the steering wheel." He said "nose" like "dose." He tasted blood on his lips. "My nose is bleeding." He pinched his nostrils to stem the flow.

"We'll find you some tissues," she said, stepping over the crackles of glass. "Come on."

CHAPTER
30

Inside it was dark, but at least lighter than the total dark of the bunker they'd been hiding away in for the last three months.

Leon did his best to forget about the clothes and bones piled up outside and the few dotted around inside...and the scene that must have taken place here months ago. All ancient history now, he told himself. No more relevant or shocking than the ancient fossilized fetal-position remains of Pompeiians.

They split into two groups. Leon's mom and Mo headed one way, he and Grace the other.

Leon carried a shopping basket in each hand, while Grace led the way with the flashlight, shining it along aisles of snacks. Their van outside was filled with survival essentials: water and canned food, boxes of rice and dried pasta. Sensible, nutritious food portions designed to keep UK missile crews functional for months and months.

Nutritious...and utterly tasteless.

What had been sadly lacking over the last few months had been the sweet stuff: packs of Haribo candy and bottles of Coca-Cola. Leon grabbed a few fistfuls of candy from the shelves and tossed them into his basket.

Grace grumbled. "Your teeth will all fall out."

"Maybe," sighed Leon. "But who's gonna see, huh?" There was that small consolation: if they were the last people of planet Earth, there was no need any more for vanity.

"All the same...you don't need to binge-grab this stuff." She shook her head. "It's, like, gonna be literally everywhere. For free...as much as you want. Forever."

"It'll go bad."

She raised her thick, dark eyebrows. "Seriously? This sugary stuff is all chemicals—it'll last forever. It's the healthier stuff that won't last long." She pulled a bag of nuts and dried fruit slices off the shelf and held it up for closer inspection. Spots of blue mold dotted the inside. "See?" She put it back. "All the healthy stuff is already going moldy."

Leon's mom and Mohammed, meanwhile, were in the food mart, across from the station's coffee area, on the far side. They were each carrying a shopping basket and filling it up with their own treats. Mohammed was piling up cans of dates in syrup in his. Leon's mom decided to pick up some instant coffee and as an afterthought some boxes of crackers. She walked a little farther down the aisle and found a temptation she couldn't pass up. She placed several bottles of red wine into her basket. Mohammed heard the bottles clinking in her basket as she returned to join him.

"Why?" he asked, shining his flashlight on the wine. "You do not *need* it."

"Oh, yes I do."

"No, you do not. It does not help."

"Well, I beg to differ."

He scowled disapprovingly at her. "I have never understood why people choose to ingest a drink that is designed to provoke a toxic response in the bloodstream."

She cocked her head. "Are you doing the religious abstinence thing on me?"

"It is a common sense thing, Mrs. Button. We should keep our wits about us at all times."

She closed her eyes and rolled them, then eventually nodded. "I suppose that's true. Very sensible of you." She pulled them out of her basket and placed them on the rack of chips beside her.

"There are actually *practical* reasons behind the tenets of my faith."

"Really? How about polygamy? Forced marriage?"

He cocked his head. "That dates back to the time of the Crusades. There were many more widows than there were men back then. It is... It *was* meant to be a practical measure. A *charitable* thing."

"A form of enslavement, more like."

He shrugged. "That is all gone now, old customs, prejudices—"

"And religions?"

"If there are other survivors out there, it will be a new world. Maybe a better culture will be born from this."

"For better or worse."

"Maybe more tolerant."

She looked longingly at the bottles of wine beside her. "Maybe one that allows the occasional glass?"

"Moderation in all things is a good thing."

She laughed sadly. "Including moderation...as my dad used to say."

"And he may yet still, Mrs. Button. If you and your children are immune, then it is likely that at least one of your parents is also." He smiled. "I would very much hope to meet them." He picked up his basket and wandered a little farther down the aisle.

"Mohammed?"

He turned to look at her.

"*Did* you ever fight over there...in that war in Syria?"

"I told you before. I only healed—"

They heard Grace scream: one short, sharp, shrill bleat of alarm.

Leon's mom dropped her basket and sprinted down the aisle toward the pale daylight glow of the entrance, Mohammed just behind her.

"*Grace? GRACE!*"

She wove her way through the leather coffee-shop chairs toward where another flashlight beam was flickering to and fro across the low ceiling and the shelves of magazines at the back of the store.

She heard Grace yelp again before she and Mohammed rounded the end of an aisle of candy and cookies. Grace and Leon were backed up into a corner against the end of the magazine racks. Leon had one arm protectively across Grace's collarbone and shoulders. With the other, he was sweeping the flashlight's beam backward and forward across the floor.

"Leon! What happened?"

"Shit…Mom…we saw something moving!"

"What?"

"I dunno…I dunno. Something."

"Well…what? Big? Small? What?"

"Small," said Grace.

"Where?"

She pointed with a shaking finger. "There…right there! Among those b-bags of candy!"

Leon's mom turned to Mohammed, grabbed the flashlight from him, and swung the light onto the rows of bags dangling from the display hooks. The plastic packs glinted under the glare as they swung gently. Shadows danced wildly around them.

"What did you see?" asked Mohammed.

"I'm not sure… It was small…white…"

"A mouse?" He looked at Leon's mom. "We know fish are immune…maybe mice—"

"No!" Grace shook her head. "It was more like a…a c-crab…or a spider. I just saw it for a second. I w-was…I was—"

"She was reaching for a bag of those," cut in Leon, waving his flashlight again at the candy. "She was digging through them and—"

"It was h-hiding! I moved and it came out from behind and scratched—"

"It *touched* you?"

She nodded, her lips trembling as she did so.

Leon's mom started to step toward them, but Mohammed reached for her arm to prevent her.

"Let go!" she snapped. "We're immune, aren't we?"

"That is not proven yet!"

"Let me go!"

"No, to be safe...you must not touch—"

"Get away!" She shook him off and hurried forward. "Grace, where? Which hand?"

"Mom," she whimpered, "look... It was just a touch...not even a scratch... Just—"

"Show me! Your good hand?"

Grace held out the other arm, the one that had been broken. The bandages and cast had come off weeks ago; the inflammation had gone down. The antibiotics had done their work.

Her mom grabbed Grace's hand and shone the flashlight at her palm. Then she turned her hand over and saw it—the faint red stripe of a scratch. She had the flash of a memory from when she was a parent helper in Grace's elementary school: two little girls accusing each other of biting and scratching. She'd easily managed to identify the victim and the culprit from the fading red welt on one of their wrists.

Mohammed took one small step closer. "If it's a mouse or a rat—"

"It wasn't a m-mouse," Grace whimpered.

"Whatever—another animal, it could be a *carrier* of the virus. Mrs. Button, for your safety, you should not touch her." He looked at Leon. "Or your son."

She turned to look at him, her face struggling to find an

expression somewhere between outrage and disbelief. "You think I give a shit?"

She stared back at the red mark. It *wasn't* fading like a naughty child's scratch. The small, straight mark remained clear, raised, pink...and now glistening.

"Grace?"

"It r-really d-doesn't hurt, Mom. I'm OK... I'm OK..." She wasn't OK—she was terrified.

"Mom," said Leon, "we should get out of here. Get outside."

"Yes." She nodded quickly. "Yes, let's get out—"

A bag of M&M's suddenly dropped off the display hook and fell to the floor. Leon swung his flashlight down. Caught in the glare of the light, they all saw it this time, scuttling off the top of the bag and on to the floor. Small, a little bigger than a quarter, as pale and fragile looking as some peculiar figurine made from shellac. It scuttled on delicate legs, six or seven of them, as thin as wire—one way, then the other—seeking to evade the pool of light in which it was caught, but uncertain as to which way to go. It paused, reared up on its legs, and raised one leg that seemed slightly thicker than the others: a small, barbed spear with serrations down one side.

The thing reminded Leon of one of the many weird bottom-of-the-ocean creatures that had yet to be named and categorized: pale from never having experienced sunlight, almost transparent in places, and defying the norms of nature with its asymmetrical body, its odd number of legs, and its one serrated leg.

It made a noise...a soft clicking.

Instinctively, Leon's mom stepped forward and stamped on it.

Its fragile form crunched like a potato chip beneath the sole of her shoe. The sound reminded Leon of a time he'd unintentionally stepped on a snail after a heavy rain. *Why?* he'd wondered. *Why do you small idiots all decide to race across the sidewalk whenever it rains?*

She lifted her foot, and they stared down at the pale smear of slime and shards of shell on the floor. They had a moment to inspect it, a moment of silence, then...it began.

CHAPTER
31

IT SOUNDED LIKE THE HISS OF RAINFALL ON FOREST LEAVES, A tap-tap-tapping that merged into a soft and soothing white noise. It was inside the store. It was all around them.

Leon shined his flashlight around. "What's that?"

His beam of light picked out movement among the racks of candy, other bags fidgeting and swinging from the hooks. Leon's mom's beam joined his. "Oh my God, there's another one!"

"And another," said Mohammed. His flashlight was aimed opposite, running along the magazine shelf.

Leon could see them emerging into the stark light—small, pale forms—some of them larger than the crushed one, fist size, some even smaller; every one slightly different. The number of legs varied; their thickness and articulation methods varied; the size and shape of their bodies and the way they moved varied. Dozens of them—no. More. *Hundreds* of them appearing from the darkness beneath the baseboard of the store's shelving units.

"They're everywhere!" screamed Grace.

Hundreds? No, maybe even *thousands* of them, each one like a different failed experiment on how a particular ocean-bottom crustacean should look, like God creating life forms on a bad day when nothing seems to go quite right. These were his screwed-up balls of paper spilling out of the wastebasket. Leon was certain that, somehow, they had something to do with the virus. Products of it? The next stage beyond those clouds of floating spores?

The creatures began to swarm out from the racks, dislodging bags of candy that dropped to the floor like ripened fruit. They swarmed across the floor toward them. Not quickly though, walking pace at best, each creature seemingly struggling to understand how its limbs should work. Their clunky, clumsy movements reminded Leon of the YouTube videos he'd watched of various microrobots' faltering first steps.

"Get out!" screamed Leon's mom. "Everyone out!" She yanked on Grace's hand and pulled her daughter after her, running down the aisle toward the front of the store. Leon followed after them, and Mohammed took the rear, shining his flashlight backward and keeping an eye on the creatures' sluggish pursuit.

Leon's mom ran to the service station's entrance, intending to head for the glass front of the building and the smashed-in panel through which they'd entered, but she could see that the floor, glistening with granules of glass, was moving.

More of them.

"It's blocked!" she yelled.

Leon caught up with them and saw that the floor was alive with creatures. They could try for it—run over them, crushing a path through them toward the battered front of the Mondeo—but what did that mean? Contact with them, with their gooey insides? If these were virus linked, creations of the plague, they had to be infectious. Just a touch, a droplet on their skin...?

He tried to close his mind to the next thought. If so, that meant Grace was already infected. He'd had his arm wrapped around her... He was already infected. His mom was infected too.

Are we already dying?

"The other way!" barked Leon's mom. She headed right, pulling Grace with her again, away from the front of the service station, toward the even darker rear. Leon followed her.

Ahead of them was a small cave of arcade and slot machines that promised big wins. Farther back were the bathrooms: male, female, baby changing. No rear exit from the building though.

Their mom pulled Grace toward the bathrooms. "Leon! Come on!"

"No!" called out Mohammed. "We will get trapped in there!"

She didn't listen. She pushed the door to the ladies bathroom open and shoved Grace inside. She reached out her hands toward Leon. "Come on!"

"Mo's right! We'll get—"

She wasn't listening. She wrapped her fingers around his forearm and pulled him toward the open door. "Get in...get in! *Get in!*"

The creatures from the store merged with the others from the entrance. Thousands...tens of thousands of them. The floor of the building seemed to be a living carpet of pale, glistening shellac forms.

Mohammed was looking for alternative escape routes, shining

his flashlight left and right. But their only option now seemed to be the bathroom—that or dashing across the seething carpet of creatures toward the front of the building.

Leon followed Grace inside, followed by their mom, then Mohammed. Mohammed tried to pull the door quickly shut behind him, but the pneumatic anti-slam support at the top allowed the door to close at its own unhurried speed.

"Come on! Come on!" he snarled as he yanked repeatedly on the handle, jerking the door, fighting with it to close. Leon caught one more glimpse of the creatures beyond through the narrowing gap: a churning mass scuttling toward them, a carpet growing deeper as the better designed and faster-moving versions clambered over the slower-moving backs of others to reach them.

With a hiss of resignation, the door gave in to Mohammed's muscle and it *thunk*ed shut.

"Is it closed? Is it completely closed?"

Leon nodded.

"Any gaps? Are there any gaps?"

Leon shone his flashlight down at the bottom of the door. Mercifully, there was a thick rubber lip filling the space between the bottom of the door and the floor.

"They're going to squeeze under that," said Leon.

They had a moment, a few moments of silence, the tiled bathroom echoing with their rasping breaths, before they heard the soft scratching at the door. Like fingernails drawn lightly across plywood.

Their mom turned to Grace. "How are you, honey?"

She nodded. "I'm OK...OK." She looked pale. Her forehead was damp with sweat.

Leon looked at Mohammed. "We're *not* immune, are we?"

"I do not know. Perhaps."

Over his shoulders, Leon spotted a small window above the sink. Frosted glass with a wire mesh. Three feet wide and maybe one foot tall. It was there to allow a splash of natural light in the bathroom, never intended to be opened or closed. It was firmly sealed.

"We can break that glass," said Leon. "We can get out that way!"

They all followed his gaze.

"It is too small," said Mohammed. Certainly too small for him.

"Maybe it's not," said Leon's mom. She looked around for something they could use to smash through it and spotted a mop and plastic bucket. She hurried over, grabbed the mop and jabbed the wooden handle at the glass. It banged and slid into the corner of the window frame.

She tried again and left a scuff on the glass.

"I'll do it!" said Leon. He grabbed the mop from her, climbed onto one of the sinks, braced himself, and then speared the window. A hairline crack arced across it.

"That's it!" cried Leon's mom. "Again!"

Leon braced his feet once more and jabbed at the window. The crack began to widen and spread.

"Hurry! Hurry!" cried Mohammed. Leon turned to see him aiming his flashlight along the bottom of the door before slamming his foot down on something. "They are getting under the door!"

Leon smacked at the window again. This time several shards of glass clattered down into the sink. The wire mesh remained though. He slammed at the same spot again and again, more shards tumbling down as the mesh began to surrender and buckle outward.

"Hurry, Leon! Hurry!" Grace whimpered from below. "They're getting in!"

He didn't turn to look. He could hear Mohammed's shoes slapping against the floor. Leon's mom's too as she screamed angrily with each stamp. He aimed the broom handle and thrust hard. This time, the very first wire snapped under the impact.

"It's going!" he shouted over his shoulder. He went at it again and again, bludgeoning a small hole through the mesh.

"Leon!" pleaded Grace. "Come on!"

He could hear both his mom and Mohammed, stamping and stamping, calling out to each other. "There! Get that one!"

"There's another!"

"Get it! *Get it!*"

He pushed the broom halfway through the hole and now started levering it frantically backward and forward, bending the loose-end wires back on themselves.

Grace screamed. He turned and looked down to see her stamping the floor around her.

Shit-shit-shit.

He levered the broom savagely against the widening hole and it broke in half. "BASTARD!" He tossed it aside and grabbed the sharp prongs of metal with his hands, bending them back one at a time.

Leon's mom could feel the creatures clinging to the sides of her tennis shoes, digging their little spear-like claws into the nylon webbing and hanging on. Learning, learning fast, holding tight and waiting for a fleeting break in the jarring motion of her legs, then pulling themselves just a tiny bit farther up, anchoring themselves again more firmly.

She felt something needle-sharp pricking at her ankle. She looked down and saw three of them clinging to the cuff of her jeans. She swiped at them with her hand, knocking two of them to the floor. The remaining one burrowed down into the narrow space between the arch of her foot and the lip of her shoe. She stamped down hard and felt it frantically wriggling beneath the sole of her foot.

"Leon!" she screamed. "Hurry up!"

"There's a hole, Mom!" he gasped. "There's a hole!"

She kicked her shoe off. The creature clung to her sock, dangling persistently from the heel. She slammed the ball of her foot into the tiled wall and crushed it.

The floor beneath the door was now heaving with the creatures, one after the other squeezing under the rubber rim, clambering over the crushed bodies in front of them.

"Mo! We can't stop them!"

She glanced at him and saw several were pulling themselves slowly up the backs of his thighs. She swiped at them with her hands, dislodging a couple. A third clung to her thumb and started digging into her flesh with a jagged blade as fine as a surgeon's scalpel. She flicked her hand, and it flew off into a toilet stall.

"Mom! I made a gap!"

She glanced up and saw that Leon had managed to create a

narrow gap in the mesh, framed by jagged little wires that were going to cut viciously at anyone struggling to wriggle through. But he was right—it was just about big enough for Grace. Maybe even Leon too.

"Get out!" she screamed. "Get out of here now!"

"I need to make it bigger so—"

"Get out!"

"Mom! It's not big enough for you and—!"

"*Do it!*"

Leon reached his hands down for Grace. She was busy fighting her own battle, stamping bugs one after the other as they scurried across the floor toward her feet.

"Grace! Give me your hand!"

She couldn't stop. Didn't want to stop. He bent down and snatched at her arm and pulled her up onto the sink. She sat there, her legs dangling.

"Come on!" He dug his hands under her armpits and hefted her up to her feet. The sink shifted and creaked alarmingly beneath their combined weight. "Climb through!"

She stared round eyed at the jagged wires around the hole. Then nodded mutely. The alternative, staying here, was unthinkably worse. She thrust her arms through the gap, then twisted her head sideways and into the hole, feeling one of the sharp wires digging at her left ear. She wriggled through the gap until she felt the wires stabbing and scratching at her belly and found herself staring down the brick wall of the back of the building at a six-foot drop down onto weed-covered asphalt.

She was going to drop headfirst, with only the strength in her weak arms to break the impact. She felt Leon pushing her butt with one hand and grabbing her right foot with the other.

"No! Leon! No, I'm going to fall... I'm going to—" He gave her a firm shove and she tumbled out.

Leon looked back at his mom. She was stamping frantically and swinging her arms. Mohammed's lower legs appeared to be covered in the creatures, like mother-of-pearl buttons. Only these buttons were spotted with red; his blood spilling from a hundred delicate surgeon's incisions.

"Mom! You next!"

"*Get out!*" she screamed as she flicked her hands at her hair. Leon could see some of them were dangling from loose tresses of her hair like oversize money spiders. He looked down at the floor of the bathroom. A number of the creatures were converging around the bottom of the basin. He couldn't see beyond the porcelain rim, to see whether they were figuring out how to get up it. But they were going to do it; they were going to figure it out—he was certain.

She staggered over toward him, pulling the creatures out of her hair as they tried to burrow out of sight and hide in her thick locks. "Get out! Make it bigger from outside!"

"Mom?"

"Just do it!" She turned away again, screaming angrily as she ripped at the back of her head with both hands trying to locate something digging into her scalp there.

Leon tore off his hoodie, bunched it up, and draped it over the lower wires, pulled himself up, then stuck his head and shoulders through the narrow gap. Grace was outside, flapping her good hand at him to hurry up.

"Come on! Come on!"

He wriggled and pushed and felt wires stab and scrape his shoulders and back and finally, with more of his weight outside, he toppled out and fell, taking the impact on his upper back.

He lay there for a few seconds, winded, gasping to get some air back in his lungs.

Grace's face appeared above him, her long, matted hair dangling down and tickling his nose. She was screaming at him to get up.

"*Help Mom! Help Mom!*"

Still wheezing, dazed, his head spinning, he let Grace pull him to his feet. She couldn't reach the window. He just about could. He could hear Mohammed's deep voice screaming with pain. His mom's too.

He grabbed at several of the bent wires, braced his feet against the brick wall and tugged ferociously at them. They bent farther, more granules of glass clattering down on him. He fell to the ground, a twist of rusting mesh wire clasped in each hand.

He got to his feet and was about to pull himself up and look inside when his mom's hands emerged through the ragged hole. Her forearms and elbows wriggled through; then, finally, she managed to push her head out through the narrow gap.

Grace screamed.

His mom's hair seemed to be moving with a life of its own, like Medusa's snakes, churning, swaying, shifting. The creatures were swarming up over her shoulders, clambering over each other like greedy prospectors to stake a claim on any spare part of her bare flesh. Probing skeletal legs and scalpels emerged from her hairline and cautiously explored her temples, her eyebrows, looking for another handhold on which to grasp to complete their advance over her.

Blood was trickling down her face from hundreds of cuts. She blinked bloody tears and her eyes—round, terrified, and bloodshot—settled on them.

"Go!" she whimpered. "Go..."

"Mom! Come on!" screamed Grace.

Their mom struggled to pull herself through the narrow gap, managed to squeeze a shoulder through, but the top of her chest was pinned by the barbs of wire. Creatures scuttled out of the window past her and dropped down on to the asphalt, sensing fresh prey to pursue.

"Oh God... They're *digging into me!*" she screamed. A long string of blood spilled from her mouth. "Oh God...oh God..." She stared at them both before slowly slipping back. "Oh God... *they're inside...*"

She slid out of view. The last visible part of her was her left hand holding stubbornly to some of the wire mesh for a few seconds more. Then her fingers slackened and her hand dropped from sight.

PART

II

CHAPTER
32

"Settle down. Everyone...please just stop talking and listen."

What was now the community meeting space used to be the staff room. It was still lined with lockers along one wall, a whiteboard with a duty roster, and magnetized "performance smileys" stuck along one end of it.

Ron Carnegie stood at the front, wearing his dark-green Emerald Parks sweatshirt and a bright-green plastic name tag that reminded everyone, just in case they'd forgotten, that he was called Ron Carnegie and he was in charge here. Site manager, still, even if the world outside had changed beyond all recognition.

"Come along now, people. Let's not waste any more time—let's get this morning's briefing underway."

Ron looked around at those present in the staff room. Thirty-seven of them in total, including himself. Twenty-five of whom he knew *reasonably* well, or as well as a manager could get to know his own staff, though the majority of them were twenty years younger than him. Kids, really. The others were an assortment of waifs and strays who'd wandered into the park or had been found on a foraging run: the Lin family—mom, dad, and their three small kids; Freya, the gawky goth girl with a limp and a lisp; Erik, the poor chap who'd been on chemo when the plague hit—his hair was beginning to grow back now, but so, presumably, was his tumor; Christof, a Swedish graduate student with an almost-unintelligible accent who had been over here studying forestry; Dorris, a bookstore manager who'd driven into the park somehow believing it was a government virus-research center.

A mixed bag, and every one of them now his responsibility until help eventually arrived.

"Karl? What have you been seeing out there?"

Karl Mullen was the Emerald Parks engineering manager, known as "Spanners." The nickname had arrived with him from the merchant navy. It's what every ship's engineer is called, he'd explained on his first day at work. Nautical tradition an' all that. Spanners had stopped wearing the Emerald Parks uniform since the end of the world, claiming it was pointless since no one was now employing him. He got up off the end of the table on which he'd been perched.

"Not much to report again, Ron. No signs of life, I'm afraid. No airplane trails, no smoke anywhere, no car engines. Nothing." This was how his daily contribution always began. The same *nothing to report* report.

Ron nodded. "Well, let's not give up hoping, people. We can't be the only ones left. What about snarks?"

Snarks—Ron's label for *It...*for *Them*.

The term had taken hold pretty quickly, linguistic Darwinism at work. It was quick and easy to say and sounded about right for something for which they didn't have an informed name. Other names had held sway for a while—scuttlers, crawlers, bugs, wrigglers—but since those things out there seemed to be constantly changing, *snarks*, being a more generic term, served as the catchall. "Not many today, Ron. I spotted several of those bigger ones we've been seeing recently. The rat-size ones." They looked nothing like rats, of course, just roughly the same size as them. Ghostly pale, their skin was almost see-through, limbs varying in number from three to six. Recently, the snarks had started looking slightly different, dispensing with their insect-like, segmented exoskeletons and appearing with internal skeletons covered by a thin and almost transparent layer of skin.

"They skirted the perimeter for a few minutes. I think they were testing to find a way in again, but they gave up."

"Good," said Ron, satisfied with that. "As I know you're fed up with me saying, we're quite safe in here."

"But they're definitely getting bigger...so it's not always going to be safe here," interrupted a girl's voice.

All eyes, including Ron's, settled on Freya.

"I'm just saying what you're all thinking! The *snarks* are getting bigger!" She hated the word. There was that annoying hard *S* on the front that forced her to slur and made her sound drunk.

She turned in her seat and looked around at them. "How long before they get to be the size of a...I dunno...a dog or a cow? Are we still going to be able to keep them out then?"

Ron sighed, took off his glasses, and rubbed his eyes. Without the lenses on, his eyes looked like tiny, little cartoon dots. "Look, Freya, this place is as good as any. Those things, the snarks—God knows what they are, but they're not going to get in here anytime soon."

"Not *yet.*"

Maybe she *wasn't* saying what all these people around her were thinking. Maybe they wanted to buy into Ron's unflappable certainty that they were safe in Emerald Park forever.

"We're *immune*, Freya," said someone behind her. She turned around and saw it was Ron's deputy manager, Dave Lester. "Every last one of us here is *immune*. Which means, frankly, we've just got those pests to deal with when we go outside. And they squish pretty easily."

"Right now they do...but what if they get bigger? Stronger? What then?"

"Then we take baseball bats along with us, sweetheart." He got a laugh from a couple of the younger lads at the back, Big Phil and Iain, the park's two fitness instructors. As far as she could see, that pair of knuckle-dragging idiots were treating the end of the world like some kind of video game.

And...*sweetheart*, seriously? She narrowed her eyes warningly at Dave. He winked back at her and blew her a kiss. She closed her eyes, turned back around in her chair to face Ron, and flipped the finger back at him.

"Anytime, anywhere, gorgeous," he called out. He got his obligatory hyena-like guffaws from the back.

"Not even if you were the last man on earth," she replied.

"'S all right, Freya love. You can relax. I'm not *that* desperate. Not yet, anyway."

Freya rolled her eyes and tried to ignore the sniggering from his boneheaded followers. Dave was a sleazy jerk.

"That's enough of that!" said Ron. He clapped his hands together like a primary school teacher. "Freya, watch the attitude, and, Dave, please. Let's avoid the sexist comments. I still expect professional standards to be maintained here! Especially from my deputy!"

Dave shrugged an apology. "Yeah, sure. Sorry, Ron."

"Now look," Ron continued, "we are perfectly safe here. We just need to keep vigilant, keep patient...and keep taking the pills. Speaking of which..." He pulled out a Tupperware box, peeled off the lid, and handed it to Spanners. "Medication time. Will you pass that around, please, Karl?"

A good-natured groan went around as the box was passed along, but everyone dipped a hand in and took out a single capsule.

"Now...I'm looking for volunteers for a reconnaissance run tomorrow. We're getting low on a number of things, including these meds," he said. "Volunteers, please...and if we get none, then I'm going to have to pull some names out of a hat."

Freya stuck her hand up. "I'll volunteer to drive." She could use a break from the routine. Every day was the same now: three meals in the cafeteria and waiting, waiting, waiting for rescue.

"OK, thank you, Freya." Ron nodded. She could drive. Bizarrely, she was one of the few here with a driver's license. Most of Ron's staff were straight out of college and had never taken a test. Spanners had never gotten around to it, the cleaning ladies were mostly Eastern Europeans who had been bussed to work, and he had no idea about the Lin family.

Freya ignored Dave questioning her ability to drive with his pals. She might slur like a drunk, limp like an alcoholic, but she could drive perfectly well.

"Anyone else?"

She prayed Dave wasn't putting his hand up. She didn't want him leering at the back of her head in the car.

"All right, then," said Ron. "I'll pick Claire...Phil...and Iain."

Freya rolled her eyes. "Orange" Claire was the park's beautician, all nails and fake tan. And of course Phil and Iain were Dumb and Dumber.

Great.

"Good. Then we'll have you four, tomorrow morning, nine o' clock sharp, at the spa therapy reception desk."

CHAPTER

33

FREYA HARPER WAS JUST SIXTEEN WHEN HER PHYSICIAN told her and her parents she might be presenting the early symptoms of multiple sclerosis. Perfect timing for her school exams. Perfect timing for her late-starting but finally flourishing social life.

She'd always been one of the social outliers, one of the mixed bag of misfits who were pushed to the side. Not because of her MS—that hadn't happened yet—but because she was more academic than the Cool Sisters. Unlike them, she didn't celebrate being blond, bland, and inept. She didn't run around flapping her hands and gasping *OhmyGodohmyGod* when asked to dissect a frog, or curl her lip sarcastically in math and insist it was only going to be useful when she needed to count out her (future) rich soccer player boyfriend's weekly paycheck.

She didn't shave her off her eyebrows, then paint them right back on again. She didn't hitch her school skirt several inches higher by rolling over the waistband. She didn't spill her heart out on Facebook every night or do an endless procession of duck-face selfies into her webcam.

When the Cool Sisters weren't calling her a "lesbo," they mockingly called her *female* simply because she was different from them, outside their narrow-minded definition of "normal," which to those bubbleheaded idiots obviously made her gay.

She wasn't. She just wasn't like them.

It had only been in ninth grade that her brand of acerbic sarcasm had quite randomly become fashionable. The cool boys thought it was cool, all of them lining up and taking turns at being on the receiving end of her sharp tongue, guffawing together and flicking their wrists as she snarkily put them down. The cool girls tried to mimic it badly (butt-clenchingly, embarrassingly badly, truth be told), and after five long years in the wilderness, Freya was finally in.

Then along came wonderful MS.

Her increasing lack of agility, her clumsiness, had become annoying. But since she'd never been the sporty type, nor the dancer type, nor the dainty waif type, that hadn't been a major problem, and she'd put it down to being more the clumsy Bridget Jones type—her head so full of Important and Interesting Stuff that there was less of it to devote to looking out for doorframes, or corners of desks. It was when her speech started to change that Freya had become truly concerned. Her lips had begun to feel numb, like after a trip to a dentist. Over the course of a week, they went from being oddly tingly to completely numb. When she probed them with her fingers, they felt like someone else's lips.

That's when she got worried. When she spoke, she sounded as if she'd been drinking. In fact, her parents even accused her of sneaking some booze into her room. So she told them about her mouth (but not the bumping into desks—that she put down to being just plain clumsy).

They went to the doctors, and after some tests, she received that totally awesome news from her physician. The stuff about how "it can be managed; it can be slowed down. The discomfort can be minimized with prescription painkillers, but...I'm afraid multiple sclerosis can't be cured."

The whole *being cool at school* thing went south pretty quickly after that. The boys began to think she sounded weird, and the delivery of those acerbic and sharp-witted one-liners began to sound rather clunky and...well...pretty *lame.*

Secondary school popularity, Freya discovered, was a fickle mistress: any person was only one banana-skin mishap, one social gaffe, one unsightly blemish, one tuck-your-skirt-into-your-tights moment away from social exile.

That all happened six months before plague day, or *VE Day*— that's what Ron called it. *Virus in England Day.* Freya, like pretty much everyone else, had gone to bed on a foreign news story and woken up to a national crisis.

Five days later, she'd emerged from her apartment house in Kings Lynn, stepping over the remains of her parents and out into a very quiet world. She kept the memory of those first five days locked away in a compartment of her mind, the stuff of awful nightmares. She'd wondered why the virus had spared her. God knows, it had had ample opportunity to dissolve her too, but it hadn't. It had "tasted" her, spat her out, and moved on to her mom and dad. It had turned the only two people on planet Earth that she cared about and her cocker spaniel, Teddy, into a pile of mush that had spread across the kitchen and into the living room, sending tendrils up the side wall of the stairs as it looked for more victims in the bedrooms upstairs.

She'd hidden away in her room for nearly a week. Grabbed everything she could possibly eat and drink and bolted herself inside. It was a combination of the water finally running out and the first tendrils emerging through the gap beneath her door and starting to explore her room that convinced her it was time to go.

———

"Hey, what you up to?"

Freya had been window-gazing again. She did it more at night than during the day. There was something pleasing about the way the green floodlights planted around the inside perimeter of the tropicarium tilted upward and caught the overhanging branches and leaves of the mature trees outside. By day, the same view out through the glass wall looked drab; by night it looked exotic and jungle-y.

"Wotchupta?" asked Dave again.

"Enjoying some peace and quiet," she replied coolly.

He sat down on the wicker sofa beside her. "You don't like me, do you?"

She shot a sideways glance at him. He actually sounded a touch nicer than normal. His voice didn't have that assertive, hard edge to it, nor the blokey *the next thing I say is going to be funny so listen up* tone that he put on in front of his wingmen.

"I just thought I better apologize for this morning."

"What? The casually demeaning laddish sexism?"

He took a second to process that. "Yeah...that thing."

She shrugged. At least he was aware he'd been rude, even if he didn't know how to label it. "In that case...OK. Thank you."

"We've all got to live together. Maybe even for the rest of our lives. So I..."

"It's early days yet."

Dave made a sucking noise through his lips. "You're still pretty hopeful this is just a temporary thing, aren't you?"

She nodded.

"Come on, Freya. You've seen as much as anyone else." Oh, she had. More, probably. Dave, Ron, and the park's staff had all been here watching the world's final forty-eight hours of civilization unfold on Sky News. Watched the end of the world from the comfort of a luxury health spa. But Freya and the others had escaped from the virus, seen the aftermath firsthand...and, yes, it didn't look encouraging, but she couldn't believe nobody—*nobody else at all*—had managed to survive it.

"It's all gone. It's an empty world. We're what's left." Dave adopted a cornball lisping accent. "In the wake of a global apocklelixsh, they were mankind'sh laaaaasht and besssssht hope."

She was expected to chuckle at that. She didn't.

"Maybe you should start thinking about that," he continued. "That we've got to make this work. Or we're, you know, totally screwed."

"It *works* already. We have food and power and water."

"Work, as in, for the rest of our lives. We may have to be the ones that rebuild civilization. That's a huge responsibility for *us*."

He said "us" but she knew he meant "me." And he wasn't doing that cornball voice now. He was quite serious.

"For Ron," she corrected.

He nodded. "The old boy's got a ton to cope with. And I'm there to help him until—"

"You take over."

A smile flickered on his lips, which he quickly molded into a wince.

Nice save.

"I'm going to be his deputy manager for as long as he's around. Then, you know, I guess at some point I'll have to step in and—"

"Finally get your promotion to spa manager, huh?"

His expression hardened. "There are nearly forty people here now. In the future, we're gonna grow, and somebody's got to keep things orderly."

"We're gonna grow? Make babies, you mean?"

He spread his hands innocently. "That's how populations grow, last time I heard."

She got it. Got his angle.

"This isn't actually an apology, is it?"

"Yeah," he replied defensively. "I just said sorry, didn't I?"

"I may sound slightly stoned sometimes. My stupid lips get in the way, but that doesn't mean I'm a fool. If this is your clumsy attempt to hit on me, Dave, nice try, but I'm not interested."

He shook his head.

"So what's the matter? Did Claire turn you down again?"

He got up, the wicker seat creaking. "You think you're really" —he struggled to find a good word—"*sharp and funny*, don't you!"

She shrugged. "Well...at least I'm not a total idiot. I'm hoping."

"Just so you know," he snorted, "I wouldn't touch you with a bloody barge pole. I don't do charity work." He paced away into the faux-jungle inside the glass building, past the zero-maintenance plastic palm trees and ferns.

"Nice. Thank you so much for that," she said quietly.

———

Ron Carnegie was waiting at nine o' clock sharp, by the spa reception desk. The others, drafted into the foraging party, were already assembled there: Big Phil and Iain nervously swapping wisecracks, covering their edginess with bravado, and Claire, makeup slapped on thickly like a protective second skin. They'd already made a start at outfitting themselves for the trip, pulling on several layers of sweatpants, then strapping plastic knee braces and shin guards over the top.

"You're going to stay in the car, Freya, all right?"

She looked at Ron. "Of course." She shrugged. "I volunteered to drive, not to bug squash."

The two young men grinned at that. "We're the SAS," said Big Phil. "Snark Annihilation Squad."

"Don't mess about, lads," said Ron. "You're not heading out to find the snarks—you're on an errand. We need to fill up on things. Here's the shopping list."

"I need...some *things*." Claire shot a glance at Freya. Freya nodded.

Me too.

Ron handed Claire the community shopping list. "We need everything that's on here and anything else you can think of." He turned to the two young men. "And please, lads, no risks. All right? This is not some PlayStation zombie game. If there're too many of them out there, we'll try again later."

"Relax, Mr. Carnegie," said Big Phil, picking up a cricket bat. "We'll be careful." He looked at Freya. "And you're sure you're OK to drive today?"

"As we can all see, I'm no super athlete." She narrowed her eyes. "But I'm not an invalid either."

Not yet.

Phil grinned at that. Away from his "pack leader," Dave Lester, he was slightly less obnoxious.

"Now just be careful. Like I say, if there are too many out and about today, then just come back. We can try this again tomorrow."

"We'll be OK, Mr. Carnegie."

"Good. Well, then...I suppose we should get the show on the road."

He walked them to the revolving glass door at the front that led outside to the parking lot: a clearing cut out of the woods, with individual parking spots marked out with log dividers. There were only a dozen cars in it. Three of them belonged to staff members who'd been here when it all began. The others belonged to the park and had the park's swervy, green logo—halfway between a Nike swoosh and a feather—stenciled down the side. It was supposed to be a leaf, symbolizing all things natural and the exclusive hidden forest location.

He handed Freya the keys to the hybrid Land Rover. "Drive carefully, Freya. I'll see all of you back here in an hour."

CHAPTER
34

"I'm telling you, the plague was brewed up by the...uh... Al-Talibarnies," said Iain.

Freya mentally rolled her eyes, then looked in the rearview mirror at him and scoffed at that. "Yeah, right, those Taliban and their big-ass, top-secret bioweapon research facility in Kandahar."

"Well, come on, it was made by *someone*," he argued with a shrug. "A weapon designed to leave buildings and objects and machinery intact? Seriously...it's the perfect antipersonnel weapon. And, you know, they were *losing* their jee-had thing, right?"

Freya hadn't really kept her eye on the news very much before the plague came. The occasional headline managed to penetrate her inward-looking cloud of doom. For the last year she'd become preoccupied with considering her future, which was going to be a walking stick, crutches, then a wheelchair, then one day, choking to death on a cracker because her throat had decided to spasm. Her future was going to be ever-increasing doses of painkillers and muscle relaxants. So her mind hadn't really been that much on the news.

But even she knew enough to know how little Iain knew. "The Taliban and Al Qaeda are two very different organizations, Iain. They're not one thing called Al-*Talibarn*."

"Yeah, well…"

"And the war in Syria and Iraq was being fought by guys called ISIS."

"Yeah…that's them. That's who I meant."

She shook her head and looked at him in the mirror. "Moron."

"Makes sense though… They were losing it, so they decided to invent something that was going to take out everyone on the planet." Iain shrugged again. "It's not like they had any worries about dying alongside us, right?"

"'S right," added Big Phil.

"Well, screw 'em," said Iain. "They're all plague slime and we're alive. Survival of the fittest."

"You guys really get off on all this survival shit, don't you?" said Freya.

Iain shook his head. "No…I'm just as torn up as everyone else, but it is what it is. This is about survival of the fittest."

"We could be the last humans left alive in the world," added Claire.

A woodland health spa populated by thick-headed personal-fitness instructors, beauticians, a shuffling MS sufferer, and a mixed bag of waifs and strays. Freya mentally shook her head. If they really were the last humans left on Earth, she didn't hold out much hope for the future of mankind.

"Although there could be others who survived," said Claire hopefully.

For once, Freya agreed with her. "There *must* be. We can't be the only ones who've figured out how to stay immune." She wanted to add that back at Emerald Parks it wasn't exactly wall-to-wall geniuses and rocket scientists. If *they'd* managed to figure out how to beat the virus, somebody else must have done so.

She slowed down for the junction leading to the A11 but didn't bother stopping and checking for cars. One of the benefits of postapocalyptic driving was there were no other cars to worry about.

"I wish I'd learned to drive," said Claire. "I was just too busy doing my vocational tests and the beauty-therapy course up in Manchester."

"My parents made me cram for the tests," said Freya. "It worked though. Passed first time."

Maybe that was one of the other reasons she'd enjoyed her brief honeymoon period of popularity, being the first student in her class to have a car and a valid license.

What was it that jealous cow, Tanisha, had quipped? Oh, yeah. *Soon you'll be the first one driving a wheelchair, eh, Freya?*

What a lovely world she used to live in. Maybe those two idiots Iain and Phil were right to be treating this culled world like their own version of *The Walking Dead*. One big survival game now to them. "Freya! Up ahead. See?"

She nodded. On the side of the road was a swarm of the smaller snarks, ones the size of hermit crabs. They were beginning to shuffle across the road, like migrating baby turtles scrambling across a beach toward the safety of a tropical sea. Freya stepped on the accelerator and squished over them, Iain whooping with delight and craning his neck to look out of the rear window.

"Nice one!"

"Yeah!"

Freya rolled her eyes as she watched them in the mirror, both lads twisted around and grinning at the glistening, smeared tracks behind them.

"Shit, check out the snail trail!"

"Snark juice!"

"The pair of you are totally gross!" Claire chuckled. "How many d'you think we just splattered?"

Freya inwardly sighed as the three of them made their own guesses.

She caught sight of someone sitting in the middle of the road right at the last moment. She'd thought it was just another victim. Not every pile of bones they'd come across had been lying flat. Others had been drooped in seated positions. She'd even once come across one slumped across the counter in a pub, kept on his feet because he'd been wedged between two beer pumps.

She slammed her foot down on the brake, and the Land Rover swerved to a sluggish halt, lubricated by the last of the snark gunk still on its tires.

"What did you do that for?" shouted Iain in the backseat as he rubbed at his forehead. "Just banged my 'ead!"

"Umm, look?" She pointed through the windshield.

"OhmyGod!" Claire pulled herself forward to see better.

"There *is* someone else!"

243

Freya unclipped her seat belt and reached for the door handle. She felt Claire's hand on her shoulder. "What if he's infected? What if he's not immune, like we are?"

"Claire, if he's still alive after all this time...then he's figured it out too."

Freya opened the door and pulled herself clumsily out of the car. She looked back the way they'd come. There was no sign of any snarks. She walked to the front of the Land Rover and saw the person she had almost run over.

"Hello? Are you OK?"

He nodded. She couldn't figure out how old he was. A boy? A teen? Adult? He looked gaunt, shockingly pale. His dark hair was matted and unruly, his cheeks mottled with scratches. But not sick. Not with the virus. There was no doubt about that. No one ever got sick from it and recovered.

You were either immune or you weren't. Just like his mom used to say: *There's no such thing as a little bit pregnant.*

He was sitting on a backpack. Like a country hiker taking a break for sandwiches and tea from a thermos. Only he didn't have either of those things—in fact he looked as if he hadn't eaten in quite a while. He looked like some poor wretch who had sat down and just given up.

"I'm so sorry... I...I didn't see you until the last—"

"I'm OK," he said quietly, struggling wearily to get to his feet.

He sounded as if he had an accent of some kind. Irish? Australian?

Freya stepped forward and offered him her hand. He took it and pulled himself up.

"Are you alone? Are you with others?"

He shook his head. She wasn't sure which question he was saying no to. Just then she heard a shrill, panicky voice echoing from the trees beside the road.

"*Leon?*"

A young girl staggered out from the gloom beneath the branches, buttoning her jeans. Ten…maybe eleven. Like the young man, she looked pale and painfully thin. Even more unwell than the boy, if that were even possible. Long dark hair hung in greasy clumps. She stared, wide-eyed, at Freya, and rubbed a hand absently up and down an arm wrapped in old, stained, and yellowing bandages.

"Just us," he croaked in answer to Freya's question. "It's just me and Grace."

CHAPTER
35

"The reason you two weren't infected by the virus is because of these..."

Leon and Grace stared at the small, blue plastic capsule the man was holding between his thumb and index finger. "Painkillers—Tylenol, aspirin, codeine, ibuprofen...basically any kind of analgesic."

He was wearing the same-colored short-sleeved sports shirt as most of the others here and a plastic name tag: Terry Morris. They were in a small room with a single striplight glaring down from the low ceiling onto an exam table and a pair of plastic chairs. On the walls were posters on how to administer first aid and how to spot the early signs of a stroke or seizure.

Grace was sitting on the table, Leon on one of the chairs, and Terry Morris was standing beside her, in the process of unwrapping her bandaged arm.

"You must have both been taking painkillers of one sort or another when it all started. Am I right?"

Leon nodded.

"But Mom wasn't," said Grace.

Terry looked at her. "You saying your mum *didn't* get infected?"

She shook her head. "But the crabs...got her."

"She lasted until then?" He looked puzzled. "Those things came nearly two months *after* the initial outbreak. She must have been taking something during that time, otherwise..."

Grace shook her head.

"Maybe she *was*, Grace," said Leon. "And we didn't know. Mo too."

Terry shrugged. "I don't know how this works or why, but we spotted it early. Everyone who turned up here had been on painkillers of one kind or another. There's a Chinese family that turned up."

"They were all taking tablets?" asked Leon.

"They all routinely drank traditional herbal tea for medicinal reasons. Which of course has a strong natural analgesic in it. They lost their youngest child to the virus though. A baby. She was on formula milk. That pretty much confirmed it for me. It seems this plague—this virus—is unable to *digest* people with traces of those chemicals floating around in their bloodstream."

He puffed his cheeks. "I really don't know if it's limited to painkillers and anti-inflammatories. It might include other drugs like mood stabilizers or certain antibiotics. But I suspect not. Otherwise many more people would have found themselves immune. It's guesswork—I'm just a qualified nurse. Here we all pop an aspirin, a Tylenol, or an ibuprofen daily and so far that seems to have done the trick."

"Grace has been taking antibiotics...for her arm. It doesn't seem to be healing."

Terry nodded as he finished unravelling the bandage. "Oh... that's a nasty inflammation," he said as he exposed her forearm. "We probably need to try her on a different kind." He peered closely at her red skin, blotched and weeping in places. "The usual bad germs are still around and doing their thing, it seems. Infectious bacteria are still here—and still quite deadly. I presume you've also been taking some painkillers or anti-inflammatories?"

Grace nodded.

"And you too?" he said to Leon.

"I get bad headaches all the time. So I've been taking aspirin."

"Today?"

"Not for a few days. We ran out."

"How long?"

Leon shook his head. "I...I don't know. A few days. Just over a week ago maybe."

Terry frowned. "Did any of those *snarks* touch you in the last week?"

Leon and Grace looked at each other, confused.

"It's what we call 'em," Terry explained. "Unless you've got a better name for them."

"Crabs," said Grace. "Bugs."

"Walkers...crawlers," added Leon. "They seem to be changing."

"And getting bigger," said Grace.

"Yeah, we've noticed that too. Any of them touch you in the last week?"

Leon nodded. "Sure." He pointed to the scratches and cuts on his cheeks. "I don't know if they have eyes… I've never seen any eyes, but they kept finding us."

"It could be smell, sound, motion…pheromones maybe."

"They… Are they really made from the stuff that used to be people?" asked Grace solemnly. "That's what Leon and me think."

Terry nodded. "It's the likeliest answer. The virus infected clouds from the *raw material*. You saw those, I presume?"

Both nodded.

"So I suppose it's evolving. All the stuff that used to be people, cats, dogs, birds, insects—every living thing—it's using that and trying different things."

"You make it sound *smart*," said Leon.

"Nature can be pretty smart." Terry dabbed at Grace's arm with a cotton pad dipped in antiseptic. She winced.

"Tender?"

"Yes. Very."

He peered closely at a raised welt on the back of her hand. "How did you do that?"

"*Barbed wire*," answered Leon quickly. "Rusty barbed wire. I think that's how she got this infection on her arm."

He finished dabbing at her arm with antiseptic. "Well, at least that's cleaned up now." He pulled fresh bandages from a plastic pack and wrapped her arm up once again. He reached out and touched her forehead. "You're quite warm."

"I think she has a fever or something," said Leon.

Terry nodded. "I think so too. Look, I'll give you some different antibiotics and some stronger anti-inflammatories to take. It'll keep those snarks at bay, but more importantly, it'll clear up this nasty infection. We may be immune to the plague, but I'm afraid even a septic paper cut can still kill you just like the good ol' days."

He turned to Leon. "And let's get you both on aspirin again."

"I'm Freya by the way."

Leon looked up from the cafeteria table. He was getting used to this: people coming over and telling him their name and then asking him what he'd seen "out there." He and Grace had been left alone for the first two days at Terry's insistence. He said they both needed some rest and feeding. They'd been assigned a guest chalet to share inside the vast glass house, and Grace was still feeling very poorly and feverish, although it seemed like the infection in her arm was beginning to get better.

He recognized Freya as the girl who had nearly run him over. "Leon," he said, offering her his hand.

"Well, duh, I know," she replied. She grasped his hand and shook it. "Seems like I'm in the back of the group to pester you with an avalanche of questions."

He shrugged. "That's OK. There's not much I can answer though. It sounds like me and Grace haven't seen anything you guys haven't already seen."

Freya set her tray down on the table. "Just like meals in the school cafeteria."

It was *heated* food. Sure it came from cans—nothing came freshly picked anymore—but it was food heated in a saucepan, a luxury as far as Leon was concerned.

She settled awkwardly into the chair. "You're looking a lot less like roadkill now."

He laughed. "I'm feeling better, thank you."

"How's your sister doing?"

"She's a lot better than she was. I think we were both in a pretty crappy place when you nearly ran me over."

Freya picked up a fork and speared one of the ravioli in her bowl. "So what's your meds story?"

"What?"

"Your medication story?" She blew on her food. "Quite a few here are alive and well because…uh, because we *weren't* well. We're all pill chompers. We survived the initial outbreak because a lot of us were on one med or another at the time." She nodded at those people not wearing the park's uniform. "The staff, on the other hand, survived because they were isolated and stayed inside the tropicarium. But the rest of us…we were just lucky to be sick at the time."

The tropicarium, Leon had learned, was the name for this large glass-house structure that contained the pool, the hot tubs, the sauna, the chalet cabins, the plastic palm trees and plastic orchids, the artificial grass. The place looked like a tropical paradise, except none, or at least very little of it, was actually real.

"Grace had a broken arm and I get headaches. So we were both on painkillers at the time."

"Terry said your mum survived for a while too?"

Leon nodded. But that was all he gave her on the subject. What had happened had happened five months ago. It felt like much longer.

Three months they'd spent back down there in that dark

nuclear bunker, working their way slowly through thirty-year-old rations. Just him and Grace, surviving, simply existing like cave dwellers. They'd been in shock, Leon realized, what the U.S. Army called PTSD. Losing his mom felt like years ago. On the other hand, it took only a question, a smell, a word...to bring her right back and make it feel like yesterday.

"Hey, it's OK," said Freya. She touched his hand lightly. "We all lost someone. I don't talk about my parents either. Subject best left with the wrapper on."

"Yeah." Both he and Grace had done a lot of crying. Sometimes together, but mostly he'd done his crying when he was sure she was in some fitful sleep.

Leon glanced up at Freya, looked at her closely this time. She was pretty in an imperfect way: her ears stuck out just a little; her jaw tapered like an almond, giving her a slightly weak chin. Her mouth worked sluggishly, making her words garbled, and she moved around cautiously, like a person driving someone else's car for the first time.

"So, in case you're wondering about my slurred speech...I'm not *drunk*. I was diagnosed with MS about nine months ago. It's why I sound like this. Why I feel so friggin' exhausted all the time."

"Oh. I'm sorry. That sucks."

"Or it doesn't, depending on how you look at things. If I'd been a well girl, I suppose I'd now be part of some disgusting, pale, slimy, crabby thing." She smiled nonchalantly. "Girl with early signs of MS versus gross bug thing...no brainer, really."

Leon noticed the older man who was in charge here, Carnegie if memory served him, coming over to join them.

"How are you feeling this morning, Leon?"

"Better, thank you, sir."

He smiled at the formality. "Terry tells me your sister has a nasty infection, but he's put her on some pretty robust antibiotics?"

"Yeah. She's feeling better already."

"You were both in a pretty sorry state when they brought you in. Terry said you guys were borderline malnourished, dehydrated. He thought your sister might have scabies."

Leon nodded. "We...uh...we didn't cope very well."

"Well, look, Leon, you're going to be perfectly safe here. We have a contained, sealed, safe environment. Power and food and water for as long as we're going to need it."

"How long do you think that will be?"

Ron smooshed his lips like a car mechanic totaling up an estimate. "Who knows?"

"The authorities, or, you know, whoever's left out there and still functioning," cut in Freya, "are gonna need some time to get their act together before they start reaching out."

Ron nodded. "We might have to dig in and cope on our own for quite some time."

"So you keep saying," said Freya. "That is if anyone *does* come."

"The authorities have contingency plans for all kinds of disasters, Freya. There'll be an emergency authority hub somewhere outside London. If we've managed to get by OK, I'm sure the prime minister and the cabinet have too." He turned to Leon. "And your president and his people I imagine are just fine too, but I can expect it's going to be quite some time before a major relief effort gets going."

ALEX SCARROW

"Dave thinks the whole world is dead and gone...that it's just us left." Freya turned to Leon. "He's Ron's *assistant*."

"*Deputy manager*, Freya," Ron chided her gently. "I think Dave is overly pessimistic. There'll be relief efforts happening eventually."

Leon nodded. "I'm sure you're right, Mr. Carnegie."

"Anyway...we're just going to sit tight here for now. Freya?"

"Ron?"

Leon noticed him stiffen at her cheeky familiarity. "Why don't you show Leon around the tropicarium?"

"I might just do that, Ron."

CHAPTER
36

GRACE LAY ALONE IN THE CHALET BEDROOM. THE CURTAINS OF the small window were closed, and only a trickle of diffused daylight leaked into the small room. She felt weak and hot, her mind slipping in and out of consciousness, not sleeping but not truly awake either.

She had a fleeting dream about much happier times. Back in their New York home. Christmas, that's what it *felt* like. There were decorations and a tree in the corner of their living room. Of course it was Christmas. Leon looked so much younger. Maybe ten or eleven. He was tearing the wrapping paper off a large Star Wars Lego set, squawking with delight. Weirdly, in the dream, she was the same age she was now. Twelve. That kind of made her the big sister.

A part of her fevered mind appreciated the irony of that. Leon had stepped up after his mom had died. He'd been doing his best to be an adult. Doing OK, under the circumstances. She knew she'd be long gone if it hadn't been for him. So, now, in this pleasant dream, it was nice, if weird, to see him as a little kid once more.

She was unwrapping a new iPhone. Her mom and dad were there, smiling at each other. Her foggy mind couldn't figure out whether this was a dream or a memory or somewhere in between. She was *older* than Leon...a dream, then.

Gramps and Grandma were there too. They'd come down from Connecticut for Christmas and were cooing and enjoying watching the little 'uns.

A perfect, perfect dream.

———————

Inside Grace, a colony of cells, alien to her body's immune system, was doing its best to survive. A desperate struggle now that their world, the inside of Grace, had become a biochemical war zone.

The immune system was fully mobilized and ready for a fight. These invaders had entered their world, and they were on the prowl through the bloodstream, hunting down the unwelcome bacterial imposters who'd set up camp there. Busting down their cell walls when they found them, tearing apart their reproductive machinery.

These unwelcome invaders had a name in the universe outside: *Staphylococcus aureus.*

But there was another invader, much, much smaller, and it too had taken up residence. To these tiny life forms, the war between *Staphylococcus* and the immune system was a war between giant beasts, elephants locking tusks, while meantime, they crept like mice around their vast, stomping feet.

This second invader was infinitely smaller but dangerously similar in structure, not like other viruses—just strands of DNA floating in a perilously thin casing—but these virus-hijacked cells were *complete*. They were life forms capable of their own life cycle. The biological war of giants was of no concern to this virus, except that it was stirring up this world's, this microcosm's "little police"—the lymphocytes and macrophages. They smelled blood and were out and about in great numbers doing their part to help the giants take down the bacterial invader, looking for kicked-in cell walls into which to race, to raise havoc inside.

The virus was lying low for now, going dormant. Time to find a safe place to go to sleep until things calmed down.

———

Elsewhere, on a human scale, a hundred miles away stood a building on the outskirts of a medium-size countryside town. A three-story building that was built in the middle of the nineteenth century, with large delivery archways at the rear for horse-drawn carts to deliver payloads of barley and hops. Once upon a time, the building had hummed with activity, producing hundreds of barrels of real ale, called Butcher's Best. In recent years, it had been doing the same job but on a much smaller scale. An old building now, it had been ripe for tearing down and redeveloping before the virus hit, but like a stubborn old man, it had persisted and remained standing.

The building's basement was enormous: a storage cellar that had once been designed to store thousands of barrels was a labyrinth of low archways, tunnels, vacant wooden barrel racks, and, until a few months ago, a thriving colony of rats.

A very different colony inhabited this space now.

In the darkness of this old brick cellar, safe from the uncomfortable penetrative UV rays, it was warm. Almost tropical.

There was life down here.

A sea of life.

An *ocean* of life.

To a casual observer, the basement floor appeared to be a seething cauldron of brown broth. It could have been mistaken for a sewage treatment tank, except that it didn't smell of feces. The odor could be described as meaty, cabbage-y...the smell of a school or hospital cafeteria or a soup kitchen.

The virus had converged here, in a good place. In microcosmic terms, this was a city. A megacity. A place where many hundreds of thousands of minicolonies had merged to share their experiences, their data.

Their knowledge.

And now sections of jigsaw-puzzle DNA were being played with, assembled to see what they could form. In the darkness of the brewery basement, yet another genetic template was emerging from the crusty surface of the broth. An ambitious project this time, something much, much bigger than before. Over several hours, a small dimple in the surface of the broth became a molehill, then a hump the size of a pitcher's mound. Its form became more complex, more refined, took on definition and complexity. Beneath the surface, billions of cells passed along chemical messages. Between them, they agreed on roles and formed a brittle skeleton-like frame. Some formed sinew-like material; others, a facsimile of muscle tissue.

Finally, after many hours, the hump had become an organized subcolony that could begin to articulate and move. The crusty surface tore open and a creature that bore just the vaguest resemblance to a cow staggered to its seven feet. Some legs worked as they should; others were withered and uncertainly formed. The creature's head had the wedge-like shape of a cow's. A noise emerged from its mouth. Not the deep mooing of a cow, but a warbling, mournful shriek that sounded as chilling and unpleasant as the cry of an urban fox.

It staggered clumsily, wading drunkenly through the broth.

On the wedge-shaped head, an experimental organ attempted to function, a glistening, dark orb that emerged from beneath a protective flap of membrane. One eye, blinking and rolling in the darkness. It detected a hazy pinprick of light coming through the floorboards above—detected the light...reported its presence down an optic nerve to a subcolony of cells that had combined to form another very simple organ about the size of pinhead.

The beast staggered another step, then finally collapsed back into the broth. Not a cow, not even close...but getting there. It was an incredible result that would be logged and stored in the collective memory of this basement city. The very complicated optic organ and the other organ, a simple brain, had worked successfully together.

The short-lived creature began to break back down once again into the soup from which it had been made. This process was a lot quicker than the assembly. Cells rejoined the larger community, exchanging protein messages.

An hour later, the DNA packet responsible for creating a viable eye, optic nerve, and brain tissue had proliferated across the entire basement of the brewery, and several hundred small, articulated crablike creatures emerged from the soup, following a guiding tendril up the stairs to the ground floor, out of the delivery archway, and into daylight. Some of them began to scramble across the ground on their thin pincer legs, sniffing for the outlier tendrils of a sibling colony; others dissolved in the sunlight and became small balls of fluff, like dandelions gone to seed, waiting for a stiff breeze to carry their spores away, each one containing news of this wonderful development.

CHAPTER
37

12/3

Dad, you out there still? You <u>still</u> alive? It's been almost seven months. The general feeling is that the world is actually totally screwed. No country survived intact. There's no one left to pick up the pieces. But maybe there are lots of other survival centers like this one, still going.

We found one of them. Or, more accurately, they found us. They're holding out at this luxury, forest health-spa place. It's basically a big plastic greenhouse with gyms and Swedish saunas and hot tubs and a small swimming pool inside. The place is sealed up like a drum. Virtually airtight, like some kind of Mars colony outpost. That's how they survived: none of the virus could get inside. In fact, it's a perfect survival stronghold. They've got solar-power panels, a wind turbine, and even a diesel generator, so they're all set for power. Food and water isn't a problem. When we need more, we send out a van to the closest supermarket and fill it up.

Catching the virus isn't a problem either, Dad. We're all immune here. Now I know why. It's not hereditary—it's chemical. It's painkillers... That's the cure! Which I guess means there's more of a chance that you're still alive. See, I thought it was hereditary, which meant if we got our immunity from Mom then the chances of you being immune too would be hugely unlikely. So, if it's drugs... you've probably figured that out too. And as long as we keep popping pills we're safe from catching it. That's one thing taken care of. Check. The other's not so easy...

There's the things this virus is making. They call them <u>snarks</u> here. I don't know if other survivors are getting the same weird creatures we are—we've got these small crablike things. Every one of them seems slightly different. Now and then you get bigger snarks. The biggest thing we've seen so far was the size of a cat or a small dog.

I get the feeling the virus is trying to make new species, but it can't do the big stuff... yet. Shit. Can a virus really do that? You know, think, plan, strategize? The idea of that really scares me.

12/8

Grace's arm is all healed up now. She was sick for so long. I really thought she was going to die when we went back to the bunker. I thought the snark virus was inside her, but just taking its time breaking her down. Turns out she must have gotten an infection from something else.

Terry fixed her up by the way, Dad. He is a staff member here at this place. An ex-British Army medic turned male nurse. There's another guy who's an ex-army engineer, called "Spanners." Then there's the manager, Ron Carnegie. I think he's what you'd call one of those stick-up-the-ass types. He's a nice old guy, but everything's by the book, health 'n' safety and stuff. And his sidekick is this survival blowhard called Dave. I guess you know the type... Yup, they have 'em over here too.

The rest of the staff here are all much younger. They're all jocks and phys-ed types. Friendly though. Anyway, I wanted to specially mention Terry, since he's the guy that you need to thank for Grace (if you ever get the chance).

12/21

I had a totally WTH of a nightmare last night. It was pretty bad. I saw it all again, Mom being overrun by those little crawly things. You know what her last words to me were? (Of course you don't.) Well, I'll tell you: "They're inside me."

Uh-huh, you read that right. "Inside me."

That's what keeps coming back to me the most. But, my God...she could feel those little bugs cutting through her and getting into her body. I don't want to think about what that felt like. I try not to think about it, but, seriously, I get no friggin' say in what I get to dream about. Jeez. I do NOT want to go out like that.

"She seems very popular," said Freya. She turned to Leon. "Everyone loves her."

They watched Grace helping a couple of the spa's grounds-men, Carlo and his young apprentice, dig up the decorative flower beds and the plastic palm trees. Mr. Carnegie had suddenly gotten a bee in his bonnet about self-sufficiency and turning the unused faux flowerbeds into genuine vegetable gardens.

"After all," he'd said at yesterday's breakfast briefing, "we're living in a giant greenhouse. Come on! Who wants to eat some-thing *fresh* instead of canned?"

He'd addressed that to an audience who were decades younger than him and were used to the *ping* of a microwave. Leon guessed it had more to do with boosting morale than dealing with nutri-tion, something to keep his young staff busy. Grace was among them. She'd managed to find a pair of kitchen rubber gloves from somewhere and was making them all giggle with her *City Girl Does Rural* act, hamming up her Big Apple accent, groaning about the muck on her gloves and curling her lips like a drama queen, relishing the attention, the good-natured head shaking and eye rolling from the others.

"Everyone always loves her," Leon replied. For the first time, he realized he'd said that with just a little pride, not the way he would have in the past, sarcastically and layered with resentment. He smiled. "She's a natural at it. She didn't just chatter at school—she *networked.*"

"Unlike you?"

"I'm the contrast, right?" He turned to Freya. "The sibling who's, like, the total opposite, the miserable loner."

"No! Just...you're quieter. I'd say a thinker rather than a talker."

Absently, Leon ran a hand through his dark hair.

Freya snorted at that.

"What?"

"You! That! Doing the whole romantic, mysterious outsider thing."

"Huh?"

She mimicked him, running a hand through her hair, narrowing her eyes, jutting her chin, pursing her lips, and staring off into the middle distance. "The whole brooding poet act."

Leon closed his eyes and shook his head. "Ah, did I just do that?"

She nudged his shoulder with hers. "Only works with *pretty* boys, I'm afraid."

"Charming." He frowned as he thought about something. "What do you guys call a dog? Oh, yeah...I'm a 'minger,' right?"

She smiled at his pronunciation of the word. He'd made it sound like *ginger*. "I love it when you Yanks try on our accent for size."

"Except I'm not a Yank. I'm a Brit."

"Bollocks to that."

"No, seriously. I was born in England. Mom comes..." He dipped his head for a moment, then started again on a different tack. "I've got English grandparents. I went to elementary school here. I have a British birth certificate an' all. What more do I need to be one of you Brits?"

"Drop a few *H*'s and *T*'s, bruv...know wha' I mean?"

"Right, so you guys all talk like that when no one's looking?"

"Yeah. Wicked, innit?"

Leon winced. "Half the students in my college speak like that."

"College? What, like, degree college? I didn't think you were *that* old."

"No...no. Sixth Form college. Same as U.S. high school. I'm, like, seventeen."

Freya looked surprised at that. "You look younger but act older. So I had you as a really young-looking university-age kid."

"I hate looking so young. Maybe when I'm in my fifties I'll finally get to shave."

"Leon, seriously, it's the right way around. Better than looking older and acting all immature. Too many man-childs around."

Freya watched Grace puttering around, offering unneeded advice and being generally no real help at all. "I often find myself wondering about how all the famous people have got on."

"Huh?"

"You know, the Hollywood royalty, the billionaires, the catwalk models, the rap stars... Normally the real world never touches the likes of them. They live in their comfy bubbles and every now and then reach out to us with a tweet or an Instagram, usually something stage-managed. I wonder whether they all escaped to some mystery safety island somewhere in the Maldives...or whether I just squished one of them in the car last time we went out."

Leon laughed.

"Life's lottery winners," she sighed. "They usually come out on top."

"I bet most of them were chomping pills of one kind or another." He nudged her. "Hey, maybe we'll meet celebrity survivors."

"Oh God, kill me now."

They watched Grace tiptoeing across the earth bed, trying not to soil her pink tennis shoes, one uprooted plastic carnation in her gloved hands.

Standing to one side of the volunteers and watching them work was Dave Lester.

"Come on, boys and girls, put your backs into it!"

"Now, *he's* the kind of douche that always survives," Freya said, nodding his way. "I've seen his chalet room. He has posters of girls in skimpy bikinis holding big guns." She cocked her head. "Just great."

Leon watched him. Watched what he was gazing at. Claire was squatting down at the side of the garden. Dave was admiring the tattoo at the base of her spine.

"The guy seems like a total sleazebag."

"Tell me about it. He's made a crack at pretty much every female in here...except Mrs. Lin. Even *me* a couple of times. You know what his charming chat-up line was?" She didn't wait for Leon to shake his head. "My job is to be making as many babies as possible now." She narrowed her eyes. "Thank God he's not the one running things here."

CHAPTER

38

GRACE REALLY DIDN'T DREAM VERY OFTEN. HARDLY EVER, IN fact. Leon once said it was because she had absolutely zero imagination with which her unconscious mind could fool around. In return, she'd said she'd rather have zero imagination than zero personality.

Shots fired—she won.

But she'd definitely just had one. A horrible dream. She turned over in her bed and looked at Leon. Gray light was seeping into their chalet, but it wasn't yet dawn and he was fast asleep and snoring gently.

"Leo..."

She tossed a cushion across the gap between their beds. "Jeez! What the...?" He jerked awake in his bed and turned to look at her, bleary eyed. "God, Grace...what did you go and do that for? I was sleeping!"

"I just had a nightmare."

She saw him roll his eyes.

"Well, just... For God's sake, just try and forget about it and..." He stopped midsentence when he realized she was crying. "About Mom?"

She nodded.

He sighed. "Do you need, like, I dunno...a hug or something?"

She nodded quickly, didn't wait for a further response from him. She tossed the sheet back, hopped across the space between their beds, and curled up beside him, nudging him backward to make some space for herself.

Leon put an arm around her narrow shoulders. He could feel them shaking. "Whatever it was...it was just a bad dream, OK?"

"Mom came here," she whispered. "She came here to this place. She came to the front entrance..."

"Just forget about it. Just a dream, kiddo," he mumbled sleepily.

"Leo, oh God... She was being chased by those crabs. I couldn't open the door to let her in."

He squeezed her shoulder. "OK, maybe that does sound like a pretty shitty nightmare."

"She kept saying, 'They're inside me... They're inside me,' and I couldn't open the door..."

"Shhh..."

Grace became quiet, but he could feel her sobbing, trying to be as subtle as possible about it, but her shuddering shoulders gave her away.

"Shhh...it's OK. It's OK."

Jeez...what do I say? 'Cause it isn't OK. It isn't even close to OK.

"She's gone, Grace. She saved us. She died knowing we were all right, we were safe. That kind of thing means *everything* to parents, right? The kids are everything that matters to them."

Grace turned over to face him, a tress of her dark hair stuck to a damp cheek. "What if she *didn't* die? Maybe she got out? What if she's looking for us right now?"

Unlikely. Very unlikely. *She died.* He knew that. And hope, the kind with which Grace seemed to be wrestling, was like feeding the grief troll, feeding the pain.

"Maybe it's, like, a premonition or something, Leo?" Her wide eyes challenged him to say different.

Leon shook his head. "Listen, Grace...dreams aren't premonitions. They're not warnings or omens, they're just...I dunno, the brain firing randomly. Like you know sometimes when a slow, clunky laptop boots up? Sometimes you get a flash on the screen of the last game you played or the last website you visited? Grace, a dream is just your brain sort of trying to make a story from random stuff your sleeping mind throws around."

She seemed to wilt slightly at his explanation.

"You don't want to do this, Grace...hope for something like that. 'Cause it won't happen. She's gone."

She turned over, presenting her back to him again. "I miss her so much."

"Me too."

The pillow rustled as she nodded her head. "You won't ever leave me, will you?"

"Don't be an idiot. I'd be lost without your funky fashion tips."

He felt her giggle at that.

"And your advice on my nonexistent love life."

"You're totally terrible at that."

So true. He'd never had a girlfriend. On the other hand, Grace traded boyfriends like Yu-Gi-Oh! cards. He suspected her definition of *boyfriend* was something of a gray area. Holding hands, once, in a crowded playground, probably counted as that.

"Although"—she turned to look at him, smiling now—"my *may*-dar says Freya *may* just like you."

"You think?"

"I think."

She was silent for a while, long enough for Leon to be convinced she was done talking and might let him actually go back to sleep, when she turned to look at him once more. "What's *wrong* with her?"

"She has MS."

"What's MS?"

"Remember that older kid, Clay Baumgardner, in the apartment down from ours?"

"Uh-huh. The red-haired guy?"

"Yup, well…pretty much the same thing he had. I think."

She was quiet again for a while. Leon guessed she was trying to remember what he'd looked like, how he'd started walking with a cane, then later moved to a wheelchair. How quickly his condition had deteriorated. "That so sucks," she said sleepily. A minute later, she was breathing deep and regular, fast asleep and hogging most of his single bed.

CHAPTER

39

Freya liked it out here on the spa's roof terrace. It extended above the ground-floor gym, a two-story protrusion out from the side of the large rectangular glass box of the tropicarium. The virus's "mode" had changed from being clouds of particles to a liquid with weblike feeler tendrils, to small experimental crustaceans that seemed unable to do anything more adventurous than scuttle across the ground. And since there'd also been no signs of those clouds of particles for months, Ron had declared this open space safe.

The terrace was covered with an almost-convincing carpet of artificial grass, surrounded by a safety rail from which flower baskets hung. It had a clear view across the woodlands. Over the tops of the shorter trees, she could see the glint of the park's small artificial lake, the two clay tennis courts, now dusted with the dead leaves that had fallen from the overhanging maple trees.

Nature, well at least the *flora* part of it, still had its busy schedule to keep to. Winter was finally here, leaves had fallen in order to make a squishy nuisance of themselves, and the air had a pleasing chill to it.

She hung her laundry on the line strung out across the roof garden. Although this park had electricity, Ron was determined to preserve it for more important things than washing and tumble drying. The turbine and the solar panels provided enough for everything else, but the gym below her, full of energy-draining treadmills, and the laundry room in the basement remained locked and unused.

"Laundering clothes and maintaining personal hygiene," Ron had reminded everyone recently at the daily breakfast briefing, "is still very important and is everyone's personal responsibility."

Freya didn't mind this particular chore. It was a chance to be outside, to get some alone time and some fresh air, to feel the sun on her face...and to be perfectly safe while doing that. The Snark didn't seem to be able to make things that could climb or fly...yet.

The Snark? She shook her head at herself, at the name she used for the plague.

She realized, in her mind, the virus had evolved into a single entity, a thing...with a name. Like a person. It reminded her of a beat-cancer campaign from a couple of years ago. How cleverly the advertising company responsible for those TV ads had *personalized* the disease, made a million unlinked clusters of tumorous cells into one big punch-in-the-face-able bad guy. The cancer character had had a name: *Vincent*, a chain-smoking douchebag with slicked-back hair, grayish skin, and, oddly, an Essex accent.

And now the virus had a name: *Snark.* And he was a douche-bag too.

"Screw. You. Mr. Snark," she muttered as she reached into the basket for her bedsheet.

"Potty mouth!"

Freya spun around, staggering slightly, reaching for the back of one of the deck chairs to steady her balance.

"Oh…it's you."

Dave sat down casually on a chair nearby. "Offer still stands, by the way."

"What's the matter, Claire turn you down *again*?"

"No," he replied defensively.

"Have you tried any of the cleaning girls yet?" There were three of them, the cleaners. They spoke about five words of English between them. She wasn't sure if they were Polish, Romanian, Hungarian, or Czech. "You never know, with the language barrier an' all, they might not have figured out you're a complete idiot yet."

"You're a sarcastic cow, aren't you?"

"Hey, it's my superpower." She shrugged. "I use it only for good though."

Dave's hard face creased with an insincere smile. "Hey, do you want a hand?"

She didn't. She wanted him to go. But before she could answer him he clapped his hands slowly.

"Oh, my, 'give me a hand,' that's so-o-o hilarious! Did you write that joke all by yourself?"

The sarcasm whistled over the top of his head. "No. It's an

oldie." He got up from the chair. "Here, I'm gonna help you with that sheet anyway."

"Thanks, but I'm fine...honestly."

He ignored that and grabbed two corners from her. "You need to double it over or you'll take up too much space on the line."

She had been going to do that. The line was already covered with other people's bed linen and clothes.

He advanced toward her, arms spread, one corner of the sheet in each hand. Very close. Far too close. She took the corners from him quickly. "There." He smiled.

His hands were free...and hers weren't. He placed one hand on her hip, the other on her right breast. "Come on, Frey—"

She dropped the sheet and tried to push him back. "No!"

His arm slid from her hip, around the back of her waist: a hold on her, a very firm one. "Come on...just a bit of fun."

"I said *no*... Now piss off and let me go!"

He scrunched his hand on her chest. Painfully.

"Ow! You're hurting me!"

"Come on, Freya. Just a—"

She jabbed a finger, hard and straight, into his right ear.

He recoiled, let her go, and cupped a hand to the side of his head. "Ow! That *hurt*!"

"So did that," she said, rubbing her chest. "You really are a complete shit, Dave."

He took his hand away and stared at a small smear of blood. "Bitch."

She rolled her eyes. "Don't be such a baby. I poked you, that's all."

He stepped forward, grabbed her wrists, and pushed her back so that she lost balance and collapsed on to the deck chair. He swung a leg over and sat on her. Pulled her arms down to her sides and planted a knee on each wrist.

"You really don't get it, do you?"

She bucked and wriggled, but his weight was too much. His hard knees ground into her wrists painfully. "Get off me!"

"It's all new rules now, Freya. No more of that political-correctness garbage. It's *survive in the jungle* time. Just us... You better get used to the idea."

"Get *off me!*"

"Now, then." He started to tug her tucked-in shirt out of the waistband of her jeans and lift it up.

"*Hey!*"

Dave looked up and saw Grace standing in the doorway carrying a plastic laundry basket.

"What are you *doing* to Freya?"

He quickly pulled her top back down. "Just messing." He got off her, stood up, and offered Freya a hand. "Just play wrestling."

Freya kicked at his hand. "Get away from me, you pig!"

Dave shrugged. He muttered quietly to her, "Ron won't be running things forever."

The words chilled her. Not just an observation—it was a barely concealed threat.

He strode across the terrace to the door, looked at Grace, and winked. "You too... You're not too young, *princess*," he muttered under his breath.

"I'm going to tell Mr. Carnegie what I just saw," said Grace.

He pushed past her and headed down the stairwell. She watched him go, then hurried over to Freya. "You OK?"

Freya nodded, mutely, then began to sob. Grace sat down beside her, put her arms around her shoulders, and held her tightly. "There, there," she cooed, rubbing her back.

She may only have been twelve, but she knew when another girl needed help.

———

"Well? Dave? What have you got to say about this?"

Dave looked at everyone assembled in the cafeteria. All eyes were on him, waiting expectantly for his explanation.

"I *knew* something like this would happen." Dave shook his head angrily. "No," he sighed, "I didn't bloody well *attack* her."

"I said," Freya cut in, "you *assaulted* me."

"Ron"—he turned to his boss—"seriously? Are we doing this?"

"I want to hear what you've got to say."

Dave rolled his eyes and sighed again. "She was up on the terrace hanging her laundry. She backed up against one of the deck loungers and tripped over the footrest end." He looked at Freya. "You all know what she's like—she's clumsy. I went over to give her a hand...and she got really shitty with me." He looked at his audience. "You know what she can be like...really *arsey*. She told me to 'eff off.' Said I was looking for any excuse to grope her. And that's when little Miss Princess turned up out of the blue and decided to get the wrong end of the stick."

"Grace said you lifted Freya's shirt up."

"I was pulling it *down*, because yes...it was up. She was

struggling on that deck chair like a flipped-over turtle. I was just trying to—"

Iain and Phil laughed.

"All right, you two," snapped Ron. "Keep it down."

"I was a complete sucker, trying to be helpful to her." He snarled. "That won't happen again, I'm telling you."

"You really are a lying weasel shit bag," said Freya. "Everyone knows what you're like! Ever since I turned up here, I've seen what you're like—hitting on anything with a pulse."

"Quiet now, Freya," said Ron. "You've had your say. It's Dave's turn."

"You want to know what else he said?" She didn't wait for Ron to reply. "He said Grace wasn't too young for the same treatment either." Freya shook her head and stared at him. "Yeah, I heard that. You really make me want to vomit."

"Is that true?" asked Ron.

Dave's face creased up with incredulity. "Jesus! She's a kid! Of course I didn't bloody say that!"

"Oh my God, you lying shit! You lying piece of—"

"All right, all right!" Ron raised his hands to hush them both.

Dave shook his head. "You really are a piece of work, aren't you? Throwing an accusation like that at me—"

"*Quiet!* The two of you!" Ron snapped.

They both clapped their mouths shut. No one had heard Ron's voice sound like that before.

It was quiet. Grace broke the silence though. "He's the one who's lying, Mr. Carnegie."

Leon grabbed her hand to shush her.

"Look." Ron absently scratched at the back of his neck and grimaced. "Look, Dave...I really can't have someone around, on my team, who I can't trust with our guests. There's a disciplinary process that I have to—"

"You can't kick him out, sir!" shouted Iain. "Not based on what *she* said! You know what she can be like!" He looked at Big Phil to back him up, but he merely offered a noncommittal shrug.

"Uh-huh." Freya shrugged. "Like, you know, because that's what I do for a hobby...make false accusations of assault."

Dave was emboldened by the support. "Ron, look, this is crazy. We've all got to work together, you know? Stick together. I..." He puffed out a breath. "Look, we're probably it. All that's left. Just us. Alone. Here."

"All the same, Dave, there are rules of conduct and—"

"Ron! This isn't a holiday spa anymore! We aren't Emerald Parks employees anymore!" He pointed at Freya, nodded at those few in the audience not wearing green tops. "And they're not our bloody *guests*!" He turned back to Ron. "We can't piss around anymore and pretend it's all going to get back to normal! The game is *survival*, mate... Do you understand?" He laughed. "Jesus, look at us. We're having a crappy *disciplinary hearing*!"

Leon watched Ron still vigorously scratching the back of his neck. Still wincing and sucking air in between his teeth.

He's going to back down. He could feel Grace trembling with rage.

"Now...just...Dave...just calm down. Please. No one's getting kicked out. No one's getting fired—"

"Fired?" Dave laughed. "From what? From our *jobs*?"

Leon noticed some heads nodding in the cafeteria and realized that the only reason Mr. Carnegie was still in charge here was that no one had figured out yet that someone else *could* be. That, or maybe it was the rumor that Mr. Carnegie kept a gun locked up in the top drawer of his desk. Spanners told Leon that somebody had found one, on one of their shopping trips, and Mr. Carnegie had put it out of the way for safekeeping.

"Look, I think for the sake of peace and order here, the best thing is for you two to give each other a wide berth." He gave Dave, then Freya a firm, headmaster's stare. "Is that perfectly clear?"

Dave shrugged. "Suits me, Ron."

"Freya?"

She laughed dryly. "Sure. Why not? I mean...how many females' testimonies equal a male testimony? More than two, apparently."

"Now, Freya...I've had enough of this bickering! Dave, you're on warning from me! Do you understand?"

He smirked. "Sure...OK."

"And, Freya..."

She huffed and walked past Ron, not bothering to stay and listen to any more. She paused for a moment in front of Dave. "You touch a hair on Grace's head, you even look at her funny, and I swear, I will ram a skewer into your ear next time."

CHAPTER
40

The Congolese Jungle

Beneath tall red cedar trees with their broad, waxy leaves—a canopy that filtered out the light so much that the jungle floor below existed in an eternal emerald-green twilight—it was unnaturally quiet. Six months ago, this Congolese jungle would have echoed with twittering and tweeting, the haunting cries of howler monkeys, the incessant *chee-chee-chee* of insects. Now, like everywhere else, the only sound was the stirring of leaves, the creaking of ancient branches. Without the movement of wind, the world would have been wholly silent.

But not lifeless.

The jungle floor was very far from barren. Here in this place that once upon a time, a million years ago, had been the cradle of humanity—the place where one species of primate had learned that coming down from the trees freed up their dexterous hands and their minds—here, it was a cradle for a brand-new ecosystem.

The jungle floor as we would recognize it was long gone, buried beneath a dark-brown, leathery blanket. The blanket ran smoothly, lifting in humps here and there, faintly marking the topography below: fallen trees, dips and rises in the ground.

In several locations, the leathery material had hardened into a firm, resinlike material, and tall stalagmites, like termite mounds, emerged from the soft blanket. Copying the behavior of the trees, they speared straight upward, reaching for the sunlight. But, unlike the trees, there was intelligence at work, deploying a more effective method of reaching the sunlight. These stalagmites reached only halfway up, tapered to a point, then formed thin, sinuous "ropes" of material that swayed gently as they ascended toward the canopy of leaves overhead.

In the brilliant sunlight above the canopy, the ropes thickened and became bloated pink and sepia balloons that looked like the intestines of a pig comically inflated to ridiculous proportions. The balloons swayed gently in the breeze, their taut, thin membranes glistening in the sunlight, thousands of them up there, like tethered party balloons, collecting the solar energy, converting it inside themselves to a sugar solution that was then transferred back down the ropes to feed the hungry megacolony below.

Every now and then, a balloon gently broke free and floated away, its useful life as a solar collector coming to an end and now assigned the role of a spore container, to be carried aloft to a higher altitude, where it would eventually rupture and release its cargo.

On the jungle floor, this megacolony was one of the very first. Consequently, it was one of the most *mature*. Billions of years of evolution by our standards had accelerated here to mere months. Beneath the brown blanket churned a glutinous ocean: cells arranging into clusters large enough to store libraries of DNA packets—many of these packets assembled by trial and error into almost complete genomes. Groups of clusters cooperating and merging to become super-clusters capable of not only storing data, but—like the simplest of digital AI—processing that data. Making decisions.

Strategizing.

The "plan," for want of a better term, was embedded and encoded in the chromosomes of every single cell in this vast ocean, every one of them entrusted with knowledge of the goal, but each too simple on their own to understand it.

The plan was stratified; it came in levels of complexity. The simplest to understand and the most important level of the plan was the basic expedient of survival—procreation. An easy enough concept for simple cells to grasp.

But with the creation of billions of clusters came the emergent ability to read just a little farther down the encoded to-do list. The instructions were to store and collate the newly acquired genetic data, to try to reassemble the life forms it had consumed and destroyed.

This megacolony had made great strides on that front. It had reproduced some very impressive life forms, large ones that required the complicated assembly of resinous skeletal structures, articulating limbs, muscle tissues, nerve endings, support systems of organs. But, ironically, it was the simpler things it struggled to replicate. For example, it seemed so many life forms appeared to want to cover themselves with linear arrangements of dead cell tissue, compressed to form a protein it didn't quite understand—a useless protein that seemed to serve no purpose. A protein we would call *keratin*.

For a while, all was still in the quiet jungle; then the leather blanket bunched up with movement from below—something stirring. Eventually, the leathery skin ruptured, and out of the soup emerged a modest-size creature. Its brown eyes blinked at the green-filtered sunlight. Its small mouth opened and closed, a chattering noise emerging from its lips. Slender arms ended with delicate, five-digit hands. The creature pulled itself out of the mush and took several testing, loping steps across the leathery skin, bouncing gently like a toddler on a trampoline.

The prototype monkey moved as one would expect it to, walking on its tiny knuckles and dainty feet, its long tail curling, twitching, and waving. Behind those all-brown eyes, optic nerves fed information to a walnut-size brain. Instinct, *copied* instinct, helped the creature move. It headed for the nearest tree, leaped from the trampoline surface of the skin to the rough bark of the trunk, its small hands reaching for knots and grooves to hold on to. It scampered up the side of the tree at first, slightly ungainly and awkward, like a wild animal shaking off the tail end of a tranquillizer, but by the time it had reached the spreading branches, it was moving like a monkey should.

From a few feet away, it was an utterly convincing facsimile. It might even have fooled a zookeeper if it had been thrown into an enclosure filled with the same species. It certainly would have fooled young visitors making faces at it through a cage's mesh. But looking closer, much closer, it would have become apparent that this monkey had no fur. Instead, its skin was colored to mimic the millions of strands of keratin it had trouble duplicating.

Washington, DC

The building from the outside was instantly recognizable, having once been the iconic backdrop for so many movies, perhaps looking a little scruffy though; the front lawns needed mowing, the rear rose gardens were competing with unpoliced weeds. But the building was still very much an icon. Inside, however, a much younger colony than the jungle one was finding its way. Down the dark-blue carpets of the hallways of power, thick veins of the virus meandered, occasionally dipping into side rooms and offices, probing, investigating, hunting for organic morsels. A central, much thicker vein, protected by a hardened leathery membrane, snaked down the hallway to the office at the far end, thickening as tributaries joined in from side offices.

The double doors stood wide open and led into an oval-shaped room with tall windows beyond a dark maple wood desk that looked out across those scruffy, untended lawns.

The room would normally have been bright with sunlight. But the windows were now almost entirely coated inside by a thin, sepia-colored membrane, like stomach lining stretched out in a tannery to dry. The membrane filtered the light coming into the room, rendering the space a deep bloodred, bathing it in a womb-like glow.

The floor was concealed by a thick mattress of organic soup eight inches thick, again topped with a thin, protective membrane. The walls displayed networks of impressionistic arterial artwork—veins, branches, tributaries—like a projected map of the road network of a truly industrialized country.

The polished maple desk, the blotting pad, the two phones, one linked to an exchange on the mezzanine floor, the other linked directly to the Pentagon—the very same old-fashioned phones once used by a man named Kennedy to talk to a man called Khrushchev—were covered by thin, dark, threadlike strands of the material that had dried and died. Nothing useful here...just a smooth plastic surface that ignored the virus's probing.

This colony was at a less mature life-cycle stage. Its cells had formed smaller clusters that were now beginning to exchange the genetic data they had gathered. Simple scuttling-creature experiments had been attempted successfully, and their ghostly, pale, almost-translucent forms shifted and twitched in the hundreds as they dangled from the tall, dark-blue drapes by the window, like bats clinging to a cave roof.

New York City

In a large open-plan office with floor-to-ceiling glass windows that looked down on the streets and lesser skyscrapers of Lower Manhattan, there was very little of the virus to be seen. Scuttling explorers from a supercolony sixty floors below had found their way up to the top floor and managed to infect and disassemble the few humans who'd been taking refuge there. Apart from them, this floor had been slim pickings with little more than its modern, clean, expensive office furniture and corporate, gray-blue carpeting, and the virus had long since departed, leaving behind a dozen or so piles of clothing, bones, and tufts of indigestible hair.

There were cans of uneaten food stacked against a wall, several dozen gallon bottles of watercooler water, left unused. Unrolled sleeping bags lay on the floor, and in a cardboard box was a stack of cans that had been opened and scraped clean, their contents eaten.

The people who'd been holding out here had been prepared. They'd taken steps, and if the world had been a fairer place, they would have deserved to have survived for their efforts. But none of them was unhealthy; none of them was struggling at the time with any aches or pains, sprains or even minor headaches. Health conscious and fitness overachievers who ate their vegetables, skipped dessert, and did Pilates at least twice a week, they had no need for painkillers, anti-inflammatories, or antidepressants.

These lucky, or *unlucky* few, had been up here and holding out for weeks, maybe even months, observing the empty streets below, the empty blue skies above, watching summer become autumn, become winter. Hoping desperately for a sign that they weren't alone. That there'd be hope of a rescue.

Outside one of the broad windows, a sheet flapped and snapped in the breeze, words painted boldly in red on it.

13 SURVIVORS HERE! SEND HELP!

There'd been no one left to read it and no one left to care. New York was dead, America was dead...the world was dead.

One body, a skeleton held almost completely intact by a two-hundred-dollar designer shirt and dark trousers, was slumped in an office chair, turned away from its desk to look out over the city. The body was slouched like a lethargic teenager in front of a video game console, skull tilted at an uncomfortable-looking angle, resting against the left collarbone and topped with a buzz-cut of dark hair.

Empty orbital sockets stared forlornly out at the panoramic view of the necropolis.

In one skeletal hand, palm upward, nestled a dead cell phone, stained and encrusted with a dried residue of blood. In the other, a handgun.

A single, very tidy hole marked the left temple.

On the desk lay a scrawled note, a couple of lines scribbled on a legal pad. A goodbye written by a shaking hand.

I'm so sorry for everything.

I tried to survive. I love you both.

CHAPTER

41

1/13

Dad, the weirdest thing happened this
morning. I woke up without a headache!

LEON HAD BEEN GETTING MORNING HEADACHES FROM EVEN
before the day his mom and dad had their big right-there-in-the-
kitchen meltdown. The doctor at the Lincoln Medical Center had
said it was probably stress-induced. That's what the physician in
London had said too: Leon's parents splitting up, the pressure of
moving to a new place, the anxiety of school exams, hormones,
and that kind of teen-angst stuff thrown on top. The doctor told
him she saw so many more stressed-out teenagers these days than
she used to, and having regular morning headaches was a pretty
mild problem compared to some of them. She'd told him that one
day the headaches would probably stop without any warning. Just
like a plantar wart that, one day, despite all the expensive oint-
ments and creams...y'know...just *goes*.

He'd woken up this morning, eyes still closed, listening to Grace murmuring and whimpering in her sleep (he'd never known before how much sleep-muttering she did!), opened his eyes, and realized his head—for the first time in God knows how long—was completely clear. He lay there on his bed and listened to someone on kitchen duty banging pots and pans on the far side of the tropicarium, the sound of Vivaldi's *Four Seasons* being played over the PA system, and finally Mr. Carnegie announcing breakfast time.

And he realized he felt...OK.

Totally weird thing, Dad.

He scribbled in his journal.

I feel fine. Is that wrong?

Leon looked at those words written down on the page and then scribbled them out. It felt bad writing that down. It was as if he were saying, "Yeah, eight billion people died six months ago, but, hey, at least *I'm* feeling better."

Me and Grace are doing OK. This place is safe and pretty well organized, and I think we're going to make it. Plus, I'm not a hundred percent sure about this, I may be reading the signals all wrong, but I think Freya likes me. She's different, Dad. You'd like her. I

*think Mom would have liked her too... She's
kinda sparky.*

He looked at "sparky" and wondered what that actually meant. It seemed to sum her up though: she was funny, ballsy, smart... and mature. Not mature in the sense of being all solemn and awfully sensible about things, but *emotionally* mature. Knowing what people were *really* saying when they talked. She came up with some pretty clever stuff.

Leon realized he might possibly be falling for her. He'd wanted to take a swing at that creep Dave. He trusted Freya and Grace's version of what had happened. Mainly because he'd seen with his own eyes Dave's wandering gaze like a fumbling freshman's fingers. He'd watched him, listened to the little sarcastic asides to his wingmen Phil and Iain. He acted like a king in waiting. Waiting for Ron to make some big mistake, to trip and fall, or more likely be pushed. He wondered if all that kept Dave from staging a coup was his knowledge of that one gun locked away in Ron's desk.

It had been three weeks since Dave had tried groping Freya, and Mr. Carnegie's botched solution that they should just stay out of each other's way had surprisingly worked so far. Apart from the occasional glares across the tables at mealtimes, the peace had been kept, but Leon couldn't help wondering how long their current little world was going to last. He wondered if a rescue from someone somewhere was already underway, or whether they were all alone and at some point would find Ron's regime being replaced with Dave's.

"The guy's a complete dick," said Spanners. He lit his crinkly, self-rolled cigarette again. For the third time, Leon noted. "I served with a first lieutenant on a ship who was like him. Treated the Taiwanese crew like dirt. Dave's bad news."

He blew smoke out, and the breeze carried it quickly away across the roof of the tropicarium. Ron didn't permit smoking anywhere inside the complex, which was one of the reasons why Spanners volunteered to do watch duty pretty much all the time.

"You were in the British Navy?"

Spanners snorted. "Nah, merchant navy. Container ships. Second engineer mostly. Good laugh some of the time."

"Those big ships?"

"Oh yeah, they're *big*." He snorted again. Leon wasn't quite sure when he did that whether he was laughing or just clearing his nose. "There was this one time, when we cleared our berth in Hong Kong, when we lifted our anchor..." He looked at Leon. "Big anchor, right? I mean, the size of a car. And each of the chain's links the size of a washing machine or something... Anyway, we were drawing the anchor in, and we found bits of the rigging of a junk tangled in among it."

"Junk?"

"Fishing boat. We must have dropped it on them. Sank the poor buggers. I don't know if we killed anyone. I hope not."

"*Jeez.*"

"Yeah, big ships. Ten-mile turning circle. That's why they never stopped if someone went over the side. No point. Plus it cost too much in diesel and time."

Leon scanned the horizon with the binoculars. There hadn't been any signs of the virus in more than a week now. The last sighting had been one of Spanners's: a bloom of spores floating like a twist of campfire smoke in the distance.

"Do you think the plague is over?"

Spanners sucked on his cigarette. "The infectious disease bit? Dunno... I'm gonna keep taking the tablets for a while yet. But I guess the virus stage has got to die out at some point. Stands to reason...there's nothing left for it to infect."

"I guess so."

"It's the same as zombies."

Leon lowered the binoculars and looked at him. "Huh?"

"Well, you've seen zombie movies, right? It's the same crap every time. The world gets infected and those things eat human brains for breakfast, lunch, and dinner, right? So, how come, after everyone's been infected apart from the heroes, these zombies don't, you know, all just starve to death?" He snorted. "All you'd need to do is sit tight until they dropped from hunger, right? And what about the fact they're made of decaying flesh? How do the muscles work? The tendons? How do they even digest brains and turn that into fuel if they don't have any working organs?" He shrugged. "That's why I think zombie films are a load of old crap. There's no logical framework or—"

Leon spotted something moving in the trees. A flash of something tan-colored among the rich, dark evergreen.

"—thought behind them. Might as well all be magic. Might as well be Harry Potter, or—"

He saw it again. Something moving around among the trees. "Spanners! I just saw something."

He stopped talking and looked at him. "Snarks?"

"No...I don't think so. It was brownish."

"Well, there's a lot of brownish stuff out there. You sure?"

"It wasn't leaves or branches. It was something else. An animal."

"Where?"

Leon pointed to the trees around the tennis courts. "Over there." He handed the binoculars to Spanners.

Spanners squinted as he stared through the lenses. "You sure?"

"I saw *something*." Leon shaded his eyes and scanned the trees again.

"Brown you say? Like a rabbit? Or a fox?"

"Bigger than that. You think we should raise the alarm?"

Spanners sucked on his teeth. "Maybe."

Leon caught sight of that flash of tan again. Farther to the left, in the parking lot. "There!" he said. "It's by the cars!"

Spanners swung his binoculars to the left. "I can't see anything."

"Next to the van. The green van."

Spanners aimed his binoculars where Leon was pointing. "Oh...shit, you're right!"

It was moving one way, then the other, like something lost, confused. Leon couldn't make out what shape it was or even judge precisely how big it was, the dappled light coming down and the gaps in the fir trees providing only disjointed glimpses. Then suddenly the creature changed direction again, left the parking lot, and darted into the trees.

"Lost it," said Spanners.

"It was big. Maybe it was a moose or something?"

He chuckled. "We don't have *moose* over here, lad. There's plenty of deer in the park though. Well, there were, anyway."

He spotted movement again. Something hovering uncertainly behind some bushes near the front entrance to the spa. Moving backward and forward, pacing like some frustrated predator behind the bars of a cage. Finally, it emerged into the clear space before the main entrance.

"Oh my God..."

Leon smiled. "No way."

CHAPTER

42

"PLEASE! PLEASE CAN WE LET IT IN?"

They were all gathered in the lobby beside the spa-treatment reception desk, watching the horse trotting backward and forward outside. It looked to Leon's inexpert eye like it was horrendously malnourished and clearly distressed. The animal must have remained untended for some time, maybe locked in a barn somewhere, and had only now finally managed to find a way out.

Grace was pressed up against the window waggling her hand to get its attention. "Please, Mr. Carnegie...before it runs away!"

"I don't think it's going anywhere, Grace. It needs feeding I'd say."

"Poor thing," said Claire. "It looks so hungry."

"It is starved horse," said Sofia, one of the cleaning ladies. "We *must* give it food."

Half of those present murmured in agreement. Leon couldn't help but notice the gender split on the matter: females nodding, pitying the sad creature's condition; males more likely silently considering whether they were ready to try eating fresh horse meat.

"To be absolutely clear about this...we are *not* thinking about letting it in, right?"

All heads turned toward Dave.

"I'm serious! We don't know if that thing is infected or not!"

"It must be like us," said Terry. "Immune. It could have been on some medication that rejected the virus."

"Or maybe it's been locked away somewhere and hasn't had a chance to interact with the virus yet?" said Leon. On the issue of whether they should let it in, he found himself in the odd position of agreeing, reluctantly, with Dave.

"Well, if it isn't immune, we have to let it in before one of those crabs comes out and stabs it!" said Grace.

Freya nodded. "Come on. We've all seen how quickly the Snark affects things. If it's been infected, it would be showing signs already."

Ron pursed his lips and air whistled between his clenched teeth. "To be fair, it doesn't look infected. Just hungry."

"It could be useful to us, Mr. Carnegie," said Spanners. "As transport...or as fresh meat."

Grace turned to look at him, utterly disgusted. "We are *not* going to eat it!"

"I'm just being practical."

"Ron?" Dave stepped toward him. "Seriously? We are not letting it—"

Ron scratched the back of his neck indecisively. "A horse... could be very useful."

"*What?*" Dave shook his head. "I'm not putting myself at risk just because the girls want a pet pony to ride!"

"What's the risk?" Freya answered.

Leon realized that this was the first time in weeks that she had even acknowledged Dave existed.

"We're *immune*. That horse is…or it isn't," Freya said.

"Well, I'm voting we don't let it in."

"Well, I vote we do."

He huffed. "Now there's a shocker."

"Oh God, why don't you grow a pair?"

"Cut it out, you two!" snapped Ron irritably. He wandered over and joined Grace by the window. "It looks OK to me…just very, very hungry."

"Please?" begged Grace. "If he's not immune, we should let him in quickly!"

"How do you know it's a he?" asked Ron.

She looked up at him and made a face. "Please? Can we?"

He looked again. "Ah yes…of course."

"Ron!" Dave stepped forward. "This should be down to a vote. Not just *your* decision!" He tugged at his green top. "You're not my boss anymore, mate. Or anyone else's." He turned to look for support and got some nods from Iain and Big Phil and one or two others.

"The only reason you've been in charge here so far is because you were the manager—"

"All right."

Dave was silenced by that.

"All right," Ron said again. "You're quite right. We should

probably all vote on this." He turned to address the others. "Right then, everyone...who's voting that we let the horse in?"

Grace's hand shot up. Freya's too. The cleaning ladies... Claire...Spanners. Others too. Roughly half of them. Ron dutifully counted the raised hands.

"And who *doesn't* want to let it in?"

The rest of the hands went up, including Leon's, Dave leading the way. He silently counted them. "Interesting...it appears we have a dead-even vote."

He smiled dryly at Dave. "Looks like it's my *deciding* vote that counts."

He rubbed his neck, then looked back down at Grace for a moment. Outside, the horse had ceased its incessant back-and-forth trotting and come to a rest outside the glass doors. It hung its head wearily, like a criminal resigned to its fate and awaiting a judge's sentencing.

Ron lifted the keys off a clip on his belt. "All right, then. I'll take him around the back to the service entrance." He unlocked the door, then tossed the keys across to Terry. "Will you let me in?"

———

Ron stepped outside and let out a shaky breath.

You're going to have to watch out for that young man. He's trouble.

Ron *had* been marginally inclined to shoo the horse away, cruel as that would have been. It was another mouth to feed. But Dave's challenge needed a response. Ron had been preparing himself to go against the vote and make an executive decision, to flex his authority and demonstrate who was in charge here. Luckily he hadn't needed to.

He spread his palms as he approached the horse. "All right, boy, I'm not going to hurt you." He approached the animal slowly. The horse eyeballed him warily, snorting and shuffling restlessly on its hooves.

"You poor, poor boy," he cooed softly. "Been in the wars, haven't you?"

The horse's flanks were mottled with bald patches of skin, crisscrossed with raised welts from scratches and cuts. The bare skin looked sore and dry.

There was a term for this... *Mange*, wasn't it?

The animal had no halter on it, nothing with which to lead it. Ron cautiously held out his hand and felt the hot breath coming from its flared nostrils. He'd never handled a horse before, never even stroked one. He wasn't even sure whether patting it on the muzzle like a dog was the right thing to do.

Instead, he rested a hand on the horse's neck and gently tugged at it. It complied wearily, snorting and dipping its head in surrender.

Ron led the way and the animal followed obediently. "There's a good lad."

Through the window, he saw them all watching eagerly, Grace beaming at him through the glass. He gave her a wink and then rounded the corner, the horse clopping dutifully beside him.

"Poor boy. You look hungry." He looked at the animal's large brown eyes ringed with dried mucus. "Have you been crying, lad?"

He didn't know if horses cried, as such. Probably not. "Well, you're going to be fine now… Although, what on earth are we going to feed you, hmm? I'm afraid we don't have any apples or carrots. This way, boy."

He led the animal down the side of the building, finally coming to a halt outside the double doors that led to the main storeroom. For now, they could keep it in there—it was a little bit like a stable, certainly space enough for a horse.

He knocked on one of the doors. "I'm here, Terry!"

He looked around for any sign of snarks. Last time he'd been on a foraging trip, admittedly several months ago now, there had only been those crablike things. They didn't appear to have eyes and seemed to respond sluggishly, probably reacting to scent. He couldn't see any now.

He knocked on the door again. "Terry?"

The horse snorted beside him. Like him, it was looking anxiously around.

"It's OK, boy. None of those nasty little critters nearby." He heard the jangle of keys through the corrugated metal of the shutter door. "Come on, Terry! I'd like to come in now, please!"

"Just a sec…just a sec," Terry called through the door.

The horse shifted uneasily. "Easy, boy, easy now." Ron patted it gently on the back of his neck. The mane felt odd. He'd expected the texture of knotted, greasy hair; instead, it felt like tire rubber. He looked more closely. The dark mane *appeared* to be coarse hair slicked down by grease, but it was a solid mass. He had a fleeting childhood memory of riding a merry-go-round, sitting on a white plastic horse and feeling vaguely cheated that the animal's mane was just more painted, molded plastic.

He could hear a key being shoved into the padlock on the other side. Ron rested his hand on the mane again and squeezed it. His fingers left dents that slowly vanished like grip marks on memory foam.

That's weird.

He ran his hand across the animal's flank, where the tan-colored coat was thickest. The hairs felt a little like wood grain. They didn't splay like toothbrush fibers—they presented one solid, textured surface, like the leathery hide of an elephant.

The shutter door rattled to one side.

Very weird.

He took a step back and looked at the rear of the horse, at its tail. It hung down between the horse's hindquarters, limp and lifeless.

"Sorry, Mr. Carnegie. I couldn't figure out which key it was."

Ron wasn't listening. He ran his hand down the tail. Like the animal's mane, it felt like a length of ridged, molded rubber. Not horse hair, but a simulation of it. Just like that merry-go-round horse...a solid blob.

This...thing...isn't...right.

The animal clopped slowly forward without being led, stepping into the dim interior of the storeroom.

"Hey there, horsey," said Terry.

"It's...not...*right*," said Ron slowly. He looked down at the animal's hooves just as its rear disappeared out of the winter sunlight and into the gloom beyond. He was pretty damn certain hooves were supposed to be nearly black, hard, and shiny. Instead, what he glimpsed, before they were lost to the sun, were flexing gray-red pads that, for some reason, reminded him of gym-shoe treads.

Terry was looking at him. "You all right?"

"That horse," he said again. "It's not right."

Terry shrugged. "It's not *well*." He pulled the shutter door closed behind Ron's back and locked the padlock again. The room went dark except for a crack of light coming in between the shutters and a small shard of light coming from the open door leading into the tropicarium. Terry handed back the keys. "Here..."

"The horse feels wrong," said Ron. "The hair. It feels like sponge."

"It's probably not been—what's the term?—*groomed* for months. It's—"

"Just feel it... Go on, stroke it."

"OK."

Ron could only see the faintest silhouette of the horse, standing perfectly still, and Terry's outline, stepping toward it, reaching out a hand. He heard the soft rasp of a hand running down the animal's side.

"Well?"

"That's odd... Ew... What's..."

"What?"

"Feels sticky. Is that a cut on its side...or something?" They heard something wet *spluck* down on the concrete floor beneath the animal's distended belly. "Oh great. Did it just crap?"

Ron fumbled with the jangling keys. There was a little LED flashlight on the key chain somewhere.

"Oh boy, now that really...really stinks," gasped Terry.

They heard something else splatter on the concrete. "Whoa! I think our friend's spurting diarrhea, Ron." He could hear Terry puffing air at the stench. "Jesus Christ!"

Ron found the small flashlight nub on his key fob and pressed it. The little LED bulb glowed, and he aimed it at the horse.

The animal's eyes reflected the beam like those of a fox caught in the headlights of a car.

"Oh my God...what's all that stuff beneath it?"

Ron looked where Terry was pointing. Beneath its four legs, the belly of the creature appeared to have ripped wide open and emptied its contents in a wet, glistening, pink-and-purple pile on the ground.

Ron thought he could make out organs, sausage loops of intestines, pulsating vein-covered sacks that might well have been the horse's lungs, still flexing rhythmically. The animal snorted a bloody aerosol spray from each nostril; then its legs suddenly buckled and it collapsed onto the pile of offal beneath it.

Terry staggered backward. "Jesus!"

The horse's thick neck began to deflate, the hide, fake fur, and skin wrinkling as the substance beneath spilled out of the horse's wide-open mouth, pooling into a viscous puddle that spread out across the floor.

Ron stared at the carcass, watching as it deflated like the time-lapse film of some roadkill deer being eaten from the inside out by maggots.

"It's the *virus... We've let it in!*"

Ron looked at Terry, his mouth opening and closing dumbly. "Terry? We're all still immune, aren't we?" he whispered.

Terry was staring at the collapsing body, mesmerized. "I don't know! I hope so." He looked up. "It made a horse, Ron. It made a complete bloody horse!"

"I know."

"A completely convincing horse!"

"I know!"

"Jesus." Terry stepped away from the slowly spreading pool and headed toward the door leading to the tropicarium.

"Where are you—?"

"Diesel," replied Terry. "I'm going to get a can. We need to incinerate that. All of it."

"Yes." Ron nodded. "Go. Hurry!"

Terry rushed out. He could hear the sound of the others approaching: excited babbling from Grace and everyone keen to meet their new guest. Ron reached the door and pulled it closed behind him as they all appeared.

Grace led the way, announcing loudly that she was volunteering herself as chief horse-looker-after-er. The snaking line of the curious followed her lead and made their way along the winding pathway toward the back of the tropicarium, past the sauna shacks and empty spa pools, an excited babble of voices keen to see the animal close up.

"Hey, maybe *all* horses are immune?" She grinned at the thought of Horse World—nothing but the nature-covered ruins of mankind and an endless herd of carefree horses frolicking through it.

Leon spotted Ron, backed up against the closed door of the storeroom. "Is the horse in there?"

He shook his head and remained there, blocking the doorway.

Grace look alarmed. "You didn't leave him stuck outside, did—"

"It's not a horse."

She looked confused by that. "Of course it's a horse!"

Leon noted his ashen face. "Mr. Carnegie, what's wrong?"

"We have to burn it."

"*Burn it?*" Grace almost shrieked. Her head swiped from Ron to Leon and back to Ron again. Several others gasped in horror at the thought.

"Burn it? *What?* Why?"

Ron shook his head. "It's not right, Grace... It's not...*well.*"

"Of course it's not well," said Freya. "The poor thing's starving!"

Dave pushed his way forward to the front. "Shit! It's infected, isn't it?"

Ron met his eyes, looked away, and then nodded.

"Shit! I *said* that! I bloody said it might be!"

"It can't be!" said Grace. "It was running around just now!"

Leon put a hand on his sister to hush her. "Mr. Carnegie, we've all seen how quickly this thing affects animals. It didn't look like—"

"Leon, the thing in there"—Ron tipped his head at the door he was leaning against—"it *isn't* a horse."

They heard feet pounding and liquid sloshing; then Terry appeared carrying a five-gallon plastic drum of diesel fuel.

"Oh God...no, no, no! Leon, *they're serious!*" cried Grace.

"Mr. Carnegie, what do you mean it's *not* a horse?"

Ron looked at Leon. "It's the virus. It made a *copy* of one."

"OK, that's just insane!" said Freya. "That was a real horse I just saw outside!"

Terry set the drum down. "Freya...Ron and me just saw that thing *disembowel* itself."

"*What?*"

"It stepped inside... Then it immediately started to..." He tried to find a term that worked. "*Un-make* itself, to break apart!"

"Oh, come on, that's crazy—"

"No. We've seen the virus can make crabs out of itself," cut in Spanners. "I've seen bigger things. Rabbit size...dog size."

Freya turned around. "Right, but not an actual rabbit or dog, right? Not something you'd actually *mistake* for one?"

Just then, they heard a baleful cry from beyond the door, like the sound of some animal finally comprehending the purpose of a slaughterhouse...recognizing its impending fate. They all looked at each other. "That didn't sound like a horse..."

"All right, that's enough!" Ron bent down to pick up the drum of fuel. "We're going to burn whatever's in there now. I want you all to step back. Get far back!"

Grace broke free from Leon's hold, raced forward, and grabbed at the plastic gallon drum. "No, don't! Please, don't kill it!"

"Let go, Grace."

She hunched over the drum, grasping the handle tightly.

"Leon, get your sister, please," said Terry.

Leon stepped forward. "Come on, Grace—"

"No! Leon! Don't let them kill it!"

He peeled her fingers off the drum's handle and dragged her back, kicking and screaming. "Grace, for God's sake!"

"Dave?" Ron looked at his deputy manager. "Fire extinguishers. Get two of them. I don't want to burn the whole bloody place down!"

Dave nodded and hurried off.

Freya hunkered down and tried soothing Grace. She was sobbing, her face buried in her crossed arms.

"You're absolutely sure about this, Mr. Carnegie?" said Leon. "About what you just saw?"

Ron nodded. "It...it's a copy, like a goddamn photocopy. Completely, a hundred percent convincing...until I touched it."

They heard the clanking of fire extinguishers and Dave's approaching footsteps.

"All right, then," said Ron, drawing in a deep, fluttering breath. He picked up the drum. "Terry, will you take one of those extinguishers? The rest of you, back up some more. I've got no idea how big a fire this is going to make."

"Anyone have a match?"

"Here." Spanners handed him his lighter.

"Come on, back up...everyone!" Ron shooed them with his hands. They all stepped away from the door, picking their way back past the empty spa pools into the humid warmth of the tropicarium, but all of them still close enough to watch.

Ron turned to Terry and Dave. "I'm going to splash around what I've got in here, light it and we'll give it about a minute, then we go in again and put it all out. Agreed?"

"I...uh...I'm not going in there," said Dave. "Can't we just spray it from outside?"

Ron glared at him. "Jesus Christ...just do what I said, will you?"

"Give it to me," said Spanners. He took the extinguisher from him.

Ron shook his head at his deputy. Then took another deep breath. "Right." He turned the handle and pushed the door inward.

"Here goes." He stepped into the dark storeroom, the other two following in behind him.

Leon watched them disappear through the open door into the storeroom's darkness. He was still holding Grace firmly. And she was still sobbing. "It was so beautiful," she whimpered.

"It's got to be done, Grace."

Dave had backed up and was standing beside them. "We shouldn't have let it in in the first place," he muttered angrily.

Leon could hear murmuring voices inside the storeroom, echoing out through the open door, but not clearly enough for him to hear what they were saying. He could hear the scraping of feet, the clank of the fire extinguishers, the first slosh and splatter of diesel fuel being poured out.

Then he heard, "That's not all of it?"

"Where's the rest?"

Then...

"Shit! Ron! Look out!"

CHAPTER
43

Leon heard Spanners's voice. "They're everywhere!"

Then Ron's, screaming, high-pitched with terror. *"HELP ME!"*

He heard the loud clang of one of the extinguishers being dropped on the floor and something else that made his legs suddenly feel boneless and useless: a hissing sound. In the same way a single person clapping sounds like a clap while an audience applauding can sound like rain, the hissing sounded like white noise. Leon knew what it was—he recognized it from the service station: the sound of thousands of tiny, pincer-like legs scrabbling for traction against a hard, smooth surface.

He leaped forward, hurrying toward the open door, not sure what his plan was—to help Spanners and the others get out, or to pull the door shut?

"Leon!" screamed Grace. "No!" She grabbed at the back of his shirt. "Don't go!"

And because of that, he didn't make it to the door in time.

They swarmed out of the dark interior of the storeroom, a heaving carpet of mother-of-pearl-colored shells. Bigger than the ones from the service station, palm-size bodies, but the same random configuration of legs and claws, and this time with long, antennae-like feelers, like a cat's whiskers.

The larger scale didn't slow them down. In fact, they moved faster, frighteningly fast, on legs that had been refined to move more efficiently. They made a beeline toward the nearest fresh meat: Leon and Grace. She clawed at his shirt.

"Run!"

He backed up, tripping over her. He managed to stagger around her and keep on his feet, but his weight had knocked her into the ground face-first.

The nearest of them leaped—actually *launched* itself—through the air at her prone body, landing at the top of her back.

Leon grabbed one of her flailing hands and dragged her behind him, kicking and screaming as the creature dug its barbed pincer legs into her sweatshirt and clung on. With her free hand, she tried reaching around and tugging and slapping at it, but it hunkered down in the valley between her shoulder blades, fine, jointed legs receding like a tortoise into the shell, tugging the clenched material with it, clinging on, as impossible to dislodge as a limpet.

Leon managed to get her to her feet just as the rest of the swarm caught up with them. More of them launched themselves from the ground at him. He batted one away with his hand, a hard, razor-sharp edge slicing open the pad of his thumb. He staggered backward to where he'd been standing with the rest of the group just moments ago, but they'd now broken and fled in different directions into the tropicarium. Dave, however, was still standing there, a tennis racket in his hand. He stepped forward and swung it at a crab that had landed on Leon's upper arm. It spun off, jetting an arc of pale gunk behind it and leaving behind a broken-off pair of pincer legs that continued to flex and twitch as Leon pulled them from his hoodie.

The swarm of crabs caught up with the three of them, most streaming past them in pursuit of the others, but dozens were now starting to try to clamber up their legs. Leon stamped on one trying to gnaw its way into his left shoe. Its shell crackled and spurted gunk out on to the ground.

"It's *cutting into me!*" screamed Grace. Leon looked down to see the creature that had latched onto her back had now climbed higher and had burrowed itself in her long, dark hair.

Beside him, Dave swung the racket at everything airborne, the fibers of the racket zinging as creatures spun off like well-returned serves. "Shit! Shit! Shit!" he was shouting.

We're dead this time. That was all that was in Leon's head. He was about to reach into Grace's tangled hair to try to extract the creature lodged in there when one landed on his cheek. Razor-sharp points dug into his flesh immediately. Instinctively, he let go of Grace and with both hands clawed at the creature on his face. As he tugged at it, he could feel the thing tensing, barbed hooks burrowing deeper, his cheek being tugged painfully as he tried to remove the creature from his face.

He could feel a fine articulated arm fumbling blindly for something else to latch on to. It found his nose, his left nostril and something sharp curled up inside. He could feel dozens of other crabs taking advantage of his distraction, clambering up his legs, pinpricks like kitten claws, hopscotching up toward his torso.

Leon heard himself screaming. An out-of-body voice—someone else dying, not him. He felt pricking around his waist, circling around to his back. It felt like dozens of them, it felt like hundreds, a Lilliputian army jabbing at him with tiny spears and swords, death by a thousand paper cuts.

Then it all stopped.

Very suddenly, every one of them froze. For a moment, he felt like an overdecorated Christmas tree, standing there covered with rustling, crackling creatures, poised and motionless. Then they dropped off him. One after the other, they just loosened their hold, clattered to the floor, and scuttled away.

He looked around for Grace. She was on the ground beside him, tucked into the fetal position. He saw the creature that had been tangled in her hair slowly making its way down her shoulder and hopping to the floor. One of its pale pincer arms was covered in her blood. It held that aloft, like a trophy, like a captured flag, and as it joined the others, they clustered around it, their whisker-like antennae reaching out and stroking the bloody pincer, caressing it. He had a sense they were all trying to get a sample of it.

"What's happening?" whispered Dave.

Leon shook his head. "Grace? Grace? You OK?" He bent over to look at her.

She uncurled herself and looked at him. Wide-eyed with terror. "You OK?"

She nodded. She reached around to the back of her neck and dabbed there. She showed Leon the blood on her fingers. "It...it was digging deep. I...thought...it was getting inside. I thought I was going to d-die!"

Leon turned to Dave, begrudgingly wanting to thank him for staying put and helping them, but he was staring intently at something.

"What *the*...?" said Dave.

They looked where he was looking. The swarm was heading back toward the storeroom, back to the place from which they'd all emerged moments ago. The other creatures that had rushed past them to pursue the others scuttled back too, giving Leon, Grace, and Dave a respectfully wide berth as they did. The one creature with the bloody pincer held aloft like a victory banner was right in the middle, surrounded on all sides. Protected like some timid, crowd-shy pop star amid a mob of hired bodyguards.

"They stopped," said Dave. He looked at Leon, then at Grace. "They stopped."

"*Jeez*," Leon gasped. "I know, but...*why*?" He watched the swarm converging in the doorway, clambering over each other like a haul of shellfish caught in a trawler's net.

He hunkered down beside Grace. "You OK?"

She was staring at the blood on her hands. Her blood. "I...I could feel it...trying to get in...me..." Her face crumpled, and Leon wrapped his arm around her. She sobbed into his shoulder.

He could hear the others elsewhere in the tropicarium, their voices echoing off the glass roof. "What about Ron? Terry? Did they get out?"

Freya's voice among them. She was calling Leon's name. He looked up at Dave. "Thanks for hitting that crab off me."

315

Dave was staring down at him. He'd taken an involuntary step back. "They stopped...because...of...you, or maybe it was *her*."

"What?"

"They...*tasted her*." He backed up another step. "They bloody well *sampled her*...then they stopped!"

CHAPTER
44

"What the hell are you saying?"

Dave glared at Freya. Then looked around at all the others. The staff room was normally their meeting room, the breakfast briefing room. This evening, it felt like a courtroom.

"I'm saying I saw them. They were all over Leon and Grace. They were all over the pair of them. Then they just suddenly froze. They stopped, dropped off them, and ran away."

He looked at them, sitting alone at one of the tables. Isolated by the space around them. Even Freya, in effect acting as their defense council, stood a cautious stride away from them.

"It was like they were after a *sample*. A blood sample. They got it...and decided those two had to be left alone."

"They left *everyone* else alone," she countered. "And they haven't come back since. For all we know they may have gone for good."

"Or they're still in there," said Claire. She was perched on a table, legs drawn up off the floor just in case there might be stragglers still lurking around. "With Ron...with Terry and Spanners."

Their names, mentioned again. No one so far had wanted to discuss what must have happened to the three of them.

"They're dead, Claire," said Freya. "They have to be dead."

"What if they're not?" she whimpered.

The inner door leading to the tropicarium had been blockaded. The outside door, the shutter, no one had dared go out to investigate. If it had been forced open, then good, maybe whatever nightmare was in there had scuttled off into the night.

"Ron, Terry, Spanners...they're dead," said Freya. "We've heard nothing from inside."

"Right." Dave nodded. "Those poor guys are gone."

Claire dropped her face down and shook her head.

"It's just us now..." Dave shot a glance at Leon and Grace. "And *them.*"

Grace glared at him. "Why are you doing this to us?" She looked at the others. Her eyes red with angry tears. "Why are *all of you* sitting away from me and Leo? I thought we were all supposed to be friends?"

No one answered.

"They sampled her blood...and then they suddenly backed off," said Dave. "Which means there's something different about those two."

"Like what?" asked Freya.

Dave took his time answering that. "All right...if no one else is going to say it, I'll say it. Like they're not real people."

"What?" Freya laughed cynically. "*What?*"

"Just like the horse. They're copies." He looked at the others. It seemed a smaller crowd minus the three older men. Maybe their combined age and wisdom had taken up more space than they'd thought. Ron, Terry, Spanners—all three men in their thirties and forties—had been the elders here. Now, apart from Mr. and Mrs. Lin, who hardly ever spoke anyway, the cafeteria was occupied by young adults looking for someone to take charge. Most of them in their early twenties, right now they looked like frightened children.

"Come on! You all saw that horse! We all thought it was real, right? It looked, moved, and *sounded* like a real horse! If the virus can make a horse, then why can't it make a person?" said Dave.

"You're saying it *made* Leon and Grace?" Freya shook her head. "Yeah, right. Complete with what? American accents?! Their stories? Their memories?"

"OK, then." He must have realized how ridiculous his accusation was beginning to sound. "Then maybe it's *altered* them? Maybe they got infected before we found them and it *changed* them."

"Changed them? How?"

Dave only had a shrug to give her.

"*Come on*, how?"

"To spy on us. To learn about us...what our weaknesses are?"

Freya snorted derisively again. "You really have no idea how stupid you sound, do you?"

"Well, hold on!" said Dave. "Remember...*she* insisted we let the horse in!"

"So did I! So did Claire... So did half of us!"

"And *she* wasn't going to let Ron burn it! Even when he said it wasn't even a horse. You all heard him say that, right?"

Heads nodded. "He said the thing was breaking up into pieces. And you remember she—*she*—was screeching like a tomcat for us not to burn it!"

"Oh please, Dave…she's just a little girl. I didn't want to burn the thing alive either!"

"They have to go," he said. "Both of them."

"Shit, they've been living with us for months! Grace has never… *attacked* anyone!"

"She was infected though, wasn't she? When we picked them up. She was running that fever? I said even then we should keep her separate. Even Terry wasn't sure what was wrong with her."

"Oh, for God's sake…"

"Maybe with her it was a different kind of infection? The Snark evolving the way it infects. Doing it gradually?"

"Do you have any idea how flipping paranoid you're sounding, Dave? Maybe *I'm* slowly changing into Fake Freya? Huh? Was that why you tried to grope me? To see if I'm still a real human?"

"I know what I saw! They got on her, they got a blood sample… *then they stopped!*"

He looked around. "Who wants them to go?" He raised his own hand. Only a couple of others followed his lead, Iain one of them, of course, and Big Phil reluctantly followed suit. Just about half a dozen hands.

"There you go. Outvoted. Matter resolved," said Freya. "Are we done with this crap?"

"All right, then. Who's prepared to share a chalet with them?"

Dave looked around. "Come on, stick your hands up. Who's prepared to stay with them in their room tonight?"

No hands went up. "Come on, none of you wanted to kick them out...so let's have a volunteer to spend the night with them, then!"

Still no hands.

Dave turned to Freya. "See? And *that's* why they can't stay! No one feels safe around them now."

"But no one's voted to kick them out. So what now? We keep them locked up in a storeroom forever? Or maybe we can consider that you got just a little carried away with what you *think* you saw?"

"We *test* them."

Everyone turned to look at Arletta, one of the cleaning ladies. Her cheeks turned pink, and she seemed to shrink under the gaze of everyone suddenly looking at her.

"So, you understand?" she continued. "We must know this... for sure?"

"She's right," said Big Phil. "We really should test 'em first, Dave. We can't just fling 'em outside without being sure."

Dave nodded thoughtfully. "OK...there's that. We can do that."

"Test us?" Leon stood up. He looked at Dave. He could guess where this was heading—how exactly they were going to be tested—even if the idea hadn't yet been spoken out loud.

"Look, come on...me and Grace, we're just exactly the same people as when you picked us up!"

"Isn't that the point?" Dave shrugged. "I don't know what you and Grace were like. How do we know you were *ever* real people?"

"Oh, this is just ridiculous!" Freya got up. "They're just regular people!" She steadied her balance, knuckles down on the table beside her. "Dave, please tell me you're not such a complete shit that you're thinking of doing what I think you—"

"We've got to do something! We've got to *know*...or they're gonna have to leave!"

"All right." Freya nodded. "All right, then, let them leave. Let them get their stuff and go. But, please, for Christ's sake, you can't just throw them in—"

"Throw them in the storeroom?" He shook his head. "Is that what you think I am? A psycho?" He shook his head again. "Oh, I wasn't thinking that." He looked at Leon and Grace. "We need to see what happens. *You all* need to see exactly what I saw."

Freya frowned. "So, what are you—"

"Just a couple...just a few... That's all. We put them together in one of the sauna rooms and we see what they do."

———

"Please! Please! Don't do this!" screamed Grace. Terrified, she clung to Freya's arm.

"This isn't right!" said Freya. "This is friggin' barbaric!"

Dave, Iain, and Phil had managed to capture a few of the creatures. It had been easier than they could have hoped. They'd eeny meeny–ed over who was going to have to go into the storeroom as bait, but in the end, they'd only had to crack open the door, and seconds later the nearest of the crabs had been drawn by the faint light—or maybe the smell of them—and skittered out through the gap. Iain had slammed a large plastic bucket down, crushing one of them with the rim but trapping another four or five inside.

"Let us go!" Leon struggled and tried to shake off the hands of Phil and Iain as Dave brought the bucket over. They were standing either side of him, leading him by the arms. "This is crazy!"

"Hey, just relax, Leon," Dave said, patting his shoulder. "It's just a few. It's just a handful of—"

"Me and Grace will just leave! OK? God! We'll get our stuff and go!"

"Huh?" Dave tilted his head curiously. "Why would you do that? Why would you say that? Why don't you want to do the test, huh? Unless you *know* something?"

"For God's sake, look at her!" Leon nodded at Grace. Her arms were wrapped tightly around Freya. "Grace is terrified of those things! They killed our mother!"

Dave tapped the plastic bucket. It stirred to life with the sound of scratching and rustling. They could see faint arachnid-like outlines shifting through the almost-opaque green plastic. "It's just a few. Nothing to get excited about. Nothing you can't deal with on your own." He smiled.

Leon stared at him. "Oh my God...you're getting a kick out of this, aren't you?"

"I know what I saw." His smile quickly disappeared. "I want the rest of them to see what happened."

"For God's sake...*nothing* happened!"

Dave shook his head. "Those things took a sample...and they stopped, Leon. They stopped dead, like someone just blew a half-time whistle. I'm sorry, mate, but we have to find out why."

Dave pulled the door to the sauna open. He switched on the light inside. "Just sit down in there—this won't take long."

"I'm not doing this! Dave...this is just crazy. Mr. Carnegie wouldn't have—"

The paper-thin expression of sympathy on Dave's face vanished in a flash. He balled his fist and punched Leon in the mouth. "Shut up with your stupid whining! We're doing this! All right?" He grabbed a fistful of Leon's T-shirt and dragged him into the small room. Slats of pinewood deadened his voice. "Just sit down and shut up!" He gestured at Iain and Phil to grab Leon's arms and hold him there; then he turned around. "Freya! Bring her in here!"

"No!" Freya shook her head. She looked around at the others, gathered in a semicircle around the sauna's entrance. Looked at them for support. She got absolutely nothing. "Nope. I'm not having anything to do with—"

"Claire!" he barked impatiently. "Get her in here!"

Claire stepped forward and grabbed Grace's arm. "Come on, *Miss Princess.*"

Freya grabbed Claire's wrist. "Shit! Leave her alone!"

"Let go of me, you emo weirdo!"

Freya slapped her hard and Claire recoiled, both hands clasping her face. "She hit me!" she bawled through her fingers. "You saw that! She hit meee!"

Dave stormed out of the sauna, grabbed Grace's arm, and tore it from around Freya's hips. He twisted Freya's wrist sharply. "You can leave with them when we're done here, 'cause I've had just about enough of your shit."

"Please!" cried Grace. "Please...Dave...please. I'm not a snark! I'm not a snark!"

He dragged her kicking and screaming into the sauna and shoved her forward. "We'll find out soon enough, won't we?" He beckoned Iain and Phil to let go of Leon, and together the three of them backed out of the small room and slammed the door shut.

Through the glass panel, Dave watched Grace cuddle up to her brother, tucking her legs up off the floor, onto the pinewood bench.

He grabbed the plastic bucket and held it up for everyone to see. "There's just four or five of those things in here, that's all! That's not going to kill them! We're just gonna see what they do! All right? That's *all* we're doing here. Does everyone understand?"

Heads nodded.

"Does anyone *disagree* with what I'm doing?" He glared at Freya.

"You're a total psycho," she snarled at him.

It was silent. No one else had anything to say. Through the thick glass, they could hear the muffled sound of Grace's sobbing.

"Right then." Dave snapped the clasps off the lid to the bucket. "Phil?"

Phil pulled the door open. Dave whipped the lid off quickly and swung the bucket in with both hands. The creatures that had been clambering restlessly over each other in the bottom of it flew through the air into the room, and the door thudded quickly shut behind them.

CHAPTER

45

GRACE CLUNG TO LEON TIGHTLY, HER FACE BURIED IN HIS chest, her sobs muffled.

"Shh...Grace," he whispered as he watched the creatures flip over from their backs onto their bellies on the floor.

If we stay still? Stay perfectly silent?

Through the insulated glass in the sauna's door, a flashlight shone in. It was aimed on the snarks, casting their jagged, little shadows across the wooden-slat floor. Leon could see the silhouette of several heads crowding the window to peer in.

Enjoy the show, you shitheads.

He watched the crabs, four of them, subdued for the moment. It was the first time that he'd had an opportunity to study them closely. It occurred to him that he could just get up, draw them over to him by his motion, and then stamp on them. Four wasn't enough to overpower them. Four were easily dealt with, in fact. But then that *wasn't* what this was about, was it? Instead it was about proving to everyone outside this room that they were who they said they were. That they were real humans. Not like the horse. Not copies.

The four crabs were all slightly different—different in size, in the number of appendages they had, in the configurations of their protective shells. One had a single egg-shaped shell over its top, making it definitely crab-like, while the one next to it had over-lapping C-shaped segments that reminded him of a croissant. The third one looked like a spider, with no shell on its soft body, only on its seven spindle-thin legs, and the fourth...looked vaguely like a snail with a spiraling shell like a Mr. Whippy ice cream.

Leon found himself identifying them: *Crab, Spider, Croissant, and Whippy.*

"I'm scared," whispered Grace.

"It's OK. There are just four of them. Look."

She turned slowly to look at them, sitting together on the floor, long, whisker-like antennae twitching, flexing, touching each other's. Her grasp on Leon eased slightly as she seemed to relax a little.

"What...what are they doing?"

"I don't know...sniffing the room for us?"

They seemed to be communicating through their antennae, rub-bing them together. He saw two touch, then separate, leaving, for a moment, the tiniest string of sticky liquid dangling between them.

Exchanging fluid? Is that how they talk?

"Grace...I know this isn't good...but we need them to come for us. Everyone outside is looking in. We need them to see those crabs attack us."

She shuddered. "Leon, please...don't attract them!"

"It's only four. We just need them to know we're here and come toward us. Don't worry...I'll crush them. I'll get them all."

"Oh God...they're horrible!"

She was right: they were horrific creations: all jagged, serrated edges, their ghostly pale—in places, almost transparent—surfaces lit up by the stark beam of the flashlight trained on them. He tried to make sense of how their limbs articulated, rigid crustacean sections linked by gooey strings of soft tissue. But, worst of all somehow, they had nothing that looked like eyes, nothing that remotely resembled a face.

"They're sharp," Grace whispered. "They cut. They dig—"

"Shh...relax. It's going to be fine. Only four of them. We can handle that. OK?"

He felt her head slowly nod against his chest.

"I'm going to let them know we're here...and when they attack, I'll get 'em. I promise."

He looked up at the window and saw heads crowding at it, watching. Impulsively he flipped a finger at them. *Screw you, Dave.*

"OK...OK...here goes." He stamped his foot down on the planked floor. The creatures reacted instantly to the movement, jerking in awareness and then scuttling quickly across the floor toward them.

Crap. Crap. Crap. His instinct was to yank his foot up, but for the benefit of their audience these things had to attack him. He clenched his teeth as he felt the first sharp appendages dig into his tennis shoe, then the slight tugging sensation on his jeans as the first of them began to pull itself quickly up his lower leg.

"Shit. Here they come!"

As she caught sight of the first one pulling itself up over his knee, Grace suddenly let go of him and screamed, scrambling away, pulling herself along the sauna's bench and huddling up in the corner as the creatures raced up Leon's thighs, over the waistband of his jeans and up his torso.

The snail-like one—*Whippy*—stopped on Leon's belly and its little scissorlike claws began cutting through his T-shirt while the other three continued their race up toward his neck.

In the background, through the glass, he could hear Freya or someone shouting to put a stop to this. Whippy was through his shirt now and Leon felt the sharp pain of its scalpel claws digging into his skin.

Enough.

"No!" he screamed, and swung his fist at it. The creature sensed a threat and tightened its hold on his belly, but the blow on its shell knocked it off, leaving several pale appendages clinging to the small, bloody incision beside his belly button, like the stinger of a bee stubbornly left behind.

Leon jumped to his feet and flailed to knock the other three off his chest. He managed to grab hold of one, *Spider*, and wrench it off him. The other two, sensing easier prey, leaped off him, onto the bench, and skittered quickly toward Grace, who screamed in blind panic.

Leon tossed the squirming spider-like creature to the floor, then stamped hard on it. Juice spattered out from its bulbous abdomen.

He stepped across the floor and thumped the window with his fist. "You satisfied now?"

He spun around to tackle the other two that had gone after Grace. He'd promised her he'd get them. He'd promised her…

She was frozen perfectly still, her eyes rounded in terror, her mouth agape with a scream that had stalled in her throat. Croissant and Crab were sitting on her chest, their long antennae probing her face cautiously, stroking her cheeks almost affectionately. The light of the flashlight was trained on her through the window. Her face and the two inquisitors sitting passively on her chest cast an absurd shadow on the wall.

Leon could see her whole body was trembling. Her eyes flickered toward him.

"Leon," she whispered. "Help me."

"I won't let them hurt you. Just…stay still."

And then something happened. Something Leon couldn't make any sense of as it occurred. A small lump began to grow from the skin just beneath Grace's right ear. Like a blister at first, then extending into a small polyp dangling lifelessly, then elongating to a fine tendril just three inches long. It flexed and curled and reached out, stretching toward the nearest antennae stroking her cheeks.

Her tendril and the antennae caressed each other gently, curled around each other like a tender lover's embrace.

"Oh Jesus!" whispered Leon.

"What?" Grace looked at him, saw his expression. "What? What's happening?" She couldn't see.

Leon grabbed the crab-like one and tugged it off her chest, its claws hooking on to the material of her T-shirt as he pulled, squirming in his fingers until he managed to tear it free. He tossed it on the floor and stamped on it. Then did the same to the other.

He turned to the door of the sauna, his eyes blinking in the glare of the flashlight now aimed at his face. "They're all dead! Can we come out now?"

Silence.

He winced in the glare and shaded his eyes. "I said...can we please come out now?"

The light shifted from his face, and now he could see their silhouettes crammed at the window. He could just about make out the dark ovals of mouths hanging open.

They saw it. They saw that thing on Grace's face.

All the same. He needed to say something. "For God's sake! We did your frickin test. Now let us out!"

He turned back to look at Grace, the flashlight beam full on her now. She was huddled up, face buried in her arms her shoulders shaking as she sobbed.

What just happened? It had happened so quickly, lasted just a couple of seconds...maybe he'd imagined it.

The latch *snick*ed and the door swung open. Dave was standing in the open doorway.

"You can come out."

Leon puffed out air. A tiny part of him wanted to say thanks—a very tiny part. The rest of him wanted to throw a punch at the guy for putting both of them, particularly Grace, through this.

He turned to her. "Come on, kiddo. It's all over."

"No! Just you, Leon. She's staying right there."

"*What?*"

"Come on, you saw it too, Leon. You saw...that thing on her face."

"What are you talking about?"

"That thing…the growth…her *face tentacle.*"

The word sounded comical and out of place, and Leon found himself laughing, more as a release of tension than anything else. "You're kidding me, right?"

"She grew something out of the side of her face. We all saw it."

Leon shook his head. "Oh, come on…"

But something did happen there. He blanked the thought out quickly.

"Jeez…it was playing with her hair… It was, I dunno, *curious* about her hair!"

"No, that's *not* what happened," replied Dave. He stepped to one side to look at Grace, aiming his flashlight on her. "Hey…*you!* Show us your face!"

She ignored him and remained as she was, curled up, arms wrapped around her knees, and her face buried.

"I said show us your face! *Now!*"

Slowly she moved, lifting her head up. She stared intently at the wall in front of her, showing them her profile, the left half of her face pale and pink and shining with tears.

"Look at me!" barked Dave.

She ignored him. Leon could see her bottom lip quivering and curling, her chin dimpled like orange peel. He knew that face— the time she'd been accused of smashing another girl's phone at school and their dad had been called at work about it and at dinner that night he'd demanded she own up to it, then forced her to ring the girl and apologize. *That* face.

"Grace?" said Leon softly. "It's OK…" He was still hoping that what he'd seen had been a trick of the light or his eyes playing games. "Just show him you're normal, kiddo."

She turned her head slowly toward them, revealing her right cheek. Tears were streaming down and she looked terrified. There was something else in her expression: she looked *ashamed*.

"Please," she whispered, "p-please...d-don't hurt me..."

And there it was, looking almost like a flesh-colored earring dangling below the small lobe of her ear. It curled and flexed like a kitten's tail.

"Bloody hell!" gasped Dave.

Leon felt lightheaded, dizzy with conflicting emotions—revulsion...sadness...fear. Fear—not for her, but *of* her. "Grace?"

"Leon," she whimpered, "I'm not...a monster... I'm me. It's me, it's me, it's me. Don't leave me! Please...*please*...don't let them hurt me!"

"She's...she's a snark!" said Dave. He grabbed Leon's arm to pull him back.

Leon shook his hand off angrily. "Grace? What...what's happened to you?"

"It's not your bloody sister!"

He ignored Dave. "Grace...come on, talk to me."

"I'm scared," she whimpered.

"Were you infected? Is...is that...is that what happened?"

"I didn't know!" she cried. "I didn't know, Leo! Honestly!"

"Didn't know?" Dave shook his head. "The hell she didn't know!"

"*I didn't know!*" she screamed at him.

"You were the one begging to let that horse in, weren't you?" Dave turned to look at the others crowded outside the sauna. "Wasn't she? She wanted to let that thing in! And when Ron said he was going to burn it?" He turned back to her. "You knew. *You bloody knew!*"

She shook her head vigorously, sobbing. "No. No...I...I—"

"Leave her alone!" snapped Leon. "She's crazy about horses, OK? She's always wanted one! She just—"

"It's not your sister, mate. Not anymore."

Leon swung a fist at him. The first time in Leon's life that he'd ever thrown a punch. It was clumsy, slow, and badly aimed, and it glanced off Dave's cheek. Dave retaliated with a punch to his gut, and Leon doubled over, winded.

"Get him outside!"

He felt hands grabbing hold of his shoulders. He tried shaking them off, but then a knee came up sharply and smashed him in the temple. His head suddenly exploded with white noise, and he was vaguely, dully aware of being dragged out of the stuffy sauna cabin and thrown down onto some rubber matting.

He gazed up at the glass roof of the tropicarium, everything blurred and spinning and refusing to settle into something on which he could focus. It was getting dark outside. That's the one thing he could make out. Darkness was coming.

Oh, my poor, poor Leo. You've been knocked silly. His mom's voice. From the time he'd bashed his head using a chin-up bar in the doorframe of his bedroom. *Leo...you silly boy. Are you all right?* He remembered being rushed to hospital and a doctor telling his mother he'd concussed himself and it was best if he stayed in the hospital overnight so they could watch him.

Over the ringing in his ears, he was vaguely aware of other voices in the background now. Shouts and screams and some ridiculous fight going on over something, but he was struggling to piece together what it was all about. Something important though. Something immediate. Life and death.

Thumping, banging. And a screaming voice. He knew that voice. It was Grace. She was screaming his name over and over and over. And another female voice he vaguely recognized but couldn't put a name to right now.

"You can't do this! No. Oh God! No. *You can't do this!*" He sat up, his head still spinning and now beginning to throb painfully, his ears still ringing. From the sauna he could see flashlight beams and shadows flickering around. He could hear Dave and Iain in there with her. The narrow doorway was plugged with everyone else, curious and frightened.

Freya appeared beside him. She crouched down. "You OK?"

Leon shook his head like a dog shaking off water. He pulled himself up, Freya helping. "What's happening in there?" he uttered groggily. "What are they doing to her?"

"We've got to stop them! We've got to—"

Leon pushed himself forward into the pack of bodies around the door.

"*Leon! LEEEE-ON!*" Grace's voice sounded muffled now, as if they were gagging her. He wrenched at shoulders in his way, pushing them aside to get back into the small sauna. But he needn't have bothered.

Dave appeared in the doorway with a squirming green shape slung over his shoulder. It took a second for Leon to realize it was a tarp wrapped around Grace.

"*Leon! Help me!*" her muffled voice whimpered.

He could see one of her small, pale fists poking out from the tarp, thumping ineffectually against Dave's back.

"*Put her down!*" Leon screamed.

Dave squeezed through the door, and the curious crowd backed away from him as if he were carrying a hornet's nest on his shoulder. Leon took advantage of the space ahead of him and charged forward. But once again he found himself down on the ground, blinking up at the spinning, darkening sky. Something heavy landed on his chest. Big Phil. He was straddling him and his meaty fists were holding his arms down.

"Mate," he whispered, "if you don't want the same thing to happen to you, just stay there, all right?"

Dave strode past, Grace kicking and screaming over his shoulder. He was heading toward the storeroom. He saw Freya struggling a few feet away, Claire and one of the cleaning girls restraining her like prison guards.

"Dave! You bastard! You can't do this!" Freya was screaming after him.

"What's he going to do?" asked Leon, still not getting it.

Big Phil looked down at him, shaking his head. "Just be quiet, mate."

"*What's he going to do?*"

The answer came, not from Phil, but from the sound of liquid sloshing in a gallon drum. He saw Iain walking in behind Dave, the drum held in his arms.

Oh God.

"*No...no...nononono!*" He tried to buck Phil's weight off him, but there was too much bulk for his slender frame to shift.

"Sorry, Leon. Sorry, mate... We've gotta do this."

He ignored Phil. *"DAVE! PLEASE! WE'LL LEAVE! WE'LL LEAVE!"* he screamed.

Dave carried on ignoring him and then paused by the storeroom door, waiting for Iain. Leon caught a glimpse of them discussing something; then his view was blocked by all the others making their way toward the storeroom. "Phil! For God's sake... they're gonna *burn* her! Let me go!"

He could see Big Phil didn't want to think about that. Big Phil was more than happy just thinking about keeping Leon down on the ground. "Just shut up! Mate, please?"

"Please! Please! *Oh God...please!*"

Leon could smell the diesel. He could hear it spattering the ground. He could hear Grace's muffled screams increasing in pitch.

She smells it too. She knows what's going to happen. He twisted and squirmed and Phil's grasp just got tighter as he braced himself.

"It'll be over quick."

"You can't let him do this to her!"

"It's not Grace. It's not your little sister."

"Let me goooooo!"

In the twilight gloom, he saw a glow of flickering amber. Leon caught a glimpse of flame...a twist of paper burning at one end. He heard Dave shout something over the top of Grace's muffled screaming. The crowd took several cautious steps back, which allowed him to see more. Iain quickly pulled the storeroom door open, Dave tossed the soaking, squirming tarpaulin bundle in. Iain shook the rest of the diesel fuel out inside the room, then hastily backed out.

And Dave finally tossed the flaming twist of paper in. The door remained open. A second or two passed.

Then with a soft *whump*, a rich, orange glow spilled out of the open door. Dave, satisfied the bundle was burning, slammed the door shut.

Leon heard Freya screaming…then he heard himself screaming.

PART

III

CHAPTER

46

"He's really nice. He's got a good heart. You'd like him."

Freya paused, the phone held to her ear as she stared out at the dark city from the balcony. "Yeah. Not too bad-looking. No Brad Pitt, of course. More like *Big Bang*'s Leonard. But, you know, he's really sweet."

She paused again, her head cocked, listening. "Yeah...I know. I know he's messed up inside. I *do* know that. But who isn't, right? We're all a little screwed up in our heads these days. I mean, I saw you turned into gunk. Everyone who's alive has now lost someone they loved. Everyone. We're all damaged goods one way or another."

She clutched the phone to her ear, even though it was just a lifeless sliver of plastic. Even if it had had any charge left in it, there'd be no point. There were no signals out there.

I know, Freya love...but just be careful who you attach yourself to. Boys can be so cruel...

"Oh God, I know all about boys, Mum. He's not like that." She turned to look back into the dark bedroom. She could just about see his dark form spread across the bed. She could hear his heavy, regular breathing. Fast asleep, for sure.

"He's just...well... I think *I'm* going to have to be the strong one for a while. He's broken right now. So I'm going to look after him."

And when he's better again, Freya...will he look after you? Will he stay with you when you can't walk anymore? Feed you when you can't swallow? Push you around in a wheel—

She laughed softly. "You mean will he dump me for someone way hotter? I don't think I'm facing any stiff competition right now." She stared out at the dark city of Norwich. Not a single light. Not a single sign of life. "Anyway, it's not like we're going out or anything. We're just friends right now. Survival buddies."

She lowered the phone from her ear, losing interest in talking to her dead mum. Even as just a voice in her head, a voice from the grave, she was still suffocatingly protective of her fragile little girl.

"I love you, Mum," she whispered, "but I'm a *big* girl now. I can take care of myself."

She set her dead, useless phone down on the balcony coffee table and gazed at the cluster of tea candles set in the middle, the only man-made illumination in Norwich. The apartment they'd randomly picked was in a modern-looking, converted, five-story, canal-side warehouse, which Freya imagined had months ago been occupied by groovy hipsters, urban types—all trimmed beards, slim fits, and canvas deck shoes.

By day, the river below looked like a mottled tan-and-red

mud bath. Every now and then, its thin membrane surface ruptured as gas bubbled out. By night, it looked far more interesting. Beneath the membrane, faint green swirls of bioluminescence sometimes rippled through the gloop, like a submerged aurora borealis.

Freya had been concerned at the prospect of being this close to the virus's presence. But Leon had made the point that the virus was *everywhere*. If it could make horses, even people, then it could get anywhere. Apart from the occasional swollen, intestine-like balloons floating on the breeze, they hadn't seen the virus produce anything that could actually fly, so up here in the penthouse apartment seemed as safe a place as any.

A bridge ran over the river and on the far side was a soccer stadium—Norwich City Football Club—opposite a retail park with an untouched Sainsbury's supermarket. Even though the stench inside of rotting freezer goods was almost overwhelming, the shelves were still fully filled with cans of food, bottles of soda, and boxes of painkillers that would last them for years.

Here's OK. For now.

Here would do while she waited for Leon to *return* to her.

She glanced back into the room—he was still fast asleep—then looked down at the faint every-now-and-then swirls of green in the canal below. She was no expert on mental health. She'd once known a girl at school who had been so relentlessly bullied online she'd had a nervous breakdown. That's what this looked like to her. A collapse.

Too much. Just too much.

Burning Grace alive. Hearing her screams...

Freya crushed her eyes shut and urged her mind to move along quickly.

They'd been taken by Big Phil and dumped on an exit ramp off the A11... Phil had Mr. Carnegie's gun with him. He'd pulled it out to show her and told her Dave had given him orders to "give it to 'em." And by that he'd clearly *not* meant handing the weapon over.

She'd been waiting anxiously for something like this. Not just expulsion from the park, but a tidy out-of-sight-of-the-others death for them both. Obviously Dave didn't want to be looking over his shoulder for the rest of his life.

Phil said he wasn't willing to do it—actually *couldn't* do it. He said he liked Leon and her, but they both had to go. He fired the gun twice in the air to get them walking, and probably so he could show Dave two spent rounds when he returned. Then he'd jumped in the park's car, turned, and headed back down the road, grinding the gears noisily, the car lurching awkwardly. She'd watched it until it had disappeared, concerned that Phil might have second thoughts, come back and do what Dave had ordered him to do.

The A11 led to Norwich, and Leon had said something about his grandparents living somewhere nearby. So that's what led them here.

Her mind flickered back to Grace. Skipping quickly past those horrific last few minutes, past *that* day, to the weeks and months before. Just a young girl. A precocious, sometimes annoying, but mostly cute kid. Always smiling, always making others laugh with her Little Miss Prada put-downs.

Freya wiped her damp cheeks with the back of her hand.

There was no friggin' way she was a snark.

This "slime from outer space"—as good a theory as any—had managed to make a copy of a horse. Not even a great copy: up close, touching it, the truth was apparent. But to make a copy of Grace that even Leon couldn't detect?

Bullshit. Complete and utter bullshit.

Dave had murdered an innocent girl in the most horrific way possible.

CHAPTER
47

Dave stirred the charred remains with the toe of his boot. They'd left the storeroom firmly closed until the fuel had spent itself. There were a few cardboard boxes in the place, but the rest was cinderblock walls and a corrugated-iron roof, nothing that would catch and spread—a perfect oven, in fact.

He looked up at the pale-gray sky. One of the roof support beams had been softened enough by the intense heat for it to buckle and collapse, bringing down about a quarter of the roof. The light angled down in thick shards that flickered with the last wisps of smoke slowly rising from the blackened concrete floor.

He could see chunks of carbonized matter that might once have been part of the fake horse, might have been part of the Fake Girl.

It didn't have a name now. *It* wasn't called Grace anymore... *That thing* they'd burned was now known as the Fake Girl.

Apart from checking it once after the flames had died down,

to make sure the fire wasn't going to spread to the rest of the complex, the door had remained firmly closed and locked. No one had even gone near it, as if ignoring the door meant that somehow what had occurred here days ago had never really happened.

The mood in the park had become subdued. The Chinese family had packed their things and left. Ten fewer people now lived here than a week ago, and the place suddenly felt like a ghost town. Dave had tried to get their minds off it, to lighten the mood under the new management regime. He'd continued the ritual of Ron's breakfast briefings, had even tried to get some team games going on the whiteboard in the cafeteria. But there was little appetite for it.

Screw 'em, then. He figured they'd snap out of it soon enough. *Life goes on.*

He looked around the blackened room. Some of the cinderblocks had been cracked by the heat. Beneath his boots the crisped bodies of some of those crabs crackled like unshelled prawns done far too long on a barbecue.

Nothing in this room could have survived.

He saw something on the floor, a dark lump the size of a fist. He squatted down beside it and poked at it with a pen. Soot flaked off and he saw it was the toe end of one of Fake Girl's shoes. The rubber toe-tip had melted down to a puddle, but a small fraction of the vinyl material remained and the little swoosh logo.

So damned convincing, weren't you? Complete with your tennis shoes, your little pink backpack, your...

He felt a momentary wave of nausea that he'd looked at her as human.

He stood up and turned toward the door. Iain was waiting in the doorway, not willing to take even a single step inside.

"Well?"

"Nothing left," said Dave. "It's all burned to hell."

"The roof's caved in. What if the snarks get in through that?"

Dave joined Iain. He pulled the door shut behind him and turned the key in the lock.

"We'll just keep this shut up for good." He looked down at the narrow gap at the bottom of the door. "And we'll board that gap up." He sucked air in through his teeth. "The storeroom's no good to us anyway. We'll call that 'outside' now."

It was Katrina, one of the cleaners, who spotted them first a couple of days later. She wasn't even on watch duty—that was supposed to be Louise, the girl who used to manage the tanning salon. Either Louise was asleep up on the terrace or just not doing her job.

Katrina shook her head. *Dave will punish her for not being vigilant enough.*

She'd come through to the reception area to refill the watering bucket in the ladies' bathroom. The first green shoots were showing in Mr. Carnegie's vegetable garden. Katrina now considered herself the principle custodian of the man's dream to nurture and grow their own fresh vegetables. No one else seemed to be taking an interest in it. As with everything else, a gloomy lethargy had settled over this place like a fog. Toilet buckets were not being emptied, mealtimes were becoming a free-for-all. Hopefully things would pull together again soon, but until then, Katrina was going to do her little bit and keep those green shoots going.

The last week had seen a stark change in the atmosphere of this place. The burning of that girl had affected everyone. There were two distinct groups in the park now: those who were convinced she'd been a creature disguised as a girl, and those who thought they'd all been responsible for allowing the murder of a child to happen.

Katrina considered herself to be firmly in the latter group, along with the other cleaners.

She saw the new arrivals making their way through the parking lot, just as the fake horse had done, across the gravel and cautiously toward the front entrance. She saw them both at the same time as they glimpsed her through the tinted glass wall at the front.

So there was no ducking out of sight. They now knew someone was home.

A large, slope-shouldered man and a small, much younger woman. They were pushing bicycles, their rear baskets stacked with bottles of drinking water. Unlike the horse though, they didn't look sick; they looked well nourished. Of course they did. There was food out there in abundance. Anyone armed with a can opener was never going to go hungry. Not for a long time yet.

Instead of ducking down and hiding. Katrina approached the front and waved them over. "Come here!" she shouted through the tinted glass. They walked their bikes over and lay them down just outside.

"You stay there! I go and call someone! OK?"

They both seemed to understand her. The girl nodded.

Dave and the rest of the park's inhabitants were gathered in the entrance again, just like they had been a week ago, sizing up the two new arrivals outside. This time around, there was no open discussion, no back-and-forth debate—there was no point. Dave ran things now. On his belt were two things that marked him out as undisputed leader: Mr. Carnegie's large, jangling bunch of keys and, on the other side, the gun.

They looked sullenly to him for a decision.

He felt their eyes resting on him, like hands pushing at him to say or do *something*.

"I'll go talk to them," he announced. He unzipped his anorak and felt on his hip for the reassuring grip of the gun. He unhitched the jangling keys from his belt and searched through them for the right key. He unlocked the double doors and stepped outside.

His hand remained on his hip like a small-town sheriff, ready to pull the gun out and wave it threateningly around if need be.

"Afternoon," he said stiffly.

The two newcomers stared at him cautiously. Closer to them now, he could see the man looked not quite *right*. His eyes looked squinty and watery. The hair on his head looked patchy, his scalp bald in places. The girl noticed him looking him over.

"You're looking at his hair, right?"

Dave nodded.

"'S OK... We're *real*. Steven has alopecia."

The man smiled innocently, a friendly, beaming grin that revealed pink gums and just a couple of wobbly teeth. "Hello...my name is Steven." He spoke with a whistling lisp.

"He's got special needs." The girl shrugged. "I've been taking care of him since...well, since all this went down, haven't I, Stevie?"

Dave looked at her. She looked to be about twenty, long blond hair. She was pretty even without a dash of makeup. Natural pretty.

He looked her over quickly while she was looking up at her simpleton friend.

Nice. Fit.

"My name's Dave Lester. I'm the leader here." He turned to gesture at the building behind him, at the row of pale faces peering out. "I run this place."

She nodded as she studied the front of the building. "Meg."

"You two...you're immune, right? You're not infected?"

"Oh, we know all about the painkillers. Yeah...we've been poppin' the pills all right."

Dave smiled. He liked her. She seemed straight-up. Confident. No bullshit. A bit like that sarcastic cow Freya used to be, in fact, minus the shitty up-yours attitude she'd had.

Big Phil had come back and told him that he'd done the deed. Dave had counted the bullets and sniffed the barrel. He'd fired the gun all right. No more Freya. And no more of that whining Yank kid, Leon. For all they knew, he could have been another snark waiting to hatch too.

"Seriously...we're good," said Meg. She flicked her hair, bared her teeth to him, and presented her hands. "See? We've got teeth, nails, and hair... That enough for you?"

"Right." He nodded. "OK. You know, I just have to be careful."

"We know. *It* can do people now. Pretty freaky, huh?"

He raised his eyebrows. "Well, I suppose you can come in if you want."

"Hey, who says we actually *want* to come in?"

Dave was taken aback by that. "What? Uh... Oh, I just assumed—"

She laughed dryly. "Just messing with you, Dave Lester."

He found himself laughing, liking that...liking that *a lot*. She reminded him of the kind of snarky female lead that populated teen flicks: the hot chick with a brain and all the best put-down lines. The park could do with someone like that around. Someone to liven up this godforsaken place.

CHAPTER

48

AND, IT TURNED OUT, HE WAS ONE HUNDRED PERCENT RIGHT about that. The mood in the cafeteria that evening was markedly different. New faces for everyone to get to know, to quiz about the big, bad world out there.

The girl, Meg, had little to add to what they already knew. She told them that they were the first *real* humans that she and Stevie had come across. She gave them all a brief account of their last six months, witnessing the same things they'd all seen—the "balloons," the "feather clouds," the "creepy crawlies"—and, a month ago, a completely bald man who looked as pale as a ghost, shambling around like a drunk. She'd been suspicious of him—it—immediately, and they'd given the thing a wide berth.

She told them that the whole world, as far as she knew, had been hit by the plague and was in just the same state as England. Then she told them how impressed she was by this place. Flattered Dave by telling him what a great job he'd done setting up this survival enclave. That it might just end up being the starting point for human civilization version two.

The big man, Steven, she explained, she'd found wandering around outside a nursing home. She told them all not to worry about him. Yes, he was big—and strong too—but he was perfectly harmless. He seemed to have nothing but a childlike gratitude to offer anyone who bothered to take the time to interact with him. Meg told everyone in the cafeteria that although he didn't say much, he did really cool impersonations of any cartoon characters they wanted to name.

It didn't take much to persuade him to do his party trick. His Bart Simpson soon had the small cafeteria echoing with guffawing laughter.

Dave was pleased. Finally some smiles, some laughs again. The evening with these two new arrivals felt like an important punctuation point, like a new start, a very definite line drawn beneath the unpleasantness of the previous week. More importantly, a distraction from the clear schism that had begun to develop in the park. Up until these two strangers had turned up this afternoon, Dave was becoming certain he was going to have to start waving his gun around. Lay down the law. Remind people that this was not some hippy-dippy democracy and they'd better get that into their stupid heads.

New management, new rules. Time to buck up and get on with things again.

He was pleased. And then, to make matters all the better, Meg caught his eye across the cafeteria and winked. A wink that suggested she might want to be more than just friends...given time.

Meg talked awhile with everyone who had questions for her, and then finally she was standing right beside him.

"How about you show me around? This place looks very impressive."

He made an effort not to look *too* eager to do that. He managed a casual nod. "What about your friend over there?"

"Hey, just look at him!" She shrugged. "He's having a great time showing off. Gimme a sec." She wandered over to Stevie and touched his arm lightly. He turned to look down at her. She stood on tiptoes and whispered something into his ear, and he nodded and waggled his hand at her, then went back to entertaining his audience.

She came back.

"What did you just say to him?"

Meg smiled. "That me and you were going for a little...*stroll.*"

Was that another wink there? Dave could have sworn there was. He led her out of the cafeteria and into the half light of the tropicarium. It was dark outside and several spotlights around a palm tree in the middle caught the tips of its waxy, green leaves and cast jungle shadows up onto the glass ceiling.

"This is really something," she said again.

"You know, this used to be an exclusive health spa."

"Really? It's totally awesome."

He led her around the edge of what had once been a small pool. It was now filled with soil, and bamboo canes were erected in rows. "We're going to grow beans and peas here, and potatoes and onions. No canned veggies anymore."

She nodded, studying the vegetable garden as they walked around it. She seemed to be fascinated with every detail.

"I suppose you must have seen enough yourself to realize that we have to stop waiting for a rescue and start looking after ourselves," said Dave.

"Yes. You're right."

"I'm doing the best I can to adapt it to be a real long-term survival place." He led her away from the cafeteria, past the empty spa pools and the row of sauna cabins, to the paths around the back that led to the chalets.

"Look. See? We have more growing here. Tomatoes. This tropicarium is good for them. It's perfect, really. I mean basically this is one big greenhouse." He was vaguely aware he was babbling. Talking too much.

She furrowed her brows, pursed her lips, and nodded mock-sensibly. "Excellent work, Dave. Excellent."

He stopped, looked at her, and giggled self-consciously. "Are you pulling my leg or something?"

She looped her arm through his. "No! I'm just soooo impressed with what you've achieved here! Very good work!"

He looked at her and narrowed his eyes suspiciously, still smiling though. *If* she were making fun of him, he was pretty sure—well, *hoping* actually—it was in a flirty way. "You are...aren't you?"

He couldn't make her out yet. They'd only met her just a few hours ago, and she seemed to already have everyone eating out of the palm of her hand.

She gasped theatrically. "Now why on earth would you think that I'm *mocking* you?"

"The way you're talking right now. It sounds, well, a little sarcastic."

Her manner changed abruptly. As if she'd suddenly thought of another game she wanted to play. She walked two fingers up along the inside of his forearm.

"I think I know why you let me and Stevie in this afternoon." She ran her hand up his arm. "You like me, don't you?"

Dave realized his mouth was dry. His legs felt like jelly, trembling with excitement.

"OK...OK, yeah...I, uh, think you're pretty, you know."

Her eyes rounded, wider still. "So, do you want to kiss me? Hmm?"

He laughed nervously.

"*Yes. Kiss me.*"

He swallowed. "Uh...I..."

"Kiss me, right now."

"*Right here?*" His voice was trembling. He hated that, hated sounding like some kind of teenage dork.

"Yes." She pressed her hand against his chest and gently pushed him back. He took a step backward onto the soil, almost stumbling.

"Right here...on these tomatoes," she whispered. "Right now."

Dave shot a glance across the tropicarium, toward the cafeteria. Light was spilling from the doorway, laughter too. No one sounded as if they were thinking of heading to their chalet anytime soon.

"Wow. Seriously?"

She nodded.

"Yeah, sure. OK. Yeah. O-OK," he replied, not quite believing his luck.

She tugged his shirt out, indicating that he needed to lie down on the soil. He did so obediently.

"So, how do you...want me to—"

"Shh." She put a finger to her lips. She knelt down in front of him. "You really do want me, don't you, Dave? Hmm?"

He nodded vigorously. "Yeah! But, uh...come on...if we're going to do this, we better do it before anyone comes out!" he whispered.

Her hand stole up inside his T-shirt, one finger circling lightly around his navel. "What do you think about this?" With her other hand, she gathered her long, tumbling locks into a bunch and playfully swished it like a pony flicking away buzzing flies with its tail. She tilted her head as if trying to remember something. "You like my hair?"

"Yeah...yeah...really nice...but..."

"Or what about this?" She pulled at the bunched hair, and all of it slid away from her head, leaving a perfectly smooth scalp that glistened like a pearl in the half light.

"What the...?"

She tossed the wig aside, onto the dark soil, then reached into her mouth. Something clattered around inside, and her hand emerged, clutching a set of dentures she dropped in his lap. Her lips spread wide, revealing baby gum ridges.

"What the—"

"Oh dear, oh dear," she giggled playfully in a singsong voice. "I'm not a real girl."

He dug at the dirt with his hands, attempting to scramble back from her, but, too late, something hard and sharp suddenly pierced through his navel and sank deep into his gut. He screamed, then grabbed at his belly, trying to pull out whatever had gone into him.

Her smile spread wider, skin sagging and separating like a plastic bag held over a candle, unraveling and spreading across her cheeks, toward her ears.

Dave could feel something razor sharp inside him being wiggled around, carving, lacerating his insides. He coughed a thick globule of blood onto his chin.

"She...hates...you," she singsonged softly, tilting her head. "*She*...hates you."

Her words sounded mangled and were rendered almost unintelligible by the lack of dentures and the melting shreds of her mouth.

She shoved with her hand again sharply, and it felt to him like her whole fist was inside his belly. He tried to pull her hand out, already guessing the damage she'd done fumbling around inside was enough to kill him.

She raised her other hand in front of his face, opened her fist to reveal her palm. But it looked nothing like a hand—it was deformed into the ugly, pale underbelly of some crustacean, skeletal segments flexing and overlapping, surrounding a birdlike mouth in the middle that flexed and opened like a starving cuckoo. The beak opened wide, and a head of knobby bone and cartilage surged up the tunnel of her wrist and out of the beak. It unfolded into a dozen fragile, articulated limbs, each with a fine scalpel tip. They swayed and flexed inches from his face, legs pedaling in the air.

"Please...please..." he gurgled as more blood spilled onto his chin and down his shirt.

She cocked her bald head, curious. Her face was disintegrating rapidly. All that was left now was the bridge of her nose, her eyes, her forehead. Her eyes were still startlingly pretty, glistening and staring intensely at him. Beneath them, either side of the bridge of her nose, the flesh was breaking down: skin, muscle, tendons, and bones wilting, drooping into pliable, swinging ribbons of gelatinous material that was busy deciding what it wanted to become next. Pieces swung free and dropped to the soil.

Dave's dizzy mind was going into shock—an endorphin-flooded shutdown. The merciful exit reflex of a dying body. His eyes focused blearily on the dozen fragile limbs that were kicking the air impatiently just in front of his face, a spider-leg ballet, each one seemingly eager to get to work on his flesh.

From somewhere far away, he suddenly heard a chorus of screaming voices, the sounds of struggle and panic, chairs being kicked over, smashing glass, and a deep, keening cry like whale song.

"Meg," or what was left of her, had studied him long enough. She thrust her arm forward, and those flexing legs made contact with him and started to burrow into his cheeks and his eyes. The very last words he heard, slurred and moist, words that sounded as if they'd escaped the grinding mouth at the bottom of a kitchen blender, were...

"You. Burned. Me."

CHAPTER
49

She studied his corpse lying across the soil bed. His blood looked as black as ink in the half light, like an oil spill on a beach. His body was already being worked on by the parts of her that had broken away and disassembled into "gatherers": a dozen or so small, simpleminded creatures with articulated limbs that had begun to snip and cut at his flesh, breaking it down into raw material to be absorbed as fuel.

The rest of the girl, this temporary construction, stood up.

The "intelligence cluster" of cells that were overseeing this particular mobile colony had pieced together the genetic template from a human who had once genuinely been called "Megan," who had once lived a life in a place called "Thetford." Who had once been considered "pretty" by every young guy she'd met. Who wanted to be a thing called a "model," but until circumstances improved had to be satisfied with being a "hairdresser."

This intelligence cluster was a mature one, several billion cells that had organized themselves into a firm and very permanent *core*: a structure that was able to process chemical data at a high enough level to think, to strategize, to reason.

In this sprawling new ecology of the virus, of colonies and sub-colonies, mature clusters and immature clusters, it was high in the hierarchy. If not yet a king, then it was a king in the making. The cluster had already made great strides in decoding its own DNA, to delve deep and begin to understand itself, to read most of the way down its programmed to-do list, the mission statement with which it had been born.

The primary stages of its mission were now complete: establishing a foothold, consolidating, proliferating, spreading, securing its existence. The secondary stages were now in full flow: piecing together the fragments of the world it had picked apart, like a clumsy houseguest hastily attempting to repair a fragile and expensive broken Ming vase. It was learning so much about the things it had destroyed, how rich and varied the life templates were in this world. For example, how the simple task of locomotion came in so many different forms, how things wiggled, slithered, crawled, climbed, jumped, flapped, hopped, sprinted. So much complexity in this place, so much *speciation*.

It had learned that one particular species was extraordinarily dominant. A species in many ways very much like itself; a species capable of studying, reasoning, adapting. This particular intelligence cluster had carefully and patiently read this species' construction manual, its DNA, and attempted many times to make viable reconstructions until it had finally, despite the difficulty of mimicking the dead-tissue structures, the things made from keratin protein, had finally gotten it right.

"Megan" and "Stevie" had been convincing enough to fool these creatures.

What was left to learn about this species was how its own intelligence clusters worked, that solid-state organ comprising billions of cells linked together by pathways that could strengthen and weaken according to necessity. This intelligence cluster had learned how to make a copy of this organ, but now it was very keen to learn how this curious species *used* the organ.

Among the many fragments of consciousness that had once been human beings, this particular intelligence cluster had a guest staying with it for now. A recent addition to its library, a *complete* recreation of a consciousness. For the very first time, it had established a direct link with this intelligent species at a *chemical* level. The language it understood best. Someone from whom it could learn so much. The guest had a veritable treasure trove of data to share: images, sounds, smells, thoughts, feelings, things that this entity called "memories."

The guest entity also had a name... *Grace.* Talking to Grace was difficult. She was only just beginning to comprehend this biochemical language.

[...presentlyexperiencinghighlevelsof{>€#€€#^#€€}-substance in your {#%^>€$>€>}-cluster. Explain to us the high presence of chemical. Is this what you refer to as "emotional state"?...]

He burned me. He killed me.

[..."killed," accessing your definition...]

[..."killed" is "permanent cell deconstruction"?...]

Yes...he killed me.

[...you are no longer in "killed" configuration, Grace...]

[...you are now REMADE...]

ACKNOWLEDGMENTS

A big thank-you to my agent, Veronique, and my editor, Venetia. The former for helping me keep my sanity, the latter for rewarding my insanity and encouraging me to dig deep.

The inspiration for *Plague Land* came in part from a film I saw when I was *very* young (too young probably). It was a 1950s Japanese B-movie called *The H-Man*. One image from that movie was permanently burned into my nightmares: the sight of a bundle of clothes spread out on the ground and viscous liquid bubbling from the trouser legs and shirt cuffs. Liquid that used to be a human being. I can't remember the story... It probably wasn't great, but that particular image stayed with me.

It just goes to show that nothing in life is wasted. No experience, no smell, no vague, half-recalled memory. We writers are sensual magpies. We hoard what we see, hear, and smell... and from those things, we produce stories like these. I hope, dear reader, that I cause you some sleepless nights...and I hope (for the budding writers out there) that forty years from now you'll "magpie" a grisly moment from these pages.

ABOUT THE AUTHOR

Alex Scarrow used to be a rock guitarist. After ten years in various unsuccessful bands, he ended up working in the computer games industry as a lead games designer. He now has his own games development company, Grrr Games. He is the author of the best-selling and award-winning TimeRiders series, which has been sold into over thirty foreign territories. He lives in East Anglia and is currently working on the sequel to *Plague Land*.

Visit his website at alexscarrow.com.